Praise for JESSICA SPEART's
RACHEL PORTER MYSTERIES

"A highly enjoyable series."
Chicago Tribune

"Fresh and close to the bone. [Speart's] characters
breathe with the endlessly fascinating
idiosyncrasies of living people."
Nevada Barr

"[Speart] takes readers to all sorts of interesting
places . . . She has a real flair for bringing
colorful characters to life on the page."
Connecticut Post

"Each of Speart's books is a great read."
Pittsburgh Post-Gazette

"Chills and laughs galore."
James W. Hall

"The author portrays the stark atmosphere . . .
vividly . . . There are plenty of appealing characters, not
the least of which is Rachel herself."
Publishers Weekly

"Rachel Porter . . . is a very good traveling companion."
Boston Globe

Rachel Porter Mysteries by
Jessica Speart

JESSICA SPEART

BLUE TWILIGHT

A Rachel Porter Mystery

AVON BOOKS
An Imprint of HarperCollinsPublishers

This is a work of fiction. Names, characters, places, and incidents are products of the author's imagination or are used fictitiously and are not to be construed as real. Any resemblance to actual events, locales, organizations, or persons, living or dead, is entirely coincidental.

AVON BOOKS
An Imprint of HarperCollins*Publishers*
10 East 53rd Street
New York, New York 10022-5299

Copyright © 2004 by Jessica Speart
ISBN: 0-06-055952-7
www.avonmystery.com

First Avon Books paperback printing: September 2004

Avon Trademark Reg. U.S. Pat. Off. and in Other Countries, Marca Registrada, Hecho en U.S.A.
HarperCollins® is a registered trademark of HarperCollins Publishers Inc.

Printed in the U.S.A.

10 9 8 7 6 5 4 3 2 1

ACKNOWLEDGMENTS

Thanks go to Dr. John Emmel, Dr. Gordon Pratt, and Dr. Richard Arnold, for providing insight into the world of butterflies; Renee Pasquinelli, Senior Ecologist with the California Department of Parks and Recreation, for leading me to the last known location of the Lotis blue butterfly; Katy Tahja of the Gallery Bookshop for helping to uncover Mendocino's secrets; USFWS Special Agent John Mendoza, who has never backed away from protecting endangered species; Carol Fuca for taking care of my "wild things" while I'm away; and to USFWS Special Agent Sam Jojolla, whose friendship and tireless dedication to our natural resources is invaluable.

Praise be to you my Lord
with all your creatures

The Canticle of the Creatures
ST. FRANCIS OF ASSISI

BLUE TWILIGHT

One

Damn Mister Softee. I couldn't get the ice-cream truck's canned kiddy music out of my head, its jingle playing over and over in endless fashion. I'm not really sure why—possibly because I was driving a van that looked exactly like it. The only difference was the company name printed on the side. It had been lent to me by an air delivery service, along with the courier uniform I now wore.

Cultivating my informant had finally paid off. I'd worked hard to establish a bond, exhibiting patience and concern by playing his "shrink for a day." I'd gone so far as to take his calls in the middle of the night, listening as he babbled on, his stories fueled by a combo of drugs, booze, and paranoia. In return, I'd learned that a package invoiced as toys would be coming in from Singapore; only its actual contents were endangered Burmese star tortoises.

The case was cut and dry. The box had arrived at Customs and had been X-rayed. Toys lay on top, while tortoises packed in plastic containers were secreted beneath a false bottom. The creatures spent their days and nights in the dark, waiting to be sold on the black market for five thousand dollars a pair.

I'd rushed to an airport warehouse, slit open the box, and marked each tortoise's shell with a UV pen. Then the reptiles were resealed inside their portable coffins. My plan was to deliver the package to the "toy store" and track where the torts went, nailing as many perps as possible in the process.

I'd performed similar "controlled" deliveries before; but something was different this time. Getting back in the van, I found that my mouth was inexplicably dry, my hands trembled on the steering wheel, and a dull pain ate away at the pit of my stomach. My heart raced with each passing mile, thumping hard against my chest as I turned onto the exit ramp; harder as my target came into view.

Pulling up to the curb, I grabbed the box and walked toward the store, my limbs feeling heavier than ever before. By now, the Mister Softee tune had permanently wormed its way into my brain, its tinny music pure auditory torture.

I knocked and someone opened the door. I never saw a face; just the barrel of a gun like a gaping black hole. Its mouth filled the entranceway, consuming time and space. I broke into a cold sweat and screamed *NO!* only to realize that it was already too late.

A shot rang out, piercing the air. It ripped through my body, lifting me off the ground and throwing me onto my back. My mind shrieked and my head slammed against what felt like pavement, my teeth jostling about like loose plastic beads in a baby rattle. The commotion echoed in my ears and my body ached, as if it were being kicked.

"Fight back, damn it!"

The voice barely made a dent in my consciousness, floating toward me from somewhere in the background. It was the sharp jolt of a full-frontal kick that shattered my daze, jerking me out of my head and back into reality.

"For chrissakes, Rachel. Snap out of it!"

The nightmare was happening again. I wasn't outside, garbed in a courier's uniform. Rather, I was in a gym, dressed in sweatpants, tee-shirt, and sneakers, with my hair plastered against my back and a rivulet of sweat trickling down my chin.

"What are you trying to do? Get your ass kicked on purpose?"

There was no time to think, much less react, as a foot planted itself in my stomach like a conquering flag. I was flung against a wall, causing a shock of pain to radiate throughout my body. Morbid Angel's music pounded in the air, replacing Mister Softee's theme, and the room lights flickered on and off in a blatant attempt to distract me. The ploy worked, giving my attacker time enough to land another solid punch. Everything moved in slow motion as a fist flew toward me, only I couldn't fend it off.

Then a stranger's voice hissed in my ear as two hands locked themselves tightly around my throat. That was enough to bring me fully to attention.

"What good are you, Porter? You'd never have been able to protect the courier that was killed all because she was mistaken for you."

"No!" I yelled.

I raised my right arm and swiftly pivoted to the side. Then ramming an elbow down hard, I broke my assailant's grip and jerked his hands from my throat. All restraint was shelved as I then grabbed hold of his shoulder and drove my knee into his stomach in a series of short, explosive bursts. It was pure exhilaration to finally release the frustration that had been building inside me for months.

I showed no mercy, but slammed his jaw twice with my open palm. His mouth guard flew across the room as I continued to pummel the man. I moved hard and fast, until a pair of arms wrapped themselves around my body and pulled me off. Breaking free, I turned to deliver a roundhouse punch only to be stopped in midair as two strong hands grabbed hold of my wrists.

"Whoa, Rambo! Calm down. You've beaten up your sparring partner quite enough."

My instructor's face slowly came into focus.

"Krav Maga is a method of bare-bones street fighting to be used for defense; not as a license to commit murder. You should have reacted this way immediately, and not waited to have the crap kicked out of you."

I pushed a strand of red hair from my eyes while struggling to catch my breath. "Yeah, I'll try to remember that."

"He's right, chère. Keep in mind that someone in this family has to stay healthy."

I glanced over to where the love of my life, Jake Santou, sat in a chair cheering me on. He smiled while shifting his weight, but I caught his grimace of pain. It only made me love him all the more.

I'd nearly lost the man nine months ago. Santou had been on a military flight that crashed in the Florida swamp, leaving five dead and two survivors. He'd barely made it out alive, yet managed to drag a badly injured fellow FBI agent with him. Then he'd gone back inside the wreck and hauled out the dead, refusing to let the swamp swallow them up. After that, the two men had held out nearly eighteen hours, waiting for rescuers to pinpoint their location and reach them. It had felt as if my own life hung in the balance while waiting for word. I'd never been more relieved than when it was finally confirmed that Jake had been found alive.

Santou was proclaimed a hero, but it came at a price. His injuries ranged from a leg broken in three places to a pinched nerve in his back and numerous scars. The result was that he still needed a cane to get around and had been confined to desk duty. All that could be dealt with, as far as I was concerned. The only thing that mattered to me was that Santou was alive.

He motioned and I quickly walked over to him.

"What was the problem out there, chère?"

Though I hated to tell him, there was no getting around it.

"The nightmare. It happened again. I guess my mind must have wandered, because I was sucked back into the same old thing. That's why I didn't respond at first."

Santou nodded, as if he understood all too well. "Yeah, that's not unusual. You've just got to learn to let it go, Rach."

He squeezed my hand and all my aches, pains, and fears momentarily dissolved. Then I headed over to my sparring partner.

"I hope I didn't hurt you."

Tanner responded with a grin. "Hey, that's what padding is for. I'll just use a little extra next time."

"Great. Then I can strike back even harder," I teased, becoming aware of the sweat sliding down my back. "I'm going to take a shower," I called to Jake.

He nodded and gingerly stretched his legs, as though they were fine pieces of china. By now we'd both been through enough to realize that neither of us was immortal. That was the bitch about getting older: having to acknowledge that anything can happen and you might not survive.

I jumped in the shower and soaped up, rubbing hard to wash away the dirt, sweat, and unwanted memories—only some recollections aren't so easy to get rid of.

What good are you, Porter? You'd never have been able to protect the courier that was killed all because she was mistaken for you.

No matter how hard I tried, there was no keeping the ghastly events of the controlled delivery out of my mind. Jose Abruzo's face loomed before me even now as a sheet of water rained down on my head. I should have known better than to trust an informant that not only looked like a rat, but actually turned out to be one. Jose double-crossed me by playing both sides, warning the smugglers that a female federal agent was laying a trap for them.

Timing in life is everything. As it happened, the perps

were expecting a drug shipment on the very same day their reptiles arrived. A female air service courier went about her job and unknowingly delivered the drug package to them, unaware that a bust was about to take place. Figuring her to be a federal agent, the smugglers blew her away. I would have been their target had the courier been a mere five minutes late.

I'd arrived at the scene to find cops milling around a woman with red hair, lying in a pool of blood.

"That should have been you, Porter," one of the boys in blue coolly informed me. "You oughta count your blessings that you're still alive."

And I did. I counted them every day. Only nothing could wipe away the memory of the stunned expression I saw on that poor woman's face.

I shivered as I left the shower, though the air wasn't cold. Guilt clung to me tight as a second skin from which there was no escape. Once again, I'd become the Service's scapegoat, with yet another black mark added to my growing roster.

Bad choice of informant. Troublemaker. Not a team player.

Not helping matters was that I'd been removed from my Georgia post after making political waves. My actions had prompted a congressional hearing to take place, during which the Service was warned to rein in their agents. I'd been transferred to San Francisco shortly afterwards. The controlled delivery was to have been the first case at my new post.

My cell phone rang, breaking the spell of doom and gloom closing in around me.

"This is Dr. Mark Davis of Stanford University. Am I speaking with a law enforcement agent?"

"Yes, this is Special Agent Rachel Porter."

"Well then, I have something you should be interested to

hear. I've been hiking the area to check which butterflies are out this early in June."

"That's terrific. Thanks for letting me know," I responded, ready to hang up on yet another West Coast wacko.

"Hold on a minute. I'm not yet finished," he sharply retorted. "I ran into some idiot that's digging up plants and netting every bug in sight, a few of which are highly endangered. I suggest you get up here immediately."

"Back up a second. Where exactly is 'here'?"

"San Bruno Mountain State Park. You *do* know where that is don't you?" the professor responded in annoyance.

Academics. You had to love them. Why did they automatically assume the rest of us were a good notch below them in intelligence?

"Yes, I know where it is."

How could anyone possibly miss it? Thousands of people drive by San Bruno Mountain every day, their attention drawn to the words SOUTH SAN FRANCISCO: THE INDUSTRIAL CITY branded in large white concrete letters on its southern slope.

"Good. Then you must also know that the mountain is sole home to the Mission blue butterfly and the San Bruno elfin."

"And who is this again?" I questioned, deciding to throw some of my own weight around.

"Dr. Mark Davis. I specialize in endangered butterflies at Stanford University's Center for Conservation Biology."

Each word was delivered in concise bite-sized syllables; their effect, that of a sharpened axe chipping away at my self-esteem.

Up until now, I'd worked the mega-fauna glamour cases—gators, manatees, primates, and grizzlies. Had it finally come down to dealing with bugs? Perhaps Fish and Wildlife was doing a better job of reining me in than I'd re-

alized. To top it off, I didn't know all that much about butterflies—a fact I was loathe to admit.

"Fine. Where should I meet you?"

"I can't wait around. However, I'll provide you with an
exact location and physical description of the subject. By the
looks of it, he doesn't plan to go anywhere soon. The of-
fender has a cooler with him, as well as a backpack and a
shovel."

It sounded as if Dr. Davis had watched one too many
episodes of *Law and Order*.

"Okay, I'll head there now."

"Don't hang up. I'm still not through," Davis instructed
like a true professor. "Does the name John Harmon ring a
bell with you?"

I didn't appreciate the feeling that I was being tested. As
the over-made-up rocker Alice Cooper used to sing, *School's
out forever*. In which case, I had no intention of jumping
through hoops for this professor.

"Never heard of him. Why? Should I have?"

"I would think so," Davis haughtily replied. "Not only is
he a colleague of mine, but you people hired him to trek to
Mendocino and do a final search for the Lotis blue before
officially declaring it to be extinct."

"The Lotis blue. I take it that's some sort of butterfly?"

"It's not *some sort* of butterfly," Davis disdainfully repeated my words as though they were verbal dirty laundry.
"It's the *rarest* butterfly in all North America."

Okay, so I'd failed that test. I hate it when I don't know
something.

"Sorry, but my job doesn't entail dealing with consultants.
If there's a problem, I suggest you take it up with the division of Fish and Wildlife that hired your friend," I responded, silently kicking myself for being ignorant of a
creature so close to extinction.

"You damn well *should* be concerned. *Especially* since you're law enforcement," Davis sniped.

"And why is that?"

"Because no one's heard from Harmon since he began his search in Mendocino over two weeks ago. Not his wife, his children, his parents, or any of us here at the university. It's as if he virtually disappeared off the face of the earth."

For a moment, all I could think was how odd that a man sent to search for a missing butterfly should now be missing himself. Then the chill that had previously nipped at my skin returned—only now it was stronger than ever.

Two

I quickly dressed and walked back into the gym to give Santou the bad news.

"Sorry, but I won't be able to spend the afternoon with you after all."

"Don't tell me. An emergency call just came in," Jake guessed with a shake of his tousled curls. A lopsided grin crept over his face at the sight of my disappointed expression. "That's to be expected, chère. After all, it's your turn to cover Saturday. Don't worry about me. I'll find something to keep myself amused."

"Who said it's you that I'm thinking about?" I teased, while leaning in to plant a kiss on his cheek.

Santou turned and caught my lips with his own. It's true; sometimes we don't know what we have until it's almost gone. All I knew was that I didn't ever again want to imagine my life without him.

"I'll drop Jake off at home if you have to head out," my sparring partner offered. "Who knows? Maybe he'll share some strategy tips that I can use during our next Krav Maga session."

"Don't you dare tell Tanner anything to give him the upper hand," I jokingly warned.

"You know me better than that, chère. I wouldn't dream of it." Jake chuckled.

"Yeah, yeah," I responded as we all walked outside.

I furtively watched as Jake ever so carefully climbed inside Tanner's vehicle, before jumping into my own Ford Explorer and taking off.

The morning fog was just beginning to lift. A few rays of sun dappled the city streets, stitching in and out of clouds. I made my way past tourist-choked Union Square, down Market Street, and then on to Highway 101. All the while I wondered if my I'll-do-as-I-damn-well-please ways had finally been curtailed. Ever since my transfer to San Francisco, I'd been consigned to dealing with bad-boy duck hunters and wayward tourists trying to sneak in illegal items. Now I found myself chasing after some joker running around on a hilltop netting butterflies. It was at times like this that I toyed with quitting Fish and Wildlife and joining the FBI.

I took the Cow Palace exit and drove through an area that few tourists rarely ever see. Hidden on the outskirts of the city are garbage dumps, a slaughterhouse, cemeteries, and toxic industry. The visual blight continued all the way to San Bruno Mountain, where identical row houses marched up its slope like troops of invading clones.

I chose to ignore the decay and focus instead on the last bit of wilderness clinging to life on the city's southern edge. A huge shoulder of rock, San Bruno Mountain dominates the skyline as it floats above a sea of urbanization. I wound my way up the mountain and parked in the designated lot. Then striking out, I hiked toward the meadow as Davis had instructed.

Elderberry trees gave way to stands of eucalyptus before opening onto a prairie of grassland. A profusion of California poppies, scarlet pimpernels, and buttercups intermingled in a colorful palette to create a thick floral carpet. The honking of horns, chatter of people, and ringing of cell phones gradually receded into the background, replaced by the stri-

dent call of a red-shafted flicker. I glanced up to where a
Northern harrier soared lazily in the sky, unperturbed at being the source of so much fear.

Looking around, I wondered if Mr. Butterfly might not
have already left, when a figure began to take shape in the
distance. I walked toward it and the form slowly morphed
into that of a man. He was just as Davis had described
him: overweight, short in stature, and sporting an unkempt
bush of red hair. In addition, the guy looked as though he
hadn't changed his clothes in over a month, but lived in the
same rumpled short-sleeve shirt and baggy shorts day in
and day out.

Drawing closer, I saw that the fabric gaped open where
buttons were missing and that his shirttail hung partially out
of his pants. The man had a backpack and shovel. However,
the cooler that Davis had mentioned was nowhere in sight.

I decided to pass myself off as a hiker, figuring it would
be easy enough to do. I never wear a uniform. Besides, this
was Saturday—a time when poachers rarely expect agents to
be on the prowl.

"Hi," I said with a smile and approached.

Mr. Butterfly gave me the once-over, and then swiftly
glanced around.

"Yeah. How you doing?" he muttered, pulling a pair of
binoculars from his backpack.

He placed them against his eyes and looked up at the sky,
swinging his head left and right, as if following the Indie
500. Such a grandiose show of birdwatching deserved its
own special reward.

"Would you mind telling me what kind of bird that is up
there?" I questioned, pointing skyward.

The Northern harrier sailed majestically above us, as if
also awaiting the answer.

"Sure. That big-ass bird is a bald eagle. You know, like our national symbol. Why? What's the matter? Don't you recognize it?" he cockily responded.

So much for Mr. B passing himself off as a birdwatcher. Still, I had to give the guy an A for sheer ballsiness.

"No, I'm afraid I didn't, but thanks for filling me in. I guess I don't know all that much about birds," I responded, playing along.

Mr. Butterfly lowered his binoculars and visibly relaxed. "Oh yeah? So what *do* you know about?" he flirtatiously asked.

"I know it feels good to come up here and get out of the city after working with computers all week," I bantered and coyly stretched. "Besides, it's a way for me to meet other people who also enjoy nature."

"Yeah, I like nature plenty, if you know what I mean," he retorted with a wink. "So what are you? One of those dot commers that's managed to hang onto a job?"

"Only if you call sporadic temp work a profession. The truth is, I'm going to be in trouble soon if I don't find something else to supplement my income."

My new friend made an obvious show of checking out my figure. "Hell, you're a good-looking woman. It shouldn't be hard for you to come up with a way to make a few extra bucks. Tell you what. I'll give you a twenty to do a little communing with me and nature right here and now."

"Watch it. I'm not that kind of girl," I laughed, sorely tempted to practice my Krav Maga on him.

It was then I noticed the tattoo on his arm. The design was of the perfect Playboy Playmate: a smiling, eager female with a perky pair of breasts. The cartoon figure was nude but for red high heels and thigh-high stockings. More than likely, it was the most enduring relationship with a woman that this guy would ever have.

Mr. Butterfly followed my gaze and playfully flexed his biceps so that the girl began to dance.

"So, what do *you* do?" I asked.

"Oh, a little of this and that. Mostly buy and sell stuff that I get at storage auctions. You know, those places where people keep their things when they have too much crap. Of course, they lose it all once they stop paying the rent. It's amazing what kind of shit you can pick up there. Everything from refrigerators to furniture to family heirlooms."

"And where do you sell the items? At flea markets?"

"You've gotta be kidding me. Standing around all day is for dumb-ass suckers. I'm a techno kinda guy myself. I go eBay all the way."

"That sounds interesting. So then, what are you doing up here with a shovel?" I asked, gesturing at the spade by his side. "Digging for gold?"

Mr. Butterfly chuckled, and then his face lit up. "You know what? This just might turn out to be your lucky day."

"How so?" I asked, dragging my eyes from his tattoo. I wondered how Miss Perfect's body would look when the skin on his arm began to sag. It seemed only fair that she should have to undergo the same trials and tribulations as every other woman.

"Because I think I've got a way for you to make some extra bucks. You'd also be helping me out."

"I already told you, I'm not that type of girl."

Part of me hoped he'd make a move, just so I could slam the guy to the ground and teach him a lesson.

Yeah, yeah. I know. You're a nature girl. So nature girl, how do you like butterflies?"

"I think they're very pretty."

"That's jim-dandy. But do you *know* anything about the little squirts?"

"Just that they fly from flower to flower."

"How'd you like to learn a whole lot more?"

"What for?" I asked, wondering where he was headed with this.

"Because they're worth big bucks." He held out his hand and grinned, exposing a chipped tooth. "The name's Mitch Aikens and I'm about to save your ass. Say hello to your new part-time employer."

"Wait a minute. What do I have to do?" I cautiously responded, having been caught by surprise.

"Relax, nature girl. I already told you that I do a little of this and a little of that. One of them is to breed and sell butterflies. All you've got to do is learn to be daddy's little helper. So, are you gonna tell me your name now? Or am I supposed to guess?"

"Sally Peters," I replied, making up the name as I shook his hand.

"Sally, huh? Whadda ya know? It must be fate. That's the name of my little sweetie here," he said, pointing to his arm.

Tattoo Sally's breasts bounced up and down as he again flexed his muscles. "I love it when she does that," Aikens said with a satisfied sigh.

No doubt about it. She was definitely the right woman for this guy.

"Okay, Sally. Here's the deal. I don't have time to raise these butterflies all by myself, what with everything else I've got going. Eggs are hatching 'round the clock, and they're demanding little buggers. Wait till you see. Those caterpillars can eat you out of house and home like there's no tomorrow. So what say I pay you to dig up certain types of plants and you feed the suckers for me? What the hell. You said you like nature, right? Well this'll give you plenty of time outside. Then you can go back to my place and make a few extra bucks. Just think of it as watching the beauty of

Mother Nature at work. Whadda ya say? Not a bad gig, huh?"

How could I refuse when this guy was nice enough to set my trap for me?

"Just one question. Is all this legal?" I asked, playing the part.

"Absolutely!" he exclaimed, raising his hands in a show of innocence. "Dealing in butterflies is the latest hot thing. Haven't you heard about those companies selling thousands of them to be released at special events? They're raking in a cool billion bucks a year and it's all perfectly legit. Hell, what I'm doing is small potatoes compared to that."

I'd heard plenty about it, all right. Live releases, in which hundreds of butterflies are set loose at bar mitzvahs, memorial services, corporate events, and even divorces, are a growing trend. Forget about tossing rice. Hurling butterflies has become the "in" thing to do when attending a wedding.

The gesture is meant to celebrate hope, transformation, and new beginnings. However, there are those who vehemently disagree. Experts from lepidopterist organizations to the National Audubon Society have declared war on the practice, branding it the "dark side" of butterfly popularity, and little more than a smokescreen for profit. Far worse is that it's a dangerous form of environmental pollution.

Butterfly populations are already plummeting due to poaching and habitat loss. The release of farmed butterflies only further complicates matters. Not only are migration patterns disrupted, but they spread disease among their relatives in the wild, while havoc runs rampant within their genetic makeup.

If that's not enough, ranched butterflies tend to be badly injured during shipment, so that they arrive at their destinations dead and dying. They tumble out of beribboned boxes with wings tattered and torn—all because they're viewed as nothing more than pretty ornaments.

"I'm not in that league, of course. My business is on a much smaller scale. I like to think that my specimens appeal to the discriminating collector. Which means I can't pay you a whole shitload of money. Unless you happen to stumble upon a rare butterfly or find some of its eggs. Then we'd be talking a whole different ball game."

Aikens let the suggestion dangle, clearly waiting to hear my response.

"Well, I take it that's why you're in the business of raising butterflies. To make money, right?"

"Correcto-mundo, nature girl. I can tell you're a fast learner. In which case, you might want to know how to use this little beauty."

Aikens whipped out a small aluminum tube that opened into a collapsible net. "Those of us in the biz refer to this as a National Park special." A Cheshire cat grin spread across his mouth, as if he were about to reveal a secret.

"Why is that?" I asked, knowing it would make his day.

"'Cause that's where you use it; in places where you can easily get caught. Okay, let's say I hear someone coming. Watch this. Whammo, bammo! The net instantly folds back into the tube so that I can quickly stash it away. That's just one little trick of the trade. I'll teach you others as we go along. But right now let me show you what kind of plants I want dug up."

The shovel bit into earth as Aikens tore out live plants and left bare holes in their place. I didn't tell him that such activity was illegal. He'd find out soon enough.

"Piece of cake, huh?" he remarked, stuffing a silvery bush with spiky blue flowers into his bag. "You're gonna have so much fun that you'll probably end up paying *me* just to let you continue. What say you follow me home now and I'll show you my setup?"

I began to traipse after him, when Aikens turned and tried to thrust the shovel into my hand.

"Here, carry this for me."

"Why? Am I being paid yet?" I retorted.

He stared at me and then broke into a chuckle. "I gotta tell ya, you got moxy, babe. I think we're gonna get along just fine together."

We headed back to the parking lot where Aikens homed in on a mini-Cooper as red as his hair. It would have been easy enough to guess which was his vehicle. The license plate bore the logo RED ELF, while a bumper sticker slapped on the rear fender bemoaned, WHY MUST I BE SURROUNDED BY FRICKIN' IDIOTS? Best of all was the I'm-having-a-bad-hair-day troll doll skewered on its antenna.

Aikens threw his shovel and backpack into the car, after which he pulled out an ice chest and showed me its contents. There were no sandwiches and sodas inside, but rather an array of butterflies, each shrouded in its own glassine envelope. They lay perfectly still, looking like colorful little corpses.

"Are they dead?" I asked, captivated by the rainbow assortment.

"Nah. I just gave them a tiny pinch on the thorax to stun them for now. That way they won't squirm around and damage their wings. I'll throw them in the fridge, and then the freezer, once I get home, to finish them off. Here's another tip for you. That's the best way to get perfect specimens."

I gazed at the lineup. Some butterflies were reddish orange, while others appeared copper brown with a purple sheen. Then there were those that had diagonal bands of yellow and black on their wings. Only one small butterfly was iridescent blue and lavender in color. There was something mesmerizing about the bug, even though its wingspan was only about an inch. I wondered if this was possibly the Mission blue butterfly that Mark Davis had told me about. Then I realized what I found to be so bewitching.

The world was now at a crossroads where even a tiny winged creature such as this tottered on the brink of extinction. I'd heard of butterflies referred to as barometers for the health of the planet. If so, what did the future hold for us as human beings? That thought remained with me as Aikens closed the lid.

Three

I followed the Red Elf toward Daly City. Its dense cluster of houses tumbled down the hillsides as if floating on a river of lava. Aikens parked in the driveway of a ticky-tacky dwelling with pink plastic flamingos and a black jockey holding a lantern on its front lawn. I got out of my Explorer and brought up the rear, strolling along a gnome-lined walkway to the entrance.

Talk about your eclectic mix. A suit of armor stood in the hallway guarding an array of Danish, Gothic, and Spanish this-looks-like-it's-been-through-a-bullfight furniture.

"Pretty cool, huh?" Aikens said, proudly showing it off. "Everything comes from storage units. I always keep the choice stuff for myself."

His sense of design was certainly unique. I promptly named it "eau de mishmash." The place definitely made me feel better about my own thrown-together digs.

It was then I caught sight of something moving toward us from out of the corner of my eye. Half tumbleweed/half sootball, the mobile mass of unkempt knots and fur never veered from its course. I'd have guessed it was Cousin It from *The Addams Family*, but for the fact that rather than two legs it had four.

Whatever it was sashayed up and rubbed against me. *How could a Brillo pad possibly move?* I wondered. Then the critter raised its head and purred. Whadda ya know? It was a walking, talking hairball. I bent down to pet the cat and my fingers got stuck in its fur.

"Hey, Ma! I'm home! We've got company, so make sure you're decent."

Ma? Aikens had to be joking. The man was far too old to be living with his mother. Besides, what sort of woman would put up with this mess?

I found out as Ma Aikens shuffled into view. Rail thin, the woman was an animated scarecrow dressed in jeans and a denim jacket, with a pair of terrycloth flip-flops on her feet. A cigarette, consisting mostly of ashes, dangled from her mouth. But it was her face that demanded my attention. This was why hairdressers, makeup artists, and plastic surgeons existed. Her kisser was puckered and lined from too much sun, smoke, and general unhappiness, while a lump of peroxided straw sat like a nest on top of her head.

"Do me a favor, kiddo," she said by way of greeting. "Marry my son and get him the hell out of here already, will ya? It's the only way I'll ever get this place clean."

Ma Aikens snickered at my startled expression.

"Tell you what. I'll make you a cup of coffee first. How's that sound? Come with me into the kitchen."

I did so out of sheer curiosity. It was well worth the trip. All the appliances—none of which had seen the wet side of a sponge for nearly forty years—were original, dating back to the 1960s. The hairball followed along. Jumping up, it licked at scraps of hardened food so old they'd become a permanent part of the stovetop. A package of chopped meat, long defrosted, sat waiting to be opened on the counter. I wondered if it was for tonight's dinner, considering that it was queasy gray in color.

Ma Aikens threw a teaspoon of freeze-dried coffee, half of which stuck to the spoon, into a stained cup. "It'll just take a few minutes for the water to boil. This stove doesn't work as well as it used to."

No problem there. I wasn't in a rush, since the kettle was blanketed in a layer of cat hair.

Aikens stuck his head in the doorway. "Hey Sally, stop dawdling and come into my bedroom. I want to show you the setup."

Ma Aikens flashed a gap-toothed grin. "That's my boy. Mitch doesn't waste a minute once he finds someone he wants."

In that case, I was grateful not to be the object of his desire.

"Go ahead. I'll bring your coffee in when it's ready. And don't worry. I promise to knock first," she said with a wink.

Oy veh. Who ever said there's somebody for everyone? I was tempted to ask where Pa Aikens was, but was afraid she might actually produce him.

I tiptoed around an obstacle course of junk on the floor, while following Mitch down the hallway.

He opened a door and we entered what appeared to be the room of no return. Had I not known better, I'd have sworn a bomb had gone off in the place. Clothes were strewn across almost every square inch of space. I stepped over boxes containing old watch crystals that, I imagined, Mitch was trying to sell on eBay.

My nose twitched at the whiff of a strange odor. It wasn't Lysol, food, or perspiration, but the stench of mildew tinged with cat urine. I traced the moldy scent to a decrepit computer chair, while the Brillo pad of a cat did his business in a this-has-never-been-emptied litter box. Had I really planned to work for Aikens, I'd have immediately upped my price.

"Don't pay any attention to the mess. You'll be working in an adjoining room."

Aikens pretended to cut a path through the morass with a machete as we made our way across the floor.

"Stay the hell out of here, Snowball!" he yelled at the feline, who tried to slip into the next room with us.

The cat hissed as Aikens slammed the door in its face.

I was relieved to find myself standing in a space relatively clean in comparison to the rest of the house. Lights were mounted in a row on one wall. They shone down on dozens of different receptacles, among them Tupperware containers, ice-cream cartons, and disposable paint buckets. Each had a swathe of chiffon netting draped over the top, as if it were a blushing bride hiding beneath a wedding veil.

"Let me give you a quick blow-by-blow of what's going on here," Aikens suggested. "I stick all butterfly eggs in the fridge for about three months at a temperature below forty degrees. That gets them to hatch into tiny larvae the size of pinheads. After that, I put roughly eighty of 'em in a yogurt container, where they begin to feed. Once they start to grow, I divvy them up into groups of twenty each. The main thing to remember is not to overcrowd the larvae. Otherwise they'll turn into nasty little cannibals. As for these overhead lights, they're all on timers so you don't have to worry about 'em. I've been doing this gig long enough to have gotten the process down to a science. The caterpillars do best with about sixteen hours of light and eight hours of darkness each day. I also maintain the room temperature and humidity to help them grow faster."

Aikens wasn't fooling around when it came to rearing butterflies. He had his own mini-factory for producing "hatch 'em, feed 'em and freeze 'em" winged specimens. I peeked into one of the paint buckets and found that a hole had been cut in its bottom to accommodate a large potted plant. The resident caterpillars were voraciously gnawing away at the leaves.

"Once the eggs hatch, you've gotta be with them on a regular basis for months at a time. They need constant attention, care, and feeding to keep them from getting disease. That'll also be part of your job," Aikens added.

We moved on to a fourteen-by-ten-inch plastic container in which a group of mature larvae were hungrily munching away on a pile of clippings. A symphony of tiny jaws could be heard chomping up and down if I stopped and held my breath. The crunch of vegetation followed the beat, beat, beat of larvae masticating in syncopation.

Aikens noticed that I was listening and softly chuckled. "Amazing, isn't it? Just wait until they all begin hatching and feeding. Sometimes I can actually hear them chewing up a storm as I walk into the house. I always thought it would make a great horror flick. Caterpillars growing into giant mutants that eat people, pickups, buildings. You know, everything in sight."

He picked up a small paintbrush and walked over to an aquarium where a bunch of pudgy caterpillars squirmed around.

"You're gonna have to do this too. So, watch closely, 'cause you don't want to hurt the little fellas."

Aikens meticulously cleaned inside the tank while carefully moving caterpillars out of the way. No wonder the guy needed help. This was a twenty-four-hour, around-the-clock job.

"Okay, now look at this," he said, pointing to one of the larger occupants. "This caterpillar's nearly ready to go into chrysalis. That's kinda like hibernation, or a cocoon stage. You'll see what I mean as we proceed with what I like to call my PBS nature tour."

But rather than continue on, Mitch suddenly leaned forward.

"Whoa, hold the phone. What the . . . Aw shit, I don't goddamn well believe this!" He spat and angrily stomped his feet.

"What's the matter?" I asked, unable to spot anything wrong.

"It's these damn parasitic wasps! Get a load of this, will ya?" Aikens instructed, jabbing a finger at the caterpillar.

Bending down, I placed my face close to the glass. I saw nothing unusual at first. Then my eyes opened wide in astonishment. A small wasp had somehow developed inside the caterpillar and was now gnawing its way out.

"How did that happen?" I asked, both repulsed and mesmerized by the sight.

"Outside, of course. Where else? I picked up this batch of larvae on San Bruno Mountain after they'd already hatched," Aikens explained in disgust. "A lousy parasitic wasp must have landed on the back of this caterpillar and laid a bunch of eggs under its skin. The offspring have it made in the shade after that. They grow up eating their host from the inside out, kinda like noshing on a Hungry Man meal. Pretty gross, huh?"

I didn't respond, but continued to watch as the insect ripped through the caterpillar's skin and slowly emerged out the side of its body. However, that wasn't the end. The already grotesque now took on even further nightmarish proportions. The wasp was closely followed by a band of its brothers, in the insect equivalent of the movie *Alien*. The stunned caterpillar gradually collapsed in a lifeless heap, having been turned into nothing more than a shell.

A rush of chills swept over me—and the debauchery still wasn't done. Having eaten their host alive, the little murderers now turned and stared at me with large buggy eyes, as though I might very well be their next victim. I stood up and backed away in revulsion.

"Yeah, I hate when that happens too. Kinda makes you wonder about God's sense of humor, doesn't it?" Aikens asked and slammed his fist down hard on each wasp. "Die you miserable little bastards," he intoned, grinding away until they were nothing but a smudge of dust. "I don't like to kill any of God's creatures, but nobody screws with my babies."

Then he wiped his hands clean on his pants.

"All aboard for the next stop," he said and motioned for me to follow.

We journeyed over to a large aquarium that held adult butterflies flaunting their wings in full glory.

"So, then you *do* keep some of them alive," I murmured, feeling slightly relieved.

"Yeah, just a choice few—until they mate and lay their eggs. Then it's off to the freezer with them. What the hell. They only live for a few weeks, anyway."

I kept my tongue in check, knowing that Aikens's head would soon enough be rolling.

"Here's something you'll find interesting. These in here are all males," he pointed out.

"How can you tell the difference?"

"I was hoping you'd ask. It's because females are wider on the bottom, of course." Aikens guffawed and slapped his thigh. "Nah, I'm just joshing with you. The easiest way to tell is by color difference. Males are usually brighter. Has anyone ever told you how they actually mate?"

I shook my head.

"Well, males search for a female just emerging from chrysalis, so that she's still limp. Her wings will be wet and are folded around her body. That's when he grabs his opportunity and quickly moves in. He flutters his wings and blows pheromones her way, hoping to seduce the little beauty. Then he presses up against her, belly-to-belly. Now she's his prey. A set of claspers pops out from his sides, which allows him to latch onto the female's body and open her wide. Then he has his way."

I found myself looking at male butterflies in a whole different light. "That sounds rather like date rape to me."

"Exactly," Aikens cheerfully agreed. "There's none of this take-me-to-dinner-and-a-movie-first crap. They just cut to the chase, the way it should be."

Aikens was turning out to be quite the charmer. No wonder the cheesy tattoo on his arm was his main gal pal.

"There's just a few more things for you to see."

He opened the door to a walk-in closet and turned on the light. Large cardboard boxes, all filled with transparent glassine envelopes, sat stacked on the floor. Each envelope contained its own perfectly preserved butterfly.

"I call this my stock room." Aikens smirked.

There had to be well over a thousand flawless little cadavers, all with wings stretched wide, as though waiting to take flight. Some were as exquisitely fragile as captive rays of light, while others resembled gaudy silver spangles on a woman's fancy gown. Then there were those black as night but for a brilliant burst of fireworks on the tips of their wings. Each competed for my attention while waiting to be added to someone's collection. It was a true testament to the fact that butterflies don't have an easy life. Rather it struck me as violent, hauntingly brief, and beset by a cycle of constant change.

"And here are my up-and-comers."

Aikens gestured toward a half dozen disposable paint buckets. All were lined with paper toweling and contained a number of twigs. However, it was the egg-shaped objects attached to them that captured my interest. Each was a perfect chrysalis. Some grew like miniscule fungi, while others were reminiscent of elongated teardrops.

But the most remarkable thing were the variety of colors in which they appeared. One chrysalis was yellow as ripe golden corn, while another resembled a crystal bead laden with orange and black spots. Also vying for my attention were shells bathed in an elegant shade of sea-foam green. A series of gold dots comprised a band on each of their ends, transforming the cocoons into precious pieces of jade jewelry. Every chrysalis was an exquisite gem. All but for one. The ugly duckling of the set had an exterior as brown and dry as a dead leaf.

"You wouldn't believe what goes on inside these little shells. The caterpillars melt down into this strange primordial goo. But the cool thing is that it's kinda like magic. You know, *hocus-pocus*, and a coupla weeks later, you've got yourself a hot-looking butterfly. There are more than a few ugly broads I know that should be so lucky. To tell you the truth, these things remind me of a bunch of Egyptian mummies cruising on a round-trip ticket to the afterworld. You'd swear they're dead, only to have 'em come back to life looking better than ever."

To my eye, it appeared as though they were snugly nestled inside little sleeping bags and floating along in the midst of a deep slumber. I couldn't help but wonder what butterflies dream about, and if we ever journey along the same celestial path.

How wonderful to take a long nap, shed your skin, and wake up to discover that you've become something altogether unique. How tempting it would be to leave one's old self behind. I envied the thought of being able to chuck my mistakes and begin anew. Of course, the downside was the risk of becoming one more bug stuck in a glassine envelope inside Aikens's closet.

My gaze wandered back to the drab, sad-sack chrysalis. Even in the insect world, life obviously wasn't fair. I made a wish that its occupant would emerge as the Cinderella of all butterflies.

"Go ahead. Touch it and see how it feels," Aikens urged, guiding my finger toward the desiccated shell.

There could be no denying that I was curious. I gave into

temptation and ran my finger ever so lightly along its rough, hard edge.

Creeeaaaakkkk!

My heart jumped at the sound of a coffin lid slowly being pushed open; only the noise had come from within the cocoon itself.

Aikens broke into a riff of amused laughter. "Didn't expect *that*, did you? There's a fully formed San Bruno elfin in there that's just about ready to pop. You disturbed its sleep, you bad girl, you. That sound was made by rubbing its legs together—which is about all the exercise that sucker's ever gonna get. Once its wings open, our little friend's off to the freezer for a good *l-l-o-o-n-ng* rest."

That did it. I'd had it with Aikens's crap, particularly in view of the fact that the San Bruno elfin was on the endangered list. Then there was the bug in Aikens's cooler. That was probably a Mission blue butterfly.

I turned to the redheaded leprechaun and skewered him with a cold stare. "Thanks for the tour, but I won't be accepting your job offer."

Aikens was momentarily taken back. Then his lips curled down in scorn. "Why not? Don't tell me you're gonna let a few little wasps scare you away. Or maybe that scratching sound gave you the heebie jeebies and you're not quite the nature girl that you thought. Of course, it could also be that you're really Miss Uptight Prissy and I somehow offended you. No, wait a minute. I know what it is—you're probably jealous because the butterflies are getting more nookie than you are. No *problemo*, doll. It just so happens I can help you out with that."

It was time to squash this troll doll like the repellant vermin that he was.

"Sorry to disappoint you, but it's none of the above." I pulled out my badge and flashed it in his face. "I'm Rachel

Porter, a special agent with the U.S. Fish and Wildlife Service, and I've just caught you in my net."

Aikens's jaw dropped in shock. "Sonofabitch! What is it with you people, anyway? Don't you have anything better to do than harass small businessmen who are only trying to make an honest living? I have a good mind to call my local congressman and raise hell about how my tax dollars are being spent!"

"Feel free. They already know how to contact me," I dryly informed him. "Except I wouldn't call dealing in endangered species making an honest day's wage."

"What are you talking about?" Aikens sputtered. "Everything in this place is perfectly legit. No way would I ever do something illegal. Not when a pain in the ass like you could be lurking behind every bush."

"Ahh. Now you're just trying to flatter me and make nice. Let me give you a piece of advice. Playing the innocent victim isn't going to work. Not when you've got an endangered San Bruno elfin stashed in the closet and a Mission blue cooling its wings in your ice chest," I bluffed, hoping my guess was correct. "You're in deep trouble, Aikens. This is going to cost you big-time."

"I don't damn well believe this," he muttered, pile driving his fingers through his bushy mound of hair. Then he defiantly threw back his shoulders and puffed out his chest. "Aw, come on. Who are we kidding with this? Let's get real here. We're talking a few lousy butterflies. Big fucking deal. It's not like I'm hacking ivory tusks off elephants or mowing down rhinos for their horns. For chrissakes, get a grip. What do you think my pissy little crime is gonna amount to anyway? Maybe a couple hours of community service, or a minor fine at most. Worse comes to worst, I'll plead entrapment. I can see it in the papers now: 'Hardworking businessman set up by self-styled Fish and Wildlife Mata

Hari.' That oughta sell a few rags and bump up my business in the process."

I didn't know whether he was trying to convince himself, or me—but my only hope was to outfox him.

"Good thinking, Mitch," I said and pulled a tape recorder from my bag. "You might have a point, if you were just a small-time collector. There's only one problem. I have our entire conversation on tape—including your offer to pay me more money to catch protected butterflies and collect their eggs. That's illegal, whether you agree with it or not."

I was hoping that Aikens wasn't terribly savvy when it came to the law and my legal limitations. Not to mention that there wasn't any tape in the machine. I quickly dumped the recorder back in my bag before he had a chance to check.

Aikens took a moment to size up the situation, as his shoulders slowly began to slump.

"All right, all right. So let's make a deal." He finally caved, flapping his arms in the air like a pair of wings.

Whadda ya know? The ruse had actually worked.

"Listen, I'm nothing but chump change in the big scheme of things. My stuff is mostly legit. You can look inside those boxes and see that for yourself."

Instead, I gave him the evil eye—an unspoken warning not to jerk me around.

"Aw, come on, Porter. There are a lot larger fish for you to fry. Guys that deal in endangered butterflies big time, not just for a few lousy bucks. We're talking *mucho dinero*. I'm telling ya, they're selling rare bugs to the Krauts, the Japs, the Canucks, the Aussies, and a whole bunch of others. Go ahead. Name any nationality you like."

I should have known I could count on Aikens to be politically correct.

"That's not the way the game is played, Mitch. You're supposed to give *me* names. Remember? So, who are these guys?"

"Whoa, whoa, whoa. You're jumping the gun here. That's information I don't have yet."

"Gee, that's too bad. I can't tell you how unhappy that makes me." I dug into my bag and pulled out a pair of handcuffs.

"Getting kinky on me, huh? Okay, now you're turning me on." Aikens laughed nervously "So, who gets to wear them first? Me or you?"

What betrayed him was the twitching of his eye.

"Very funny, Aikens. I'm sure the bubba who ends up sharing your jail cell will get a real kick out of that one." I made a move to cuff him.

"Okay, okay! I get the point. Just give me some time and I swear I'll get you the names."

There was no question but that Aikens would receive little more than a slap on the wrist from any court should I ticket him. He'd prove far more valuable to me as an informant. The trick was to make him believe otherwise.

I let loose a sigh and skeptically shook my head. "I don't know. I'd really be putting myself on the line for you. It's not public information yet, but Fish and Wildlife has a new policy about coming down hard on butterfly poachers. It's been a number of years since the last good case and they're anxious to set an example."

"For chrissakes, Porter. I can deliver. You've gotta believe me." A trickle of sweat broke out on his upper lip.

Half of me believed him and half of me didn't. Still, I needed someone like Aikens if I was ever going to be redeemed for the botched reptile shipment. Clearly, the air courier's death could never be rectified.

"Then here's the deal. You're not to catch or raise anymore endangered butterflies. And believe me, I'll know because I intend to stop by and check."

The truth was I'd never be able to tell one type of caterpillar from another. The only giveaway would have to be what they ate, since both San Bruno elfins and Mission blues feed on very specific plants.

"Sure, no problem," Aikens agreed, his tongue lapping up a wayward bead of sweat.

"By the way, those butterflies in your ice chest? I'll be taking them with me when I leave."

"What the hell for?"

"I'm going to drive back up to San Bruno Mountain and release them."

"What, are you kidding me?" Aikens gasped, beginning to hyperventilate.

"Why? What's the problem? You said yourself that they're not dead, but only stunned. Those butterflies are far more valuable back in the wild where they can breed than lying pinned in a case in someone's collection. Oh yeah, and as for the chrysalis of that San Bruno elfin? You'd better make sure that butterfly stays alive once it hatches, because I fully intend to release it as well."

"What are you doing? You're killing me here!" Mitch protested. "You're taking all my heavy hitters. How am I supposed to pay the bills? Huh? You ever stop to think about that? Aw jeez, and I promised to buy Ma a new vibrating chair for her birthday. Those babies were gonna bring me in some much-needed bucks."

"Thanks for reminding me. That's the other thing. I want the names and addresses of those people that were lined up to buy your elfin and Mission blue specimens."

Mitch raised his hands, as if to fend me off. "No can do."

"Wrong answer," I responded in a threatening tone.

"Hey, cool your jets, Porter. It's just that I don't have any takers for the hot stuff yet."

I sincerely doubted that, but there wasn't much I could do to prove it at the moment.

"Sorry, but I'm afraid you're going to have to come up with something better. I really want to trust you, Aikens. But my boss will kill me if I walk out of here empty-handed. You've got to give me a piece of information as a show of good faith before I leave."

"You mean other than letting you take my most valuable butterflies?" he muttered.

"First of all, you're not *letting* me take them. I'm keeping you out of *jail*. Let's get that straight. Now give me a name." I menacingly rattled the handcuffs.

"Yeah, yeah. I'm thinking." Aikens scratched his chin with two grubby fingers. "Okay. There's this guy that goes by a weird handle. Calls himself Horus. Or at least that's what other collectors call him. Don't ask me why. Anyway, word has it he sells the kind of rare butterflies that no one else can find. Seems he's got the magic touch. All I know is that the guy lives somewhere here in Northern California."

"Thanks for narrowing down the territory for me. So, have you ever bought anything from him?"

"Me? No way. Uh-uh," Aikens responded a bit too emphatically. "His prices are way too rich for my blood. Besides, I've heard that he's very discriminating when it comes to his clientele. Only deals with big-money A-list collectors. You know, the kind that'll drop five, ten thou without giving it a second thought. If you're looking to nab one of the head honchos in the butterfly trade, then this is your man."

Either that, or Aikens was hoping to knock a competitor out of his path.

"That's still not good enough," I replied, yanking his chain.

Aikens stared in disbelief, as if I'd lost all my marbles. "Whadda ya talking about? I'm giving you the Hope diamond here. Didn't you hear a word I just said?"

I jangled the cuffs once more, enjoying the sensation of them in my hands.

"All right, but you better find out a whole lot more about this Horus and do it quick."

Horus, huh? He could have called himself Ali Baba or Dick Cheney for all I cared. What mattered was that this guy was going to be my ticket out of purgatory.

I picked up the ice chest, opened the door to Aikens's bedroom, and nearly tripped over the cat. The pervading stench raced into my nose, giving me a whole new respect for household deodorizing products. I decided right then and there that part of Mitch's punishment would be to make him clean up his room and change the kitty litter.

Then I hotfooted it down the hallway, but not fast enough. Ma Aikens caught me as she walked out of the kitchen with two mugs in hand.

"Hey, where are you going so soon? I just made us a coupla cups of joe. We didn't get a chance to bond yet."

"Sorry, but I'm already late for an appointment. I'll have to take a rain check," I apologized, balancing the ice chest on one knee while trying to open the front door.

But Ma Aikens had a desperate look in her eye. "Hang on there a minute. I'm sure we can work something out. Mitch isn't such bad husband material when you stop and think about it—particularly for a girl your age. After all, it's not like you're twenty-five and still have the pick of the litter."

The woman was lucky I had my hands full; otherwise, I'd have been tempted to deck her. Instead, I rushed out to my Ford, placed the cooler in the back and took off, heading for San Bruno Mountain. Only then did I allow myself to think back on what Aikens had said.

He was right. Butterfly collecting didn't have the same negative connotation attached to it as harpooning whales, killing tigers for their parts, or shooting tame gazelles on hunting ranches. But then there had also been plenty of buffalo roaming around on the Western plains two hundred years ago, until man got through with them. For that reason alone, endangered species deserve protection, and rare butterflies certainly fit into that category.

One thing that's remained consistently true is that whenever there's money to be made, wildlife has always been on the losing end—and the rarer the animal, the bigger the profit. Aikens was just one more greedy consumer plundering the resources for his own personal gain.

I finished my drive up San Bruno Mountain, parked in the lot and opened the ice chest. There on top lay the same collection of comatose butterflies that I'd seen earlier in the day. Wings spread open, they dozed in glassine envelopes, their colors even more exquisite than I had previously remembered. It became immediately apparent why people are so enchanted by their beauty. Being alone, I now took the time for a closer inspection.

I instantly recognized the monarch, a butterfly as regal as its name, with brownish orange wings outlined in black. Another one had silver patches on the underside, making me wonder if it might not be a threatened San Francisco silverspot. But the butterfly I remained most enamored of was the dainty blue and lavender specimen. Aikens had as much as admitted by his silence that this was the endangered Mission blue butterfly. How strange to be in the presence of one of the last of its kind, and know that it might soon vanish.

I gathered all the envelopes and trudged back once more to the meadow, this time carrying a treasure trove of living riches with me. The other difference was that the grassland was now golden, reflecting the glow of the gilded sun.

I sat down in the grass and spread out the envelopes before me. Then I carefully ripped them open, one by one. The butterflies slowly awoke from their deep slumber, as if magically revived by the warmth of the sun. Each fluttered its wings and took off to resume the life of which it had nearly been robbed. Only the Mission blue lagged behind to momentarily light on my arm.

I held my breath and didn't move, hoping to freeze time. Funny the games we play. I tried to make a deal with God, asking that for every moment my winged friend stayed like this the impending doom of a mammal, a bird, or a butterfly be reversed. But the Mission blue chose not to linger.

It was then I remembered a tale I'd once heard. Whisper a wish to a butterfly and it will journey to heaven, where your request will be granted. I softly murmured my heart's desire: that all those creatures I loved so much be saved. Then I took a deep breath and quickly exhaled, hoping to help the Mission blue on its way. My plan must have worked, for within the blink of an eye, the beating speck of blue vanished into the deep azure sky.

I dialed the car phone and checked my voice mail while heading home. The sole message was from my boss. He always liked to hear that the weekends were quiet. I returned his call, having decided to keep the information I'd learned to myself for now. The reason was simple. I was hoping to protect my ass.

"All clear on the western front?" Agent Brad Thomas asked, after we'd said our hellos.

"More or less," I responded. "There was just one phone call. A tip about a guy netting butterflies on San Bruno Mountain."

"Did you follow it up?"

There it was: I could already hear the tension building in his voice. Thomas had made it perfectly clear there was to be no more trouble while I remained on his watch. I'd become known as a liability within the Service that no resident agent in charge wanted to touch. Thomas was simply the latest in a long line of managers on whom I'd been dumped.

The timing for him couldn't have been worse. He'd hoped to lay low for the next twelve months until his retirement.

"The guy claimed to be innocent, so I just gave him a warning," I fudged, choosing not to mention what had really taken place. Thomas would doubtless put the kibosh on my work with Aikens should he get wind of it.

Any leeway I'd once had went up in flames along with the disastrous results of my controlled delivery. Ever since then I'd received strict orders to do nothing but write up tickets on simple violations. That being the case, I figured why give Thomas any unnecessary agita?

"Good," Thomas replied, with an audible sigh of relief. "That's what I like to hear. Things will be fine as long as you keep your nose clean."

I chafed at the words, but kept my mouth shut. It was clear I'd become Fish and Wildlife's number-one scapegoat. I could live with that. But what stuck in my craw were my boss's recent words of warning.

There are more important things than making cases.

Not to my mind, there weren't. It made me brazen enough to stick a toe into the murky waters of "things that I might be allowed to do" and see how far I could push it.

"By the way, the man that called with the tip was Dr. Mark Davis from Stanford University's Center for Conservation Biology.

"Uh-huh," Thomas indifferently responded.

So far, so good. Even better, I could hear a ball game playing on his TV in the background. Maybe he'd be distracted enough to agree to let me do some work.

"Davis mentioned that one of his colleagues, Dr. John Harmon, was hired as a consultant by Fish and Wildlife. Harmon went up to Mendocino two weeks ago to search for the Lotis blue butterfly. The problem is, nobody's heard from him since."

Apparently, Thomas wasn't as distracted as I had hoped.

"Yeah, I'd been told there was going to be a final look-see for that thing. But I'm sure if something were wrong the Mendocino County Sheriff's Department would already be looking into it. Besides, our division didn't hire him. Most likely, it was the Endangered Species Office. Let them deal with whatever's going on. He's not our responsibility."

"Well, seeing as how I've never been to Mendocino, and tomorrow's my day off, I thought I might take a run up there," I casually suggested.

"Go! Go! Go! That ball is out of here!" Thomas erupted, at the sound of a bat solidly smacking against a ball. "Yeah, fine. Play tourist all you want. Just make sure you do it on your own time."

"Out of curiosity, do you happen to know the area where Harmon was conducting his search?" I gingerly questioned, as the crowd on TV broke into a roar.

"Huh? Oh, I heard there were a few spots that were going to be checked. The person who probably knows the Lotis blue best is an entomologist up in that area by the name of Bill Trepler. The problem is, he's impossible to deal with. The old bastard despises Fish and Wildlife nearly as much as he hates endangered species."

"Oh yeah? Why is that?"

"Let's just say he's a biologist who's gone over to the dark side."

I immediately got an image of Darth Vader carrying a butterfly net.

"You want to translate that for me?"

"For chrissakes, Porter. He hires himself out as a consultant to private developers. They pay him to make sure that neither Fish and Wildlife nor endangered species bring a halt to any construction projects on their land."

"And Trepler can guarantee that?"

"So far he's batting a thousand," Thomas confirmed. "We can't get on private land without proof that an endangered species is there. Trepler's a conservation biologist with the credentials and chops to give developers a clean bill of health. I hear the guy earns around four thousand dollars a day testifying before planning commissions, in court, and making sure that environmental impact reports go their way. He's the man these guys call upon whenever they're in pitched battles over land use."

"It all sounds rather sordid to me."

"Maybe so. But then again, it's not your problem. Take my advice, Porter. You want to go up to Mendocino? Fine. Walk around town, buy a souvenir, have a nice meal. Just stay the hell out of trouble."

I didn't respond, and a moment of awkward silence grew between us.

"Sorry, Porter. I'm just blowing off steam. I'm a little anxious these days, is all. So, you caught a guy collecting a few butterflies. No biggie, right?"

"No biggie," I agreed.

My spirits sank, knowing that Thomas was probably correct. Who was I kidding, other than myself? I'd gone from high-flying cases to chasing down a guy with a net and cooler. There could no longer be any doubt that my career was going nowhere. It had been put on ice, as surely as those butterflies I'd just released.

Four

San Francisco is a city built upon forty-two hills; a sculpture of vertiginous landscape. It has eight miles of steep inclines that plummet into wide valleys, linked by roughly three hundred and fifty stairways. This whimsical package drops off at the edge of the continent and into the arms of a beautiful bay.

San Francisco is also cold in the summer and warm in winter. Perhaps that's partly why Kipling called it a mad city inhabited by perfectly insane people. From what I could tell, he wasn't far off the mark. After all, what other town could lay claim to having spawned Jim Jones and his People's Temple, along with the Manson family—in addition to being the land of Rice-A-Roni and cable cars?

Not only is San Francisco where topless dancing began, but it's also the birthplace of the Symbionese Liberation Army, the Sierra Club, martinis and Irish coffee. The city is a stronghold of tolerance, eccentricity, and individualism—which is probably why so many people liken it to those twin Biblical hotspots, Sodom and Gomorrah. Even Sara Jane Moore chose to make her assassination attempt on President Ford here on its streets. It's true. There's no other place quite like San Francisco in the world.

I'd heard it said that God had deliberately tilted the continent so that all the wackos would end up in this place.

Maybe so. San Francisco is a haven for aging hippies, beat-niks, and drag queens. Then again, I'd lived in Miami, New York, and New Orleans and had loved each of them for those very same qualities. I felt best in a city that let its residents breathe free. Besides, if it was good enough for Robin Williams and Sharon Stone, then San Francisco was proba-bly good enough for me.

I zipped through the southern end of the city and headed for the ornate dragon-crested gateway marking the entrance into Chinatown. Once there, I drove under the touristy arch-way that could have been filched from a bad movie set. The next instant, I was transported into a different world—one filled with exotic sights, scents, and sounds.

Thirty thousand residents crowd Chinatown's twenty-four blocks each day, shopping for things such as herbal teas, live birds, and fermented duck eggs. My tires rolled over scads of red paper strewn in the streets. It was firecracker debris from the last Chinese New Year celebration, held over three months ago. As of yet, no one had bothered to clean it up, believing the litter to be a harbinger of good fortune. Sweep-ing the rubbish would only have brought bad luck. Instead, storekeepers waited for the wind to blow the mess away.

Clotheslines filled with fresh laundry hung tautly strung across ornate iron balconies. Below them, restaurants tempted me with their sweet fragrance of Peking duck. More densely populated than any other neighborhood, this is home to the largest Asian population in the West. But it's only one fragment in San Francisco's seductive mosaic.

I sped up Grant and crossed Broadway to enter the old community of North Beach. A former haven for writers and artists, its population was once eighty percent Italian. How-ever, those days are long gone. Now its tiny streets are filled with an influx of Asians. No matter. Espresso machines still perk and hiss, their vapors blending with the aroma of fresh-baked sourdough bread, prosciutto and home-made spaghetti sauce—an intoxicating mixture that rushed straight to my head.

I passed signs placed by staunch locals adamant that Columbus Avenue be called Corso Cristofo Columbus. But the attempt to mark their territory didn't stop there. Utility poles were bedecked with red, white, and green stripes in honor of the Italian flag. Alas, it was all to no avail. North Beach was already well on its way to becoming a satellite bedroom community of Chinatown. As if that weren't enough, there was even a female Jewish wildlife agent living in their midst these days.

I turned right onto Union Street and drove up toward Telegraph Hill. Coit Tower loomed ahead. San Francisco's more straightlaced residents claimed the monument had been designed to resemble a firehose nozzle. But those in the know revealed it was really modeled after a prominent part of the male anatomy. What's more, the money for its construction had been donated by a notorious female cross-dresser.

I swung into the driveway of a three-story white stucco house that clung to the hill like one in a row of gumdrops. Kicking open the vehicle door, I rolled out, having already adjusted to spending half of my life on a slant.

This was where I now lived—though you'd never have guessed it by the reception. My landlady's white dog lay in its usual spot near the front door, lounging in a sheepskin-lined wicker basket. The pooch's attitude was that of a pissed-off old man jealously guarding his territory.

The only way to tell the mutt from the rug was when he snarled, revealing a set of misshapen yellow teeth. The runt was a nasty bundle of terror with rheumy eyes, thinning fur, and breath like rotten meat.

I never had to ask if he wanted a piece of me. The game was always the same. The wizened maniac waited until the very last second, and then made a lunge for my leg. Evidently that supplied him with a large-enough dose of testosterone to keep his little heart going pitter-patter.

The mutt's behavior reminded me of an old Italian godfather. The pooch shrewdly maintained his status by acting as if he were a vicious rottweiler. It was for that reason I found the dog's name—Tony Baloney—to be both clever and fitting.

I scooted around the pooch and let myself in the front door. Then I squeezed past the five-foot potted palm that stood in the middle of the floor. The hall led directly to the rear of the house, causing my Chinese landlady to fear all the good *chi* inside would escape out the back door. The palm was her own homemade version of a *chi* barrier in what amounted to an obstacle course.

I hit the staircase and began my ascent up to the second floor.

"You get a reward when you reach the top."

Terri Tune, my longtime best friend and former landlord, leaned over the balustrade looking as fetching as ever. His blond wig hadn't aged one bit. Neither had his figure, which was still lean and fit. He wore a red kimono, ostrich feather mules, and lured me on with a piña colada topped with a colorful paper parasol.

"Here you go, sweetie. You deserve this after having worked on Saturday. Besides, I heard you took quite a beating in class this morning."

"True. But I gave it back twice as good." I grinned, and reached for the glass.

"That's my girl. Why bother to work out unless you can get to kick a little ass every now and then? Anyway, the exercise is obviously paying off. You look terrific," Terri praised like a mother hen. "Now hurry inside. Jake's already polished off his first piña colada and is beginning to scarf down all the hors d'oeuvres."

I stopped dead in my tracks. "I thought we'd discussed this, Terri. You know that I don't want Jake to drink while he's taking so many painkillers."

Terri shook his curls and clucked his tongue. "If you want to go in there and lay down the law, be my guest. But you've got to remember that he's a big boy, Rach. Maybe you should give him some leeway, what with everything he's been through. After all, it's not as though he has a death wish. Correct me if I'm wrong, but we haven't had to rush to the hospital yet and get his stomach pumped. So why don't you try loosening up a bit?"

That was easier said than done. Still, I'd met with enough resistance on Santou's part to know that I was in for an uphill battle.

"Just try to keep an eye on him, all right? Believe me, Jake's not as happy-go-lucky as he pretends to be."

I hated playing the role of enforcer after Terri had flown all the way from Memphis to help me. Santou's recuperation had been slow so far, and he still wasn't out of the woods. Not when he kept popping Vicodan and Percoset as though they were Flintstones Vitamins.

The only thing making me feel less guilty was that Terri had claimed to need a change of pace. Vincent, his significant other, was crazy busy after opening a branch of his wrestling school in Miami. But the real kicker was that Terri's own business, Yarmulke Schlemmer, was in deep trouble. The company had been hit with a lawsuit, accused of stealing designs for their doggy yarmulkes.

Terri had a network of friends in San Francisco. However, he'd chosen to pay a weekly rate for the apartment directly above mine. It was dirt cheap in a city of exorbitant rents. There was a good reason for it. The place had no kitchen. As a result, Terri spent the majority of his time downstairs. It worked out well for the both of us. Not only did he help me with Santou, but my space was cleaner than it would have been otherwise. He also made sure there was always plenty of food in the fridge.

"Hey, chère. How'd it go today?" Santou asked, flashing a carefree smile as I walked into the room.

His vials of Vicodan and Percoset sat on the TV stand beside an empty glass. No wonder he was so relaxed. Jake caught the direction of my stare and scowled, letting me know how he felt about my reaction.

Santou had taken refuge in prescription drugs ever since the accident. At first it had been for physical pain. Now it was a crutch for emotional trauma.

Jake had insisted on getting back to work as soon as possible, anxious to feel normal again. What he hadn't counted on was being stuck behind a desk doing paperwork. I could always tell when his patience had reached its breaking point; he'd consume more pills and booze than usual. That's when he'd remind me of Tony Baloney. Santou would bark in frustration and Terri and I would jump, trying to find a way to help. Sympathetic as we were, his problems needed to be dealt with professionally. Though I'd broached the subject, Santou had so far stubbornly resisted.

"It was your average day. I caught some guy poaching butterflies on San Bruno Mountain and decided to flip him into an informant. I figure it'll prove more worthwhile than writing him up on a violation that will probably get thrown out of court."

I began to walk past Santou when he grabbed hold of my hand.

"You do know the upside to all this is, don't you? At least I got transferred to San Francisco so that we can be together."

There it was—the reason why I loved the man so much.

Jake turned my hand over and pressed his lips to my palm, sending a wave of heat rushing through me. Unbelievable.

The man could still make my legs go weak at any given moment. Santou knew it as well and flashed a lascivious smile, basking in his effect on me.

"Dinner is served, children. Come and get it," Terri called out, breaking the spell.

Terri's version of cooking was a lot like mine. Tonight we had chicken scallopine takeout.

"Seriously, chère. I want to hear more about what happened this afternoon," Jake said, as we sat down and began to eat.

The chicken was terrific. Boy, was Santou in for a rude awakening the day that I finally started cooking for him.

"The call that came in this morning? It was from a Stanford University professor. He not only tipped me off about a butterfly poacher, but also mentioned that one of his colleagues is missing."

"What do you mean, missing?" Santou asked, his curiosity piqued.

"Some guy by the name of Dr. John Harmon went up to Mendocino about two weeks ago on assignment for Fish and Wildlife. He'd been hired to search for an endangered butterfly. That's the last anyone has heard from him."

"There could be any number of reasons for that. Maybe he has money problems and decided to lay low for a while," Jake speculated. "Does he happen to be married?"

I nodded, remembering the information I'd been given.

"Possibly he's spending time with another woman and doesn't want his wife to know."

"Or it could be another man," Terri interjected.

"If something were wrong, I'm sure the county sheriff would know about it," Jake added.

"Great. Now you sound just like my boss."

"Heaven forbid. We wouldn't want that, what with the way you feel about him," Santou said with a laugh. "Tell you what. I'll keep my ear to the ground and let you know if any information comes through the office."

"Fair enough. In the meantime, I thought I'd take a ride up to Mendocino tomorrow. Anyone interested in coming along?"

"Hell, that's a three-hour drive each way, chère. You know my back will never make it."

I was tempted to snipe that if he went to a physical therapist and cut out the pills and booze, it would help speed up his recovery. However, I kept my mouth shut, having been through that argument only last night.

"I'll go with you, Rach," Terri offered. "I might as well see what the northern coastline looks like."

"Terrific," I said.

That would give me quality time with Terri, while Jake found out how much fun it was to spend an entire day alone. It might prove to be the wake-up call that he needed. Only when he dropped the I-can-tackle-this-problem-on-my-own attitude, and got some serious help, would his condition ever improve.

Just the possibility made me feel good enough to eagerly jump up and begin my usual slap-dash job of washing dishes. I figured why slave over such things? They were only going to get dirty again, anyway.

Terri picked up one of the plates I'd just washed and gave it the once-over.

"Sparkling clean as usual," he wryly noted, and began to scrub it himself. "Remind me to buy my own set of silverware and dishes so that at least one of us doesn't come down with a mysterious ailment that's traced back to eating off dirty dinnerware."

I remembered Ma Aikens's kitchen and had to agree that Terri probably had a point.

"Now I'm going upstairs to make myself absolutely gorgeous."

Terri already looked good enough to make me feel like who-dragged-that-inside roadkill.

"Why? Are you going out with friends tonight?" I asked, feeling slightly envious.

"As a matter of fact, I've decided to get a part-time job at one of the trendy transvestite clubs downtown. I can use a little extra spending money, what with that damn lawsuit pending. Besides, getting out will help spruce up my social life."

That was enough to set off a series of alarm bells in my head. I hadn't realized Terri planned on staying in San Francisco for quite so long. Not only that, but he already had a circle of friends in the area. Unless there was something going on with Vincent that he hadn't told me about.

Terri quickly picked up on my line of thought.

"Vincent and I had a little tiff on the phone last night. Let him see what life is like without me for a while." He sniffed. "You know how men can be, constantly taking you for granted. Well, I've decided it's time to rock his boat a bit."

I couldn't help but feel dumbfounded. Terri had never let on that something might be wrong. Was I so wrapped up with my own problems that I could no longer tell when my best friend was going through a crisis? Talk about feeling remorse. If I were Catholic, I'd have won hands-down as the patron saint of guilt.

"Just don't go getting any ideas about teaching *me* a lesson, chère," Santou teased. "My boat's already been rocked quite enough. I'd hate to have to go through another plane crash and crawl back out in order to prove how much I love you."

"Very funny," I retorted, still not used to Jake's newly morbid sense of humor.

"Listen, I've got an idea. Why don't the two of you join me? You could probably both use an evening on the town," Terri suggested.

"Count me out. All I want to do is watch TV and get a good night's sleep. But why don't you go with him, chère? It would be good for you to blow off some steam. Don't worry. I'll be perfectly fine by myself."

"Are you sure?" I asked, ready to kill myself if I spent one more night planted in front of the Sports Channel.

"Absolutely." Jake chuckled. "Anything that'll keep us from duking it out over the remote control."

Ah, domestic bliss. Who'd have ever guessed it would come down to TV programming and bickering over who should have bought an extra roll of toilet paper?

"In that case, I'll see you in an hour, Rach. Get yourself ready," Terri said, and headed upstairs.

Terrific. I was being left on my own to perform a minor miracle. I walked into the bathroom and studied my image in the mirror. Who was I kidding? We were talking a major overhaul here. The weather had turned my hair into a mop of thick frizz, and I felt as though there were caterpillars crawling on my skin. That led to a flashback of the parasitic wasps, causing a shiver to race through me. From there it was an easy leap to the movie *Alien*. I tore off my clothes and jumped into the shower, half expecting a drooling monster to pop out of my chest.

A half hour later, my entire wardrobe was no longer hanging in the closet but thrown in a heap on the bed. It never seems to matter how many garments I have, or how recently they were bought. Murphy's Law decrees that nothing should ever fit.

I finally settled on a pair of low-rider jeans and a brand-new top. However, my hair remained a sullen child that stubbornly refused to behave. I was still battling with it when

Terri walked in the room. I felt all the more fashion challenged as I caught sight of the million-dollar babe.

Terri could easily have given J-Lo, Sharon Stone, and Cindy Crawford a run for their money. He was dressed in a low-cut blouse and a tight leather skirt with a slit running halfway up his thigh. No wonder I secretly wanted to pattern myself after him. Even Santou sat up straight in his chair and took note.

"Holy mother," he whistled. "Why don't you try dressing a little more like that, chère?"

I threw Jake a dirty glance and he wisely clammed up.

"Don't tell me that you're not ready yet," Terri groaned.

I didn't admit that he was looking at the finished product.

"It's my hair. It refuses to do a thing," I complained.

"Oh, for God's sake, Rach. That's easy enough to fix," Terri scolded.

He took me into the bathroom and promptly set to work. Ten minutes later, even I was impressed. Terri had not only tamed my curls, but also transformed my top into a chic off-the-shoulder number. Then he put the finishing touches on my makeup.

"There. See how easy that was?" Terri asked, stepping back to admire his creation. "Your new mantra should be to spend less time playing with guns and more time fixing yourself up."

"Yeah, except that a make-over won't get me out of a tight spot," I smartly retorted.

"Maybe not. But then again, a gun isn't going to stop someone from thinking that you're old enough to be Britney Spears's mother. Meanwhile the proper hair, clothes, and makeup certainly will," Terri wisely advised.

I considered that to be an exceptionally low blow, until I walked back into the living room and was greeted by Santou's reaction.

"Whoa, chère! You're going to have to use the Krav Maga you've learned to fight the guys off. Just don't forget that I'm here waiting for you."

That was enough to make me feel as seductively hot as one of Charlie's Angels. My exhilaration overcame any remorse about leaving Jake at home. That is, until the door closed behind us, and my guilt kicked in. It was at times like this that I worried Santou might be tempted to take one too many pills, feeling lonely and depressed. Worst of all, it was my fault that he was in this situation. Terri had heard it all before, but I still had to vent.

"I don't care what anyone says. I'm afraid Jake's becoming addicted to painkillers. I can't help it, Terri. Seeing him like this makes me crazy. The truth is, he wouldn't have been on that plane if he hadn't transferred to Savannah. I keep kicking myself in the rear over that."

"Enough already. I know it's natural for you to worry, what with being Jewish and the *oy veh* factor. But honestly, sweetie, you've got to stop beating yourself up over this. Santou's not going to spin out of control, and he's never going to do himself in. Otherwise, he wouldn't have crawled out of that plane in the first place. Jake's just impatient to get better is all, and he eventually will. But you're both going to have to learn to relax and give it time."

Here I was doing it again—worrying about myself when Terri obviously had problems of his own.

"Thanks, Ter. Now I want to know what's really going on with you and Vincent."

I must have caught Terri off guard, because his eyes welled up with tears.

"Oh, Rach. That bastard's gotten involved with some beefy young wrestler. One of his students. Can you believe it? Christ, it's like a bad plot straight out of an old Joan Crawford film. In fact, I'm identifying with her so much these days that just the sight of a wire hanger sends me into a tizzy."

"Are you certain about this, Terri?" I asked. Vincent had seemed head over heels the last time I'd seen the two of them together.

"Absolutely. I found a sequined jockstrap in Vincent's drawer that certainly wasn't mine, and it sure as hell wasn't his size. I got so upset that I donned a brunette wig and followed the two of them after wrestling class one afternoon. Vincent took his hot new stud to a chichi restaurant in South Beach, where they drank martinis and fed each other oysters on the half shell. The only thing that stopped me from making a scene was that I looked more like Rosie O'Donnell than Madonna that day. After that, they went back to Eduardo's apartment, where Vincent spent the next two hours."

"What did he say when you confronted him?"

"Vincent lied of course. What else? Do you believe he had the nerve to tell me that they were working on a new wrestling persona for Eduardo? Naturally, I asked if that included hands-on training in bed."

I laced my arm through his. "I'm so sorry, Ter. I thought Vincent was different than that."

"Thanks, sweetie. Me too. I guess some men are just downright deceptive, no matter how decent they might seem."

"You'll meet someone who's right for you," I said, and gave his arm a squeeze.

He nodded and took a deep breath, as if to compose himself. "That's what I want more than anything else."

A tear meandered down his cheek and I dabbed it away. Terri took the worn tissue from my hand and finished it off by blowing his nose.

"It's not as if I'm asking for the world. Then again, who knows?" He shrugged and tried to laugh, but the sound caught in his throat. "What I want exactly is what you have with Santou. You don't know how lucky you are to have a true-blue guy who loves you. Believe me, they're difficult to find."

He was right. I counted my blessings again that Jake had been saved, as Terri pulled out his compact and fixed his makeup.

"It's a little too early to hit the clubs. Do you mind if we stroll through Chinatown for a while?" he asked.

"That sounds good to me," I agreed.

We crossed Broadway, also known as the Marco Polo Zone, and were whisked into a foreign land without having ever set foot in a plane. This was the area of San Francisco that I loved best. All five senses clashed in an orgy of sights, sounds, and fragrances as we found ourselves surrounded by Chinese bookstores, produce stands, pagoda-topped lamp-posts, and movie theaters. The nasal singsong jabber of Cantonese droned in our ears, while the scrumptious scent of barbecued pork made me very nearly forget that I'd already eaten dinner.

Grant Street buzzed on this Saturday night, its energy a neon high. Signs enticed us to stop in front of every store window, where Terri oohed and ahhed over tacky souvenirs ranging from Tweety Bird watches to bamboo back scratch-ers and chirping metal crickets, all authentically made in Taiwan. Not to be passed up were the "must have" laughing Buddha figurines offered at a "one time" low price of $4.99 a pop. Meanwhile, sidewalk carts stood piled high with every plastic and rubber item made under the sun, each of which was going, going, gone for the bargain price of under five bucks. It was pure catnip for tourists, who eagerly scooped them up.

Terri contained himself as we passed by two competing music shops, one of which blasted "Jenny from the Block" while the other offered the more traditional, all-time Chinese favorite, "Respect 4 Da Chopstick Hip Hop."

It was only as we came upon a Hong Kong–style dress store that Terri finally lost control.

"Just remember, shopping is always the best way to get rid of the blues. It would do you a world of good to follow that philosophy," he advised.

By the time we walked out, Terri had shed his leather and in its place donned sequins and silk. He now wore a tight-fitting, high-collared, pink cheongsam dress with a hot-to-trot dragon embroidered down the front. Being the Madonna of quick fashion change, Terri looked nothing less than absolutely stunning.

We soon found ourselves at the corner of Washington and Grant, standing in front of a tiny, dark dive. Above the door was a weary neon sign bearing the single word BUDDHA.

"I should have known this was where we would end up. What is it with you and these kinds of places?" Terri asked, crinkling his nose.

"They've got character," I replied with a grin.

"*Characters* are more like it—primarily the creepy four-legged kind. All right. Let's go in and get this over with," he acquiesced.

We stepped inside the hole in the wall and entered a room that was dusty and dank.

"Mmm, yes. I see what you mean. There's something truly charming about a bar where the service is surly and there are rarely more than two customers at a time, neither of whom usually speaks English. Then, of course, there's the background music. It's always either Kenny Rogers croaking his way through 'Ruby' or Frank Sinatra crooning 'In the Wee Small Hours of the Morning,'" Terri summed up. "Hand me a stack of those cheap paper squares that pass for napkins, will you?"

He placed a few under the leg of a wobbly stool and spread the rest across its seat. "What this place has is all the charm of an opium den, Rach."

Okay. So he was right about that. But then there were also no tourists.

We sat under a dilapidated canopy that threatened to topple upon us at any moment. But that was nothing compared to the diminutive eighty-year-old behind the bar who wore a T-shirt that read, GO AHEAD. MAKE MY DAY.

"Wouldn't you know? It's Saturday night and look who I get: the female John Wayne and Suzie Wong, herself," she needled in a thick Chinese accent.

"How do you like that? I've never been compared to John Wayne before," Terri wryly commented.

"Actually, I think she meant me," I responded.

"Okay girls. What will it be?"

"Make mine a Campari and soda," Terri replied.

"And I'll have an Absolut martini with an olive."

"Coming right up."

The old woman set a couple of Buds on the bar, flicked off their caps, and slid them toward us.

"There you go."

"Perfect," I retorted.

She poured herself a Coke, and we all clinked drinks.

Mei Rose Chang was a one-of-a-kind piece of work. Aside from bartending, she used to regularly appear as an extra on the now defunct TV show *Nash Bridges*. However, we knew her best as our landlady.

"Tomorrow I cook a big meal and you watch. That way you learn to make good food," she informed me.

"I can't, Mei Rose. I already have other plans."

"What other plans?" she asked suspiciously.

Mei Rose had been attempting to teach me to cook for months. So far, I had managed to find a convenient excuse to

escape. I'd already told her that my idea of cooking was takeout, but she stubbornly refused to give up. She must have viewed me as her ultimate challenge.

"Terri and I are driving to Mendocino tomorrow. Have you ever been there?"

"Mendocino? That's one place I don't want to go. Grandmother was sent there as a mail-order bride soon after the Gold Rush. She sailed from China on a sampan that took over a year and a half to arrive. Grandfather had come to this country thinking he would find gold and strike it rich. But when the Gold Rush ended, he still hadn't made a dime. Chinese people in Mendocino, they labored as water-slingers and cooks in lumber camps for little money. Grandfather, he worked his fingers to the bone cooking for loggers, while Grandmother took in sewing and laundry and raised eight kids. It was a hard, hard life," Mei Rose related, with a sad shake of her head. "What you want to go there for, anyway?"

"I'm looking for a man that's searching for butterflies."

Mei Rose eyeballed me. "You one strange girl."

Terri finished his beer, stood up, and smoothed the wrinkles from his dress.

"So is your friend here," she added.

"And this dive is the Taj Mahal of bars," Terri breezily retorted. "Just let me use the facilities and we'll be on our way."

Mei Rose pressed a buzzer under the counter and Terri pulled open a mesh wire door. The *click, click, click* of his high heels echoed as they went downstairs into the basement.

"I tell you once more only because I like you. Every girl need to know how to cook. Otherwise how you expect to keep that man of yours? You think you live on love alone? Pshaw!" She dismissed the idea with a brisk wave of her hand.

"Not all women have time to cook these days, Mei Rose,"

I patiently tried to explain for the umpteenth time. "They have other things to do. That's why there are restaurants."

"Look at me. I do everything. You're young and strong. You should do it, too. All I know is you better be careful, or you're going to lose that man of yours."

Hmm. I wondered if she knew something I didn't—especially after having heard about Vincent.

"Plenty other women know how to make chow fun and keep their man happy. You better learn quick, or some clever girl will come along and steal him away from you."

I fidgeted on the stool, finding that the subject made me increasingly uncomfortable.

"You be smart and listen to what Mei Rose tell you. I take you shopping and teach you to cook. Otherwise, you end up alone in this world, or with that nutty friend of yours."

I envisioned myself without Santou and nearly caved in to her demands.

What are you, crazy? Snap the hell out of it! my inner voice ranted, saving me at the last possible moment from the Sergeant Bilko of Chinese cooking.

"That would be great, Mei Rose. Only I'm way too busy right now and don't have the time."

But Mei Rose wasn't about to go down without a fight. She skewered me with a laser-sharp glare, until I felt like an enormous butterfly pinned to the wall.

"Then you better make time, missy. I know what I'm talking about."

It made me wonder what Mei Rose, herself, might have been through. All that saved me was the sound of Terri's heels coming back up the stairs. I breathed a sigh of relief as he shut the wire mesh door behind him. Even so, I could feel Mei Rose's words trailing behind us as we walked outside.

"I finally figured out why the walls and floors of her dungeon downstairs are painted blood red," Terri confided. "It's

so Mei Rose can easily clean up the mess after knocking off those tenants that are late with their rent."

"Thanks for the tip. Listen Terri, would you mind if I skipped the clubs tonight and headed back to Santou instead?"

Terri smoothed back my hair and gave me a kiss on the forehead.

"Of course not, Rach. I'd do the same thing if I were you. Everyone knows that clubs are mainly for people with nothing better to do."

This time it was my turn to blink back tears. As long as Terri and I had each other, neither of us would ever be alone. Still, he deserved to find someone to love and make him happy.

"Then I'll see you bright and early tomorrow morning," I reminded him.

I watched as Terri strolled off. Then I turned and began to walk toward home.

I was deep in thought when a chill unexpectedly settled in my bones. I quickly looked up. Just ahead stood Old Saint Mary's Church, famous for its brick bell tower. The timepiece on the tower's front reported the hour to be ten o'clock. But it was the inscription chiseled in the bricks below that was darkly menacing: SON, OBSERVE THE TIME AND FLY FROM EVIL.

It was enough to make the hair on the back of my neck stand on end. I quickened my pace with the feeling that mischief was afoot, just waiting to pounce.

As if on cue, the sound of steps swiftly approached from behind. However, I wasn't prepared for the hand that roughly latched onto my shoulder, nor the object that was thrust into my side.

"Hey, babe. What's the rush? You look too good to be all by your lonesome."

Something metal bit through my clothes and the world

changed gears, as everything began to move in slow motion. Even the streetlights flickered and blurred, just like the room lights in Krav Maga class. It was my nightmare all over again, except this time it was far too real. My pulse raced, fearing that the metal object pressing into me was a gun.

"Let'sfindsomeplacequietanddark whereenoonewillbotherus."

The words were drawn out and distorted as they reached my ears, like an old 45 record being played on 33 rpm.

"Justdon'tdoanythingstupid,andyou won'tgethurt."

The man pushed up against me. The rancid smell of his breath turned my stomach as his fingers bit into my skin and steered me toward an alley. At the same time, he removed the metal object from my side and reached for my purse. I glanced down and saw that he held a short bolt in his grip rather than a gun.

I didn't stop to think, but acted solely on reflex. Dropping my head forward, I rammed it back as hard as I could, catching my assailant on the nose. His hand flew off my shoulder. I quickly whirled around and threw a punch to his solar plexus, followed by a painful jab against the temple. The next thing my attacker knew, he'd been thrown up against a wall.

Only then did I get a good look at him. Oh, shit. I was dealing with a street kid who couldn't have been more than fifteen years old.

He clutched his chest and struggled for breath, all the while glaring at me like some poor puppy that had been wrongfully kicked. My fear instantly disappeared, replaced by a whopping sense of guilt. More than likely he was a runaway in need of money.

"Are you all right?" I asked, and took a step toward him.

"Just stay the hell away from me!" he warned, and ran off as fast as he could.

Damn it. What the hell else was I supposed to do? I thought. *Let him mug me, or possibly worse?*

But no matter how I tried to justify it, there was no escaping that I'd just beaten up a kid—one with a desperate look in his eyes. The incident haunted me the entire way home.

By the time I walked through the front door, I wanted nothing more than to fall into Santou's arms and forget what had happened tonight. However, when I got upstairs, the television had been turned off and Jake was no longer in the living room. I tiptoed in and found him fast asleep on the bed. He lay so still that I could have sworn he was dead. Then I saw the two bottles of painkillers uncapped on the nightstand beside him.

I listened to the sound of his breathing, while holding my own. Each exhalation was painfully slow, each inhalation excruciatingly shallow.

But that wasn't all. An empty bottle of scotch lay like a passed-out drunk on the floor, and I knew that his recovery still had a long way to go.

Five

I awoke to a gray, foggy day, wondering if I'd ever get used to the Bay Area weather. Rolling over, I tried to snuggle against Santou only to find he was no longer under the covers. Then I heard the thrum of the shower. The pipes behind the wall squeaked in protest as Jake turned off the water.

Adding his pillow to my own, I stretched my arms and legs, luxuriating in the extra few minutes to remain in bed. Then I caught sight of the scotch bottle on the floor, and remembered how I'd found Santou stoked to the gills on drugs and booze last night.

Jake slowly limped back into the room wearing nothing but a towel around his waist. An angry scar snaked out from beneath the terrycloth and ran down the length of his left leg. He followed my eyes with his own, probably having already looked at it a million times himself.

"I thought maybe I'd tell people that I got it fighting the war in Iraq. What do you think?"

"Maybe so," I said and smiled.

"Talk about a downer. Terri told me yesterday that my scar's going to clash with the red Speedo I was planning to wear this summer," Santou caustically joked.

"So, how's your head this morning?"

"Still there, as far as I can tell. Why?"

"Because I thought you might have tried to kill off all your brain cells last night."

Jake looked at me without a word.

"The pills and booze? It's got to stop."

"Maybe you've just got to learn to live with it," Santou peevishly snapped. A second later, he hung his head and ran a hand through his hair. "I'm sorry, chère. It's just that they help me get through the day. Believe me, you don't know what it's like."

"What I do know is that it's been nine months since the crash. You should be off painkillers by now. For chrissakes, Jake. Face it. You've become addicted. It's time you change doctors, start seeing a physical therapist on a regular basis, and clean up your act."

"And maybe you should let me handle this in my own way and try being a little more patient. You have no idea what I'm going through, and this sure as hell doesn't help."

"Fine. I just don't want to come home one day and find you dead on the floor, because I damn well don't intend to mop up the mess."

Santou glared as he grabbed his clothes off the chair and stormed out, slamming the bedroom door behind him.

"That went well," I muttered to myself, and headed into the shower.

I stood under the water and let it beat down on me, conflicted by two entirely different emotions. Part of me felt guilty that Jake was in this quandary, while the other part wanted to smack him hard across the head.

Okay, so maybe tough love *wasn't* the way to go. I took a deep breath and decided to give patience a shot. Quickly drying off, I dressed, and opened the bedroom door, determined to make up.

"Don't shoot. I'm coming out," I joked. "How about if I make us some breakfast?"

But there was no answer. I walked out to find that Santou had already left the premises.

Maybe he's complaining about me to Terri.

I decided to pop upstairs, knowing that Terri was expecting me this morning.

Though I knocked on his door four times, there was no answer. I finally resorted to using the key.

Terri was asleep in bed with his eye mask on. I sat on the edge and gently shook him awake.

"Rise and shine, Sleeping Beauty. You don't happen to have Santou under the covers there, do you?"

Terri lifted his mask and grudgingly opened one eye. "Why? Has he gone AWOL?"

"Let's just say we had a little disagreement."

"Terrific. What about?"

"I came home last night and found him knocked out, having downed a hefty cocktail of pills and scotch. Not even an earthquake would have rocked his world. I told him this morning that he needs to get professional help, because I don't intend to scrape his dead carcass off the floor."

"Good going, Rach. That was very sweet, and a surefire way to win him over." Terri snorted.

"All right, I probably could have been a bit more diplomatic. But I also wanted to get my point across."

Terri yawned. "As if you ever have a problem doing that."

He was right. I now realized I was an absolute dolt.

"So, are you still coming with me to Mendocino, or should I let you go back to your dreams?" I gruffly asked, feeling thoroughly embarrassed.

"Oh, please. The Hulk is about the only one that ever shows up in them anymore. No, if I don't get up now, I probably never will. Give me half an hour and I'll meet you downstairs."

I was sitting in my Ford, ready and waiting to go, when

Terri walked outside. To my surprise, he looked unusually subdued, dressed in a pair of black jeans and a charcoal gray shirt.

"Well, you certainly blend in with the weather today," I noted as he sat down and strapped on his seat belt.

"Yeah, in more ways than one."

"What do you mean?"

Rather than answer, Terri simply shrugged.

Great. That made two for two. Apparently, I was annoying everyone that I came into contact with this morning. I threw the Ford into drive and headed for the Golden Gate Bridge.

The fog grew thicker with each passing mile, as if we were being sucked into a conspiracy of clouds. The haze could have enveloped the Ford and swallowed us whole, leaving no trace that we'd ever existed. No one would have known any different. Certainly not early on a Sunday morning, when it seemed as though the whole town was deserted.

Not a soul was around. That is, except for the troops of homeless wandering the streets like ghosts, their numbers having surged with the burst of the dot-com bubble. Materializing out of the fog, they tapped on car windows and begged for spare change at every red light. Then they floated back into the murk like flotsam, having been discarded by the world with no more thought than that given to garbage.

So far San Francisco had seen two gold rushes come and go, the latest being the Internet boom. But the good times were now gone, having taken a heavy human toll.

We sped up Van Ness, crossed onto Lombard, and the Golden Gate Bridge soon came into view. Shrouded in mist, it mystically floated between land and water as if held there by thin air. Its orange-gold towers rose forty stories high, beckoning in a siren song of suicide to all who've lost hope.

California has long been the last stop for many who fear

they'll never make good; the Golden Gate Bridge their swan song.

Come all ye who have lost houses, wives, and jobs, experienced bankruptcy, or are flat-out broke and depressed. When everything else fails, there's still one place left to go: the most popular suicide spot in the world.

The bridge offers the ride of a lifetime, providing a four-second dive to the bottom with speeds reaching up to eighty miles per hour on impact. It's said that San Francisco is a city of dreamers and drunks. If that's true, then the Golden Gate has come to symbolize the end of the trail for broken dreams. So seductive is its call that even the founder of Victoria's Secret chose to make his final leap off this bridge.

Perhaps it was such thoughts that made me realize Terri had been exceptionally quiet so far this morning.

"How did things go last night?" I inquired, wondering if I'd done something wrong.

"Hmm, let's see. How should I put this? I wouldn't slow down while driving across the Golden Gate if I were you. It might prove way too tempting for me to jump."

"What happened?" I asked in alarm.

"It's what *didn't* happen. None of those clubs would hire me," Terri wailed.

That didn't make sense. Not when Terri had been billed as the top female impersonator back at the Boy Toy Club in New Orleans. He'd nailed Cher, Madonna, and Liza better than they usually performed themselves.

"There must be some reason. Did any of them tell you why?"

"Oh, there's a reason all right," he bitterly replied. "Do you really want to hear it?"

"Of course," I answered, though I suddenly wasn't so sure.

"It's because I'm a washed-up, out-of-touch, over-the-hill transvestite who doesn't have my finger on the pulse of the club scene anymore. In other words, I'm just too damn *o-o-o-old!*" Terri elongated the word in a long, drawn-out sob.

"That's totally ludicrous," I scoffed, feeling highly insulted. Neither of us had yet reached the age of forty. If they thought Terri was too old, what did that say about me? After all, I wasn't that far behind him.

"Did you perform Cher and Madonna for them?"

Terri nodded. "That's the problem. They're looking for someone who does Britney Spears and Christina Aguilera these days. For God sakes, can you imagine? I'd have to appear in chaps and a thong, with a snake wrapped around my neck, and grind away like a cheap espresso machine. Very classy, huh? They suggested I add Carol Channing to my repertoire and audition at a club that caters to an older clientele, instead. *Carol Channing!* What do I look like? Chopped liver for the geriatric set?"

"They obviously don't know what they're talking about," I tried to console him.

Terri pulled the visor down and examined his face in its mirror. His fingers probed every little wrinkle.

"I can't even afford a face-lift these days. Not with that lawsuit hanging over Yarmulke Schlemmer's head."

"Don't be ridiculous. You don't need one, anyway."

However, I snuck a peek in the rearview mirror at my own face. How long would it be before I broke open *my* piggy bank, hoping to scrape up enough for a few nips and tucks?

"I'm sure there are plenty of other clubs where you can work."

"Yeah. I hear they're having a cattle call for mature transvestites to perform at a local senior citizens center," Terri morosely responded. "Between Vincent, the lawsuit, and now this, I don't know what I'm going to do, Rach. I need something solid to hang on to in my life or, I swear, I'm going to float aimlessly along, just wasting time."

Time. There it was. That terrible word. I could feel it ticking away inside me like a bomb ever since my mother's death. It was a constant reminder that there was only a finite amount left, and I had damn well better make the most of it.

I looked over at Terri's expression and it nearly broke my heart. "Remember what you told me about having patience, Ter? Don't worry. Things will work out."

He half-heartedly patted my arm and gazed out the window, appearing to be deep in thought.

The San Francisco skyline faded into the fog behind us, much like an aging movie star taking refuge behind a thick, gauzy veil. Soon a tunnel came into view, its mouth painted in candy stripes like a colorful rainbow. Upon entering, we were magically transported into a California never-never land. We exited to find ourselves in Marin County, home of New Age consciousness, granola bars, wealthy stockbrokers, and aging rock stars. The headquarters for Birkenstock sandals loomed off to the west like the Emerald City, making me feel rather like Dorothy in *The Wizard of Oz*.

We continued north on Highway 101 through a landscape of rolling hills bedecked with gnarled oaks. Three huddled together in the mist, their contorted limbs transforming them into a trio of scheming witches from *Macbeth*.

From there we sped through wine country, bastion of the good life, with its carefully tended vineyards, gourmet restaurants, and stylish homes, all paid for with great gobs of money. A quick turn onto Route 128 brought about yet an entirely different change of scene.

A rural two-lane road wound through verdant mountains, its path so serpentine that my car squealed in delight rather than sensibly slow down. Soon the Ford was *shush, shush, shushing* from side to side with the proficiency of a downhill skier, twisting and turning in perfect unison with each hairpin curve.

Paul Newman, Tom Cruise, look out. I drove with the giddy exhilaration of a newbie race car driver. The only thing that kept me in check was the sight of Terri's chalk white knuckles gripping the sides of his seat.

We were next ushered into what could best be described as a redwood tunnel, with a canopy so dense it obliterated the sky. The remains of an ancient forest, the trees soared above us. Some reached up to three hundred and sixty feet in height, with hefty trunks that were twenty feet in diameter. Each redwood base was surrounded by a network of Medusa-like roots spilling over into a lush fern-filled grove. All this shadowy old growth was caressed by a ghostly fog that provided the forest with droplets of moisture. Looking around, I realized this could very well have been the prototype for Jurassic Park.

I reveled in the fourteen-mile stretch, aware that less than four percent of virgin redwood forest still remains today, and only half of that is protected. The throaty rumble of logging trucks rolling past helped bring the message home.

What took me by surprise was the whiff of salt breeze that unexpectedly tickled my nose. We reached the end of the Navarro River and turned onto a stretch of ocean road. But I had little time to appreciate its beauty as the Ford was pulled inside a dense pillow of clouds. I drove on instinct alone, aware of the precipitous drop onto the rocky cliffs and pounding surf below. The road was dangerous enough during the daytime. At night it could prove to be deadly.

A shaft of sun broke through the haze as we continued our approach, its light so bright as to be nearly blinding. It took a moment before my eyes could adjust and I was finally able to see. What appeared to be a New England village lay stretched along the bluffs, staring out toward the ocean. Perched on a craggy coastline, Mendocino was nestled in the curve of a cove, wrapped on three sides by the Pacific.

The ramrod-straight spine of a church marked the town's entrance, its razor sharp spire perforating the sky. Its stark primness was offset by a cluster of Victorian houses, all punctuated with steep gable roofs, bay windows, fanciful filigree, and porches trimmed in gingerbread.

The town seemed to hold its breath as a set of waves violently crashed and churned against the convoluted shoreline. Or perhaps the stillness was due to the wet fog blanketing every surface from the sidewalk to the water towers to the board-and-batten siding on the buildings. I wouldn't have been surprised to discover this was where the Ghost and Mrs. Muir now resided. More than anything, Mendocino resembled an old sepia photograph that had sprung to life.

"Unbelievable, Rach. You certainly know how to pick the most out-of-the-way spots," Terri murmured.

"What do you think? It looks pretty interesting, huh?"

"I'm not sure yet. I'll have to get back to you on that one. To tell you the truth, this place kind of gives me the creeps. I don't know whether to explore the town or run for my life."

"What say we grab something to eat while you decide," I suggested.

"Good idea. I didn't have any breakfast, and I'm sure you must be coming down from off your Cocoa Puff high."

I grinned, accepting the fact that Terri knew me all too well.

We drove into town and parked on Main Street. Then, following a sign, we climbed a set of rickety wooden steps up to a restaurant that overlooked the bay. The place had the feel of a hippie dive trying hard to appear casually chic. We kicked back, sipped some coffee, and ordered a couple of omelets. After that, we proceeded to study the local wildlife outside.

One resident wandered around with a furry raccoon tail hanging from the back of his pants. It gave him the appearance of a brand-new species that was half critter/half human. He strolled past a battered VW bus with tattered lace curtains strung across its scratched-up windows. A girl emerged from within wearing a denim vest and a long flowered skirt.

Our waitress delivered two how-fast-can-these-clog-your-arteries brie omelets, along with a mound of greasy home-fries. We promptly devoured them and she returned with our bill. I wondered if it was a requirement to wear over-sized camo pants, a tight T-shirt, no bra, and a belly-button ring to work in this place. A quick glance at the other waitresses revealed that it was her own bad fashion sense.

I immediately caught myself and wondered if I would have had a similar reaction just ten years ago. Then a worse thought hit me. It was a knee-jerk response to the fact that I was getting older. Terri's gaze met mine and I knew he was thinking the exact same thing. We nodded in silent agreement, as if secretly vowing to buy identical outfits and make ourselves wear them at home in order to feel younger.

"Keep the change," I said, giving the waitress a hefty tip as a form of penance. "By the way, do you happen to know where Bill Trepler lives?"

Our Lady of Camo wrinkled her nose and rolled her eyes. "That old coot?" He lives at the end of town near Portuguese Flats. But I don't know why you'd want to go see him."

"Oh? Is there a problem I should know about?"

"Only that he's one of the most unpleasant people ever to walk the face of this earth. That is unless you have a soft spot for right-wing, obnoxious jerks. Then it's a whole different story. I guess it pretty much depends on which side of the issue you fall."

"What issue is that?" I questioned.

"About turning this area into a developer's wet dream," she said, nonchalantly scratching her breast. "If Trepler had his way, every inch of Mendocino would be built up and changed for the worst. You're not here to see him about anything like that, are you?" Her eyes narrowed suspiciously.

For chrissakes, I might be a few years older than Our Lady of Camo. But no way did I look like some sort of conservative businesswoman. I took a quick gander at my jeans and sneakers just to make certain.

"No. It involves something totally different," I assured her.

"In that case, his place is easy to find. It's the one with the mountain lion skull over the door."

"The guy sounds like a real charmer," Terri remarked, as we left the restaurant and walked downstairs. "If you don't mind, I think I'll hang around town and let you see Trepler on your own. I spotted a few shops I'd like to check out."

"That's fine," I agreed, figuring he had the better end of the deal. "What say we meet inside that place around three o'clock?" I pointed to an art gallery just down the street from where we were parked.

"Sounds good to me. Break a leg, sweetie. Just remember, don't think twice about slapping him around with some of those fancy moves you've learned if he tries anything funny."

I promised to do my best, jumped in the Ford, and took off.

I drove toward the opposite end of town, taking note of all the expensive restaurants and boutiques that were scattered about. Each was quaint enough to make me wonder if Martha Stewart had been set loose in the place. Mendocino was proving to be an interesting mix of hippies, rednecks, and yuppies, with a large dollop of tourism rolled in.

Turning my head, I looked across the street toward the bluffs and, for one crystalline moment, my heart came to a stop. Striding along the cliffs was a large, imposing figure.

The man seemed to have the same startling effect on a few adventurous tourists, who quickly scurried out of his way.

Perhaps it had to do with the fact that he towered close to six feet five and wore duck boots, carpenter jeans, and an army surplus jacket. Slapped on his head was a navy knit cap, even though it was a warm June day. Long salt-and-pepper dreadlocks hung out beneath, their braids as dark and dense as the links on a ship's anchor chain. They matched the crinkly dun-colored hairs of his shaggy beard.

I could almost feel the vibration that came with each step he took, as though the earth were slightly giving way beneath his feet. A worn canvas bag and thick walking stick helped give him an air of homelessness.

He must have sensed my stare, for he turned and glowered as I slowly drove by. I slyly glanced in the rearview mirror and was taken aback as his gaze locked on mine, his eyes fierce as those of an angry bear. I tried to focus on the road, but continued to feel their glare, hot as a branding iron, demanding to know what I'd been looking at and warning me to stay away. I hurried toward Portuguese Flats, along the western edge of town.

Six

Mendocino slowly began to change. Gone were the spruced-up Victorian homes with picture-perfect white picket fences, having been replaced by tired cottages and weed-filled lots. I passed one nondescript place after another, until I finally spotted Bill Trepler's house.

Chickens meandered around an unkempt yard while rabbits listlessly hopped in and out of a hutch. Of far more interest was the car that sat parked in the hard dirt driveway. It was a shiny, brand-new, top-of-the-line Lexus.

I got out of my Ford, walked up to the front door, and brazenly knocked. But the only sound to be heard were the chickens scratching and clucking in his yard.

Go away, go away! they seemed to say, as if annoyed at being disturbed.

I knocked again just to show them who was boss.

This time they seemed to cluck, *What a schmuck, what a schmuck.*

They were probably right. This was getting me nowhere and my inner clock was becoming fed up.

I turned to walk away when the door swung open, as if of its own accord, and Bill Trepler appeared. He looked to be in his early sixties, had thinning gray hair, and dots all over his hands that fell somewhere between freckles and age spots. As for his face, it was sunburned and displayed patches of dry, scaly skin. Equally apparent was the fact that he was in excellent physical condition. The guy had arms to rival those of Popeye. Trepler clearly spent a great deal of time working outdoors.

"Whatever you're selling, I'm not interested in buying," he announced in a voice so scratchy that he must have been gargling with kitty litter.

"I'm not selling anything. I'd like some information."

"What about?" he asked, sounding as suspicious as Camo Girl.

"The Lotis blue butterfly."

The words softly floated in the air, light as soap bubbles blown by a child.

Trepler studied me, giving my presence careful appraisal.

"And why would you be interested in the Lotis blue?" he finally asked, his raspy voice bursting the bubbles one by one.

"I'm concerned with anything that's considered rare and which might prove to be a problem for industrial interests and land developers."

Those appeared to be the magic words. Trepler opened the door a little wider.

"Then it seems we have something in common. That being the case, why don't you step inside?"

I entered a hallway that looked as though it had been decorated by an old Irish grandmother. Hand-crocheted lace doilies lay strewn on every tabletop and chair, while porcelain leprechaun knickknacks were positioned just so. Keeping with the theme, the walls were painted dark green and the house had a musty smell about it. My boss had said that Trepler made four thousand dollars a day as a private consultant. Whatever he was spending his money on, it certainly wasn't the décor.

"Are you a fellow entomologist?" Trepler politely inquired, leading the way into the living room.

Holy shamrocks, Batman! The entire space was plastered in wallpaper consisting of dancing four-leaf clovers.

"No, I'm here scouting around for someone with an interest in the Mendocino area," I responded, purposely remaining noncommittal.

As far as I was concerned, I was telling the truth. After all, Dr. Mark Davis had requested that I look into the disappearance of his colleague.

"In other words, you might be requiring my services?" Trepler probed with the deft touch of a skilled surgeon.

"It's certainly possible," I concurred.

"Then let me properly introduce myself. Bill Trepler, former director of Conservation Biology at the University of Nevada. And you are?"

"Rachel Porter," I responded, shaking his hand.

"All right, Miss Porter. Why don't you take a seat and I'll give you some background on the Lotis blue."

I sank into a sofa that seemed to have no springs, its cushions enfolding me like a large cocoon.

"First of all, what do you know about the bug?" Trepler questioned, as if prepping me for an exam.

"That it was the first of six butterflies to be placed on the endangered species list and is extremely rare."

"Well, you're right about that. These days it's the rarest butterfly in all North America. One major problem is that its territory is restricted to the Mendocino area. There's no other habitat for the Lotis blue anywhere else on earth. At least, as far as we know. I believe it was Vladimir Nabokov, the novelist of *Lolita* fame, who said lepidopterists have more information about butterflies in deepest, darkest Africa than they do those living along the coastal stretch of the western U.S. from Mendocino northward. Strange, isn't it?"

"How long has this particular butterfly been around?" I asked, wanting to pump him for all the information I could get.

"The Lotis blue was first discovered in 1876, when two specimens were caught. It was described as a new species of Lycaenidae, a family that includes the blues, coppers, and hairstreaks."

I hate when experts slip into scientific jargon. My mind inevitably begins to drift.

"Okay. Then as far as collectors know, the Lotis blue has been in existence until just recently," I affirmed, determined to keep myself on track.

"Not quite. The butterfly disappeared for fifty years shortly after its initial discovery."

"What do you mean disappeared? They literally vanished?"

"Exactly."

Trepler pumped a bicep while plucking a pack of Marlboros from his shirt pocket, and I knew he was trying to impress me.

"It wasn't until 1935 that a colony of Lotis blue were once again stumbled upon by a man living right here in Mendocino, a naturalist who had no idea what he'd found. He spent the next eighteen years showing specimens to lepidopterists in the Bay Area, none of whom had a clue as to what they were, either. Finally in 1953, an entomology professor came to visit and identified the butterflies as the mysterious Lotis blue."

Trepler lit a cigarette, took a deep drag, and promptly broke into a coughing fit. I waited as he grabbed a tissue and hacked up whatever had settled in his lungs. He spit out some phlegm and looked at it. No wonder the guy was living alone.

"So, what happened after that? Did collectors come in and wipe out the colony?" I impatiently asked, wanting to move the story along.

"Absolutely not. The exact location was kept secret for that very reason. However, Professor Tilden did trade some of his samples for other butterflies that he wanted in his collection. He also gave a number of specimens to several museums. In fact, Tilden is responsible for the lion's share of Lotis blue butterflies that reside in collections today. It wasn't until years later that he revealed the location to a graduate student, who then made several trips to the site. That's when word finally began to spread. But stop and think about it. Here was a butterfly that had been seen by only four men in over a hundred years, up to that point."

"So then, this grad student was ultimately responsible for the butterfly's demise," I concluded.

"Don't be ridiculous. Of course not. He ended up working as a biologist for the Fish and Wildlife Service. In fact, he petitioned for the Lotis blue to be listed as an endangered species."

"What happened after that?"

Trepler shrugged. "Not much. Only twenty-six adult Lotis blue butterflies have been spotted since 1977. The last one to be seen was in 1983. After that, nothing."

"Where were the butterflies usually found?" I questioned, refusing to give up.

"Near their food plant, the *Lotus formosissimus*. It's a diminutive weed just a few inches high that produces a pretty little yellow-and-purple flower."

"Then what's been responsible for their disappearance?" I prodded, beginning to feel enormously frustrated.

"Who said they've disappeared?" Trepler responded with a crafty smile. "After all, they were only ever collected at seven sites, ranging from wet meadows to sphagnum bogs. Maybe people have just been looking in the wrong spots. I happen to know of a number of coastal bluffs where small marshes occur as the result of numerous springs popping up. I'll let you in on a little secret. I've seen *Lotus formosissimus* growing profusely in those areas."

Trepler emitted a throaty laugh while puffing on his cigarette. It was probably because I was staring at him with my mouth hanging open. He seemed to interpret it as a sign of concern.

"Don't worry. I'm not suggesting that you'll have a problem with development in this region. Quite the contrary. You won't. Not if you use my services."

Trepler leaned in so close that I could smell not only cigarette smoke, but also stale coffee on his breath.

"You see that car out there?" he asked, pointing through the Bay window to his driveway. "Let's just say the Lexus came as a thank-you from a very satisfied customer. That should make you more comfortable about what I'm able to deliver."

I remembered again what my boss had said. Trepler's job was to make certain that endangered species didn't bring construction projects to a halt.

"Well, you certainly seem to know a lot about this particular butterfly," I admitted.

"I know a lot about many things," Trepler responded and nonchalantly crossed his legs. "That's why I get paid the big bucks."

"Then let me play devil's advocate for a minute," I suggested. "What if the Lotis blue *were* found on a particular tract of land that my employer was interested in? What then?"

Trepler flicked his ashes into a dirty coffee cup that sat on top of an old wooden chest.

"I'd say the butterfly was just passing through the area at the time. It would be my word as an expert against people who don't know half as much." He smiled, exposing a set of stained yellow teeth.

So that was how the game was played. It couldn't have been any more clear that Trepler was a high-priced "rent-a-scientist," or what detractors had nicknamed a "biostitute."

"That all sounds well and good. There's just one problem. Rumor has it that Fish and Wildlife recently hired a top-notch conservation biologist from Stanford to perform an extensive search for the Lotis blue in this area. I hear they're also clamping down on the illegal collecting of butterflies."

"So, is that what they've turned into now? The butterfly gestapo?" Trepler snorted contemptuously. "That agency does nothing but go on witch hunts. Hell, they use a bunch of thugs masquerading as agents, who are nothing more than eco-Nazis. Fish and Wildlife's an ignorant, self-serving government group that would rather spend taxpayer dollars on trumped-up charges than focus on issues that really matter. Hell, those jokers wouldn't know a Mission blue from a Lotis blue if they tripped over one."

Ouch! That jab hit a bit too close to home. Mainly because it was partially true.

"The whole lot of them are out of control, running amok while attempting to play Big Brother," he continued to rant. "If our government had any backbone, they'd immediately shut the Fish and Wildlife Service down."

He certainly didn't bother to mince words.

"As for endangered species? Let me give you my philosophy on *that* topic."

Trepler slid an arm along the back of the couch until it was lodged directly behind my head. For one brief paranoid moment, I almost believed he knew my true identity and planned to knock me off. The Mister Softee jingle flit through my mind as I once again looked down a gun barrel and broke into a light sweat.

"Please do," I murmured, and pushed myself forward until I was perched on the edge of the seat.

"When a creature is endangered, it's usually for a helluva good reason. If something isn't smart enough to adapt and survive, then it deserves to become extinct," Trepler lectured, building up a head of steam. "I don't believe in this do-gooder Endangered Species Act nonsense that's got every frog, gnat, and fish on a must-save list, no matter the cost. Not if it means that a person can't do whatever he wants on his own damn land."

Trepler must have interpreted my silence as agreement, because he cracked his knuckles again and began to relax. Then he stared at me and slapped his knee, as if having made a momentous decision.

"Come with me into the next room. I want to show you something."

I followed him into what seemed to be an office as well as a workspace. A pile of papers sat neatly stacked on a desk in one corner, while an old oak table dominated the center of the room. Covering its surface were all the necessary accoutrements for mounting butterflies. There was a pair of scissors, along with a slender tweezers, glassine paper, a container of stainless-steel insect pins, and a bottle of relaxing fluid. A piece of Styrofoam had a groove cut through its center, making me wonder if it were some sort of spreading board. Most likely the furrow held the butterfly's body in place while Trepler worked on its wings.

Trepler didn't stop at the table, but walked over to five wooden cabinets that were lined up against a wall. Each contained fourteen shelves. He opened one of the drawers and pulled it out for me to view. The interior was a display case filled with row upon row of breathtakingly beautiful butterflies.

"Butterflies only live for about a two-week period. So, what's the harm in harvesting some of them ahead of time? Tell me why collectors should get a bad rap, when so many other factors kill large numbers of them much more efficiently. Take habitat destruction, for example."

That struck me as darkly funny, considering the role that Trepler, himself, played in it.

"Or how about suburban sprawl?" he continued. "Then there are the pesticides that people use in their gardens to keep their flowers and plants bug free. What do you think that does to them? The same goes for farmers who have chemicals sprayed all over their fields. And don't forget about automobiles. How many butterflies do you suppose end up smashed against car windshields each year? At least people get to enjoy them this way."

Maybe so. But ultimately a butterfly is a living thing. Not something to be pinched, gassed, or frozen out of existence in order to be displayed under a sheet of glass. Besides, how many more butterflies would there be if Trepler had allowed those in his collection to live and breed? These specimens had no more life to them than a colorful set of inanimate stamps.

He opened the remaining drawers and I felt slightly ill staring at what must have been thousands of impaled butterflies, each with a pin thrust through its thorax. I chose instead to focus my attention on the four tiny tags that were attached to each individual bug's leg. Trepler noticed my interest and seemed to be pleased.

"Those are labels. Would you like to get a closer look at them?"

I nodded and he lifted the glass.

"Just don't touch the wings. They're very fragile."

No problem there. I was much more interested in gathering incriminating data.

Leaning down, I discovered that every butterfly had its own story to tell. Trepler's neatly printed handwriting revealed not only the name of its collector, but also the exact date and precise location from which each had been gathered. Still other tags indicated those butterflies that had been bred and reared by hand. Their labels meticulously noted the date that chrysalis was formed as well as when the adult emerged and how it was nurtured.

I was beginning to realize how maniacal butterfly collectors actually could be. More than a hobby, it was a full-blown obsession.

Trepler replaced the glass and gently closed the drawers. Then he led me toward a large safe.

"It's not that I don't trust you, but I'd appreciate if you'd look away for a moment."

I did as instructed, listening while Trepler spun the safe's lock like the wheel of fortune.

Click, click, click! The tumbler giddily sang out.

The safe emitted a deep groan as its door slowly swung open.

Turning back around, I watched Trepler remove a small display case and reverently place it in the middle of the oak table.

"That's it right there," he revealed in a hushed tone, gesturing toward the one and only specimen it held. "The Lotis blue."

Maybe it was because I'd heard so much about the mysterious bug that I heard myself gasp, the sharp intake of breath making me momentarily woozy. My heart sped up as I gazed at what amounted to near perfection. How could something so small, so insignificant, carry this much impact? I felt myself pulled into the deep violet blue of its incredibly delicate wings, their margin outlined in a seam of black before ending in a feathery burst of luminescent white fringe.

"It's probably difficult for you to see, but a wavy band of orange spots borders the subtermen of the hindwings in between two rows of sinuous black lines."

I had no idea what he was talking about, and I didn't care.

Instead I concentrated on scrupulously examining the specimen, hoping to imprint the butterfly forever in my brain.

"The Lotis blue seems to have a somewhat mystical effect upon many people," Trepler observed with an understanding smile. "Perhaps it's viewing an object so beautiful and knowing that only a privileged few will ever be granted such an opportunity. The butterfly looks almost alive, don't you think? To my mind, preserving specimens like this makes them seem somehow immortal. Possibly that's the allure. It's as if there's no such thing as death, but rather the subject is simply asleep, having been suspended in time and space."

All I knew was that I'd become totally captivated by a winged creature as insubstantial as a piece of tissue paper.

"Remember, what you're looking at is exceedingly rare. There are only fifty specimens of its kind in existence, and almost all of those are in museums."

How odd. I noticed that the Lotis blue had only one tag attached to it rather than the usual four. It listed the date of capture and nothing else. *JUNE 19, 1975.* What a stroke of luck. Had it been gathered one year later, the butterfly already would have been placed on the endangered species list, making it illegal to own. Of course, there was always the chance that the actual date of capture had been tampered with for that very reason. If so, Trepler would have been in contempt of the law. Unfortunately, no one would ever know.

"Needless to say, this is the crown jewel of my collection. The Lotis blue is the butterfly that every collector yearns to possess."

"All right, you've succeeded in making me curious. How did *you* manage to end up with one?" I asked, deliberately trying to keep the inquiry lighthearted.

A flurry of goose bumps ran up my arms as Trepler turned his head and pointedly stared at me.

"I'm sure you've heard of what curiosity did to the cat. Perhaps it's best if you don't ask, but simply appreciate the beauty of this specimen that I've so generously shared with you."

Trepler was totally oblivious to the fact that he'd just waved a red flag in front of my face.

"If it's so valuable, then you must worry that someone might try to steal it," I said, having noticed the house lacked a security system.

"Anyone who knows anything about me is fully aware that I'd track them down and blow their fucking head off."

Not a pleasant fellow—but with a reputation that, I imagine, was highly effective. Perhaps it was time to get back to the original reason as to why I was here.

"I hate to sound skittish, but do you know if that Fish and Wildlife consultant has checked many spots in the area?"

Trepler looked at me oddly, and I was afraid that I might have somehow tipped my hand.

"Don't misunderstand. I realize you're exceptional at what you do. It's just that I'd like to know what we're up against."

"I'm telling you not to worry, Miss Porter. That should be enough. I know for a fact the fellow hasn't done diddly-squat."

"And why is that?" I asked, wondering how Trepler could be so certain.

"Because nearly all the sites where the Lotis blue were once seen are on private land, and nobody's going to grant a government lackey access. Without that, he doesn't stand a chance. Now you really ought to stop stressing about the nickel-and-dime stuff. Trust me. You'll live longer."

"Then would you mind answering just one question? Can you tell me where the Lotis blue was last spotted?"

"Sure. That would have been on Old Man Baker's property, a place he called the Sanctuary. The Lotis blue's territory was a four-acre plot of land. However, they tended to congregate around a bog about the size of this living room.

My pulse began to race and my skin felt flushed. I only hoped that Trepler didn't notice. I knew it wasn't wise to ask any more questions, but I simply couldn't stop myself.

"So then, it's possible that the Lotis blue is still around?"

I could sense Trepler begin to clam up, even as he shrugged.

"I guess. After all, they went for fifty years without being seen, only to reappear one day. Such a small, obscure species is easy to miss. Or, who knows? Could be they never disappeared at all. Maybe they just don't want to be found."

Give me a challenge, tell me something can't be done, and get out of the way. By now, I was completely hooked.

"Do you know how I can get in touch with Mr. Baker?"

"Why? You thinking of trying to catch some of those suckers for yourself? Maybe sell them to make a few extra bucks?" Trepler sarcastically questioned.

"Of course not. I just thought I might take a look at his land, is all. I want to see everything that's in the Mendocino vicinity. So, will you tell me where I can find him?"

"That's three questions so far, but sure. Have you got yourself a shovel?"

"Excuse me? I'm afraid I don't understand," I responded, feeling slightly perturbed. Trepler and his games were becoming annoying.

"You're gonna have to dig him up. Old Man Baker is dead," Trepler revealed, with a sharp bark of a laugh. "Funny thing about that. He had this old house with a dynamite view of the ocean. A great place perched right on top of a cliff. It's a helluva spot, where the waves gather together just for the fun of crashing. Anyway, seems Old Man Baker must have lost his balance and fell off the porch one day, because they found him with his neck broken, lying at the bottom of the cliff. Strange when you think he'd been living there all of his life. I guess he should have paid more attention to that last step, considering his deck had no railing. But the guy was a crackpot, anyway."

Trepler was one to talk. He seemed to gain perverse pleasure from telling the story. Otherwise, why else would he be grinning at me like a loon?

"Who owns the land now?"

"Another oddball nut. Only this one lives in San Francisco. Kind of fitting, huh? The fact is, I've never met the man. Don't even know his name. Word has it he rarely comes up to Mendocino. Just lets the land sit with a No Trespassing sign posted on the front gate. What a waste. I'm talking twenty acres. That place is begging to be developed."

"Sounds intriguing. I'd like to drive by and take a peek. Is the place easy to locate?"

"Sure, as long as you know what it is you're looking for. There's no marker or mailbox or anything like that. Just drive north out of town along Highway 1, heading up toward Russian Gulch. You'll see a group of eucalyptus trees on the right-hand side. The entrance to the Baker property lies not far beyond there. Just be sure to turn left onto the first gravel road you come to after the trees."

I caught one last glimpse of the Lotis blue as Trepler placed the specimen back in the safe, and checked to make sure it was locked. Then he ushered me into the front hallway.

"Thanks for the information. I'll be in touch," I said and began to walk out the door.

"Hold on a minute. You never did give me the name of your employer."

It was now my turn to smile. "Oh, sorry about that. It must have slipped my mind. I'm with the U.S. Fish and Wildlife Service. I'm one of those eco-Nazi special agents that you spoke so highly of."

Trepler stared in disbelief as his complexion darkened and his features became tightly compressed.

"Why, you miserable bitch," he said, with both fists clenched. "You have one helluva lot of nerve coming into my home and passing yourself off as an employee for a development concern."

"I did no such thing," I reminded him. "All I said was that I was looking around the area, which is absolutely true. It's not my fault if you didn't ask who my employer was before now. As a matter of fact, I'm playing by your own set of rules. Don't you remember? You said it plain as day when I asked how you'd obtained your Lotis blue. Your response amounted to Don't ask, don't tell."

Let him mull that over, I thought, while heading down the walkway. *It should give him some agita wondering what I'm up to.*

"And the government is surprised when their toadies sometimes turn up missing. As far as I'm concerned, your consultant got exactly what he deserved," Trepler responded, his voice slithering from behind to come up and bite me.

I froze in my tracks and slowly turned around. "What do you mean by that?"

"Haven't you heard?" He exuberantly slapped his thigh, nearly crowing in delight. "Your friend's car was found in a ditch along a remote stretch of road early this morning. Must be he ran into someone who didn't care all that much for Fish and Wildlife, either. Come to think of it, I'd be careful on that ride up to Old Man Baker's place, if I were you."

Trepler broke into a grin that split his face in two, while mocking me by flapping his arms as if they were a pair of wings. I flashed back to the spreading board, and all those drawers filled with dead butterflies lying impaled for eternity. I couldn't rid myself of the image even as Trepler stepped back inside and slammed the door.

Seven

I waited until I was out of town before placing a call on my car phone to the County Sheriff's office up in Fort Bragg.

"This is Rachel Porter. I'm a special agent with the U.S. Fish and Wildlife Service. I understand you found a car belonging to a Dr. John Harmon this morning. He's working as a consultant for us and has been missing for the past two weeks. I'd appreciate if you would share whatever information you've discovered up to this point."

"Let's see. A 1998 green Jeep Wrangler was spotted off road early A.M. today. Is that the vehicle to which you're referring?" responded a male voice, clearly reticent when it came to handing out any pertinent information.

I bit my lip in exasperation. "I'm not referring to a vehicle, but to a person. I have no idea what type of Jeep, SUV, or car he drove. Was the Wrangler registered to a Dr. John Harmon?"

"Who are you again?" the voice asked suspiciously.

"Special Agent Rachel Porter. And who am I speaking to?"

"Sheriff John Wiley."

"As I was saying, Sheriff Wiley, I'd appreciate anything you can disclose pertaining to the incident. Dr. Harmon's family and colleagues are all very concerned."

"Yes, ma'am. I already know that. They've been calling here nonstop. So I'll tell you exactly the same thing I told them. There is no 'incident.' We found an abandoned Jeep, is all."

"But that obviously suggests something unusual must have taken place. Come on, the man hasn't been heard from in two weeks," I insisted.

"Maybe to you, but not to me. Abandoned vehicles aren't all that uncommon around these parts. And I can honestly say there was no sign of foul play. Maybe you should consider contacting the man's insurance company. To tell you the truth, it appears to me that this Dr. Harmon decided he no longer wanted his Jeep and simply dumped it in a ditch. But here's what I'll do. Leave me a contact number and I'll give a holler if anything comes up that suggests differently."

By the time I was through, I'd supplied him with everything except my social security number, giving him the means to contact me twenty-four hours a day, either at work, home, in my car, or on my cell phone.

Hanging up, I ran through various scenarios of what might have happened as I drove toward Old Man Baker's property.

Santou had speculated last night that Harmon was either having an affair or possibly contending with money problems. What neither of us had considered was that he might be divorced. Perhaps Harmon was trying to dodge child support payments. Only that would have meant walking away from his well-paying job. The man was up for tenure at Stanford University, so that didn't make sense. Besides, a gut feeling told me that he wasn't that type of guy.

Damn! I'd forgotten to ask Sheriff Wiley if Harmon's vehicle had a flat tire when it was found. If so, he might have been walking back to town and possibly was attacked by a bear.

Good thinking, Porter. And what would a black bear have been doing out on the road? Hitchhiking?

Okay, so there were any number of reasons why someone might choose to disappear. But what kept eating at me was Trepler's reaction. It was almost as if he'd expected something bad to happen. The problem was that I had no proof.

I put all musings of Harmon's fate temporarily aside as a eucalyptus grove came into view. A half mile later, I caught sight of the gravel road that Trepler had told me about and swiftly made a left-hand turn.

Pebbles popped under my tires like sheets of plastic bubble wrap, each mini-explosion ricocheting in the air. Though I listened closely, there was no other sound. It would have been the perfect spot for Trepler to try and ambush me if he so chose. Then I spotted the steel gate with its No Trespassing sign tacked on the front. I parked my Ford and got out.

Redwoods soared all around, looking like husky titans with their thick, gnarly bark. Grand firs shaded the ground with umbrellas of white-striped needles. But my attention was drawn somewhere beyond, to an open meadow containing a bog, for I knew that's where the Lotis blue might be dancing through the grass this very minute. I closed my eyes and visualized the tiny phantoms for whom extinction was just a wingbeat away.

I glanced at my watch to discover it was almost three o'clock. I'd been standing at the gate daydreaming for way too long. Terri would be waiting. I jumped in my Ford and took off. Fortunately, the town center wasn't very far.

I found a space on Main Street and parked, then hurried to the store where we'd agreed to meet. Wouldn't you know? Terri hadn't even arrived yet. I hate dashing some place only to discover that I've rushed for nothing. At least there was plenty of artwork to view in the gallery.

I took my time examining all the expensive handmade furniture, glassware, and jewelry. It's depressing to see such lovely things and know there's nothing you can afford to buy. Maybe the less expensive items were on the second floor. I decided to go up and nose around.

What I found took my breath away. Enormous charcoal portraits hung on the walls, unlike any I'd ever before seen. Each was an incredibly stunning work of art. However, it was the subject matter that proved to be unsettling.

A collection of teenage girls stared back at me so intimately that I felt as if I must have surely known them. Then I realized exactly what bothered me. Each conveyed a bruised vulnerability, along with cold, calculating hardness.

Maybe it had to do with the way their lips curled seductively, or the wariness in their eyes, but the portraits were both haunting and disturbing at the same time—so much so that a chill crept through me as I studied them. I was gripped by the sensation that they looked at me accusingly, as though I were somehow responsible for their plight. More than anything, they reminded me of a group of sullen young Eves disillusioned with the world after biting into the apple and realizing that life wasn't quite what they'd thought.

Welcome to the club, I mused. *I believe it's what's known as growing up.*

I was relieved when the bell on the front door jingled, announcing the entrance of another customer. Terri walked in and I rushed downstairs to meet him, happy to escape each girl's stare.

"Hi, Rach. I certainly had a good time. It's true what they say about shopping. It *does* make you feel better. So how'd you make out?"

"Let's put it this way. The assessment that waitress made of Trepler's character? It couldn't have been more on the mark."

"A real bastard, huh?"

"He isn't my number-one choice of companion to be stuck with on a desert island."

"He damn well better not be. That would be me."

Terri put an arm around my shoulder and gave me a kiss on the cheek. "Cheer up. I got you a present."

"Ooh! Can I see it now?" I asked, my fingers eagerly inching toward the shopping bags.

"Hey, where are your manners?" Terri jokingly reprimanded. "For goodness sake, someone would think you'd been a poor kid who never received any gifts on Christmas."

"Technically I didn't. We celebrated Hanukkah."

Terri raised a knowing eyebrow.

"Okay, so we had a tree and opened all our presents on Christmas Day," I admitted, wondering what he had bought me.

Terri pulled a box from one of the bags. "Here. You might as well open it now. Otherwise, you'll just nudge me the rest of the day."

"A present? For me?" I teased, wasting no time in tearing off the ribbon and removing the lid.

Inside was a gorgeous silk blouse with a wonderfully seductive neckline.

"*That* ought to make Santou sit up and take notice," Terri mused, holding the shirt up against my frame. "I knew apricot would be the perfect color with your hair."

"Terri, it's stunning, but you can't afford this. It must have been outrageously expensive."

Terri brushed back one of my curls. "Don't worry, sweetie. What good is money unless you spend it? Besides, I came to a decision while buying the most decadent lingerie for myself. All those queens who refused to hire me last night? They can go to hell. I'm fully determined to land a class-act job that will have them kicking themselves in the ass for ever having rejected me. This shopping spree is my way of declaring my unmitigated success as a top-notch performer."

I loved Terri for lots of reasons. One being that he always remained true to himself, and never allowed anything to fully destroy his self-confidence.

We walked outside, got in the Ford, and were on our way out of town when Terri nearly jumped out of his seat.

"STOP THE CAR!"

I slammed on my brakes, my heart sliding into overdrive, wondering what could possibly be wrong.

"Okay, now back up and turn onto that street we just passed," Terri instructed.

"What's the matter?" I asked in alarm.

"You're not going to believe what I just saw."

"Are you kidding? This is all for something you spotted? For chrissakes, Terri! You just scared the living daylights out of me."

"Sorry, but wait until I show you this thing."

I bit my tongue to keep from calling him a drama queen, as I threw the Ford into reverse and turned left.

"This is it. Stop here," Terri commanded and quickly scrambled out of the Explorer.

I was still muttering to myself as I turned off the engine and grudgingly followed him to an old clapboard building. Then I gazed up at where Terri's finger pointed.

Positioned on the roof was a life-sized statue of a bearded, winged figure gripping a scythe. Before him was a weeping maiden. Holding an acacia branch in one hand and an urn in the other, she stood behind a pedestal on which rested an open book. Next to her was an hourglass, though it was impossible to tell how much sand was left inside. A broken column leaned up against the front of the pedestal. The maiden looked down in sorrow, as if passively accepting her fate, while the man's hands were tightly clasped around her long, flowing hair.

Terri was right. This had definitely been worth stopping and turning around for. The statue was both macabre and fascinating. It toyed with our imagination as we continued to stand there, spellbound.

"Creepy, isn't it?" Terri remarked, as if reading my mind. "What do you think it's supposed to represent?"

"I don't know. There are so many elements involved that it's hard to tell. I suppose it could be Father Time, what with the hourglass."

"Except the woman is crying, and that winged dude certainly doesn't appear to be very benign. He looks more like the Angel of Death to me."

"Maybe so," I agreed, growing increasingly aware that Mendocino wasn't exactly the laid-back little town that I had thought it would be.

We got back in the car and had just started off when something drew my attention once more to the headlands. There on a windblown bluff was the itinerant man that I'd seen earlier in the day. He stood tall and straight, looking like a vagabond version of Moses, gripping his walking stick and staring transfixedly out to sea.

I wondered what he was looking at, and if it had anything to do with winged messengers and crying maidens. Or if he was simply waiting for the water to part while watching butterflies flit on the breeze.

Eight

San Francisco was all aglitter as we approached soon after sunset. I liked to think the city was celebrating our return. But then I had plenty of time to muse, what with being stuck in traffic with a bunch of Beamers, Saabs, and Mercedes. My Ford jockeyed for position with the best of them as we inched our way across the Golden Gate Bridge. It seemed as if the entire Bay Area was attempting to make it home all at once. This was the ritual Sunday night re-entry back into town after the weekend exodus.

We drove back along Lombard, turned down Van Ness, and wended our way over to Union as if we'd been living here all of our lives. Pulling into Mei Rose's driveway, I booted open the car door and rolled out, fully aware that we'd arrived home at a good time. Tony Baloney was out of his basket, having been safely tucked away for the night.

Terri and I were already discussing which take-out menu to order from as we began our climb up the stairs. But wait! A wonderful aroma was emanating from my apartment.

"What do you think? Maybe Santou decided to cook up some of his special gumbo and surprise us," Terri suggested.

"Could be," I replied hopefully.

We opened the door and walked inside, only to realize the fragrance was closer to that of a Chinese restaurant. Then I caught sight of Mei Rose jostling pots and pans about in my tiny kitchen. She wiped the perspiration from her forehead and glared at us.

"Shame on you two, leaving Jake all alone like this," she clucked. "What you expect him to eat? The man needs food in order to gain back his strength. Otherwise how he ever supposed to get well?"

I glanced over at where Santou lounged in his recliner chair, grinning from ear to ear. He reminded me of a human version of Tony Baloney as he ate a bowl of home-made wonton soup, clearly taking pleasure in being pampered. He finally acknowledged my accusatory stare.

"What could I do? Mei Rose insisted," he offered up in self-defense.

Mei Rose proclaimed her annoyance by clanging a metal spoon about while whipping up an assortment of dishes, and continuing to give me the evil eye. What a feat.

"That's it. Tomorrow you come shopping with me. It's high time you learn to cook," she advised, with a warning shake of her finger.

"But I can't. I have to go to work!" I protested.

"Early, early morning before your job. No more excuses," Mei Rose stubbornly retorted, holding her ground.

It was clear that she wouldn't take no for an answer. Besides, my stomach told me this wasn't the time to pick a fight. Instead, I took a deep breath and plunked myself down in a chair as Mei Rose brought out a feast, setting each dish on the table before us.

There were pork dumplings, sesame chicken, steamed seabass, Chinese vegetables, and a big bowl of chow fun. Yum, yum. Quiet momentarily reigned as we proceeded to dig in. That is, until the apartment buzzer rang.

"Are you expecting anyone?" Santou asked, spearing a second dumpling.

"No," I responded, already knowing I'd have to be the one to run downstairs and answer the door.

Even Terri didn't bother to look up. Maybe Mei Rose was on to something. Food certainly did bring everyone together—which is precisely why God invented restaurants in the first place.

"That last dumpling is mine," I said, staking my claim before leaving the table.

Some day I'd convince Mei Rose to invest in an intercom system. Until then, I'd just have to consider this to be my exercise.

The doorbell buzzed again and Tony Baloney joined in the fray, his bad-ass bark as squeaky as the lid being pried off a rusty tin can.

"You go get 'em, killer," I encouraged, figuring that would give the pooch enough adrenaline to keep him going for the rest of the year.

I opened the front door to find Eric Holt standing outside.

"Rachel, you look terrific," he said, and gave me a kiss.

Eric was the kind of man that every woman fervently prayed would be straight. Tall and lean, with high cheekbones to die for, he was also charming and rich, with impeccable taste in clothing, and an eat-your-heart-out George Hamilton tan. Eric had been smart enough to invest in the high-tech boom and make a fortune in the stock market. But his true genius lay in getting out while the going was good.

"I hope it's not a problem that I'm dropping by like this. I was in the neighborhood and thought I'd say hello."

I doubted that his visit was quite so unintentional, but was glad to see him, anyway. We'd only recently met, though Terri had known him ever since his Boy Toy days.

Eric had also lived in New Orleans at one time. He used to go to the club to watch Terri perform. Back then, Eric was straight—or at least that's what he'd told himself. The Boy Toy had been his first venture into the gay world. He viewed himself as a patron of the arts and had considered it to be safe. After all, what could be more inspiring than watching someone like Terri transform himself into a dozen different divas every night of the week?

A few months later, Eric had been brave enough to take the leap and come out of the closet. It was news that his wife of five years wasn't terribly happy to hear, being that their marriage also involved a child. Even so, the relationship had managed to survive a while longer. Terri never learned what prompted the final breakup, though it wouldn't have been very hard to guess. Whatever the reason, it proved enough to make Eric pack his bags and skedaddle—all the way over to Europe.

During that time, he and Terri not only stayed in touch, but also managed to visit each other on a regular basis. Still, it had come as a surprise when Eric moved back to the States after a breakup with his partner of ten years. He'd chosen to settle in the Bay Area about eight months ago. It was probably one of the reasons why Terri still hadn't gone home. These days, Eric worked for a surviving Internet company and lived about an hour south of San Francisco.

"Have you eaten yet?"

Eric shook his head.

"Good. Then come upstairs and join us for dinner."

He appeared to be a bit reticent. Then I remembered the first time we'd met. He'd come to my place for dinner and eaten my chili. It had obviously been an experience that he still couldn't forget.

"Don't worry. Mei Rose did the cooking tonight."

"In that case, I'm totally there," he said with a grin.

Terri jumped up from his seat and gave him a hug as he walked in.

"Eric! I can't believe it. I haven't seen you for months. I felt sure you must have gotten bored with me."

"Don't be silly. Something just came up, is all. I was out of town for awhile."

"On vacation?" Terri asked, with what sounded like a tinge of jealousy.

"No, family business. Things have been crazy ever since I came back. Nothing we need to talk about at the moment," Eric said, making it clear that the subject was temporarily off-limits.

"Good. This is meal time," Mei Rose declared, filling a plate and placing it in front of him. "Now eat," she instructed, sounding like the Chinese version of a Jewish mother.

"So, how's the Internet business going these days?" Santou asked, having lost more than his fair share of money in the stock market plunge.

"Things are actually looking up. The good news is that our books aren't cooked, and advertising revenues are beginning to boom again. The bad news is they're keeping me busy as hell. Hopefully that will change after I've been there a while longer."

"Terrific. Who knows? The way it sounds, I might eventually make back some of my money before I kick off," Jake quipped.

He reached for the container of Percoset by his side, only to have Mei Rose sharply slap his hand.

"You finish eating first before you take that stuff. Otherwise it make you sick," she reprimanded.

A look of shock flashed across his face and I held my breath, wondering if Santou would blow. There was no question but that he'd become dependent on the pills. Instead, I found myself amazed as he backed down and sheepishly nodded his head.

"In that case, how about some more chow fun?"

Unbelievable. Mei Rose was proving herself quite the force to be reckoned with.

She headed downstairs after dinner while Terri and I began to clean up. It was then that I was surprised yet again.

"Why don't you two sit down and visit with Eric while I wash the dishes?" Santou offered. "I don't want you thinking I'm not good for anything around here."

"That's the furthest thought from my mind," I assured Jake, as he slipped an arm around my waist. It was almost like having the old Santou back again.

"Actually, I'd like to go out for a drink if you don't mind," Eric said, coming to stand beside Terri. "I haven't had a chance to explore this area of town very much and it's a beautiful night. I'm not looking for anything fancy. Just a simple, quiet place with local color and not a lot of tourists."

"Sure, go ahead. Terri knows a few spots he can take you to," I replied, gracefully bowing out.

"Why don't you and Jake come along?" Eric suggested.

"Thanks, but washing dishes is about all the excitement I'm up for tonight," Santou joked.

However, I heard the edge in his voice, and knew that he didn't particularly care for Eric.

"I think I'll stay with Jake. Besides, the two of you have some catching up to do."

"I'd really like it if you'd join us, Rachel," Eric insisted. "I could use a woman's perspective on something that's going on in my life right now."

"Go ahead, chère," Santou urged. "There's another ball game on TV that I'm planning to watch."

But I suspected Jake really wanted me out of the way so that he could take a couple of Percoset in peace.

"Maybe it's best if I stay."

"For chrissakes, Rachel. Don't you trust me anymore?"

Santou irritably snapped, as Eric and Terri edged their way toward the door.

"Frankly no. I'm beginning to think that you're out of control," I bluntly whispered, sorely tempted to hire Mei Rose to stand guard over him.

Santou dried his hands on a dish towel and threw it down. I waited, not knowing exactly what to expect, as he drew closer. To my relief, he placed a finger under my chin and brought my face up to meet his.

"I promise not to take any more pills tonight. What's more, I'll be fully awake when you arrive home. How does that sound?"

"Terrific," I responded, truly wanting to believe him.

"All right then. Go out and have a good time."

I couldn't help but feel anxious as I walked out the door and left him behind.

"How long has that been going on?" Eric inquired as we stepped outside.

"What do you mean?" I responded, choosing to play dumb.

"Santou's addiction to pain pills. I saw the vials of Vicodan and Percoset. That's pretty heavy stuff."

"Yeah, you're right," I reluctantly acknowledged. "He's been taking them ever since the plane crash. Jake says he's in too much pain to stop."

"That's probably bullshit. If not, he might need another operation. In either case, you'd be smart to get him off those drugs as soon as possible considering his personality type."

"How do *you* know so much about it?" I asked, curious.

"I had a little addiction problem myself when I was coming to terms with being gay."

"I never knew that," Terri said, sounding surprised. "But then I also didn't know right away that you had a wife."

Eric glanced down at his feet, as though to make sure they kept moving one in front of the other.

"Then I suppose Santou hasn't told you that we were in the same drug counseling group back in New Orleans, either," Eric revealed. "We were both hooked on cocaine in those days."

"What? You're kidding. No, he hasn't," I responded, feeling somewhat astonished. "Of course, he doesn't like to talk about it all that much."

No wonder Eric had so easily recognized Santou's problem. Maybe that's why Jake didn't care for him. I thought about that as we strolled down Columbus Avenue, before allowing myself to be seduced by the neighborhood.

Six square blocks make up the heart of North Beach, every one of them packed with calzone joints, trattorias, and an overabundance of coffeehouses. We passed Café Roma, which proudly promoted its coffee as being "Black as Night, Strong as Sin, Sweet as Love, Hot as Hell."

"That sounds exactly like what a good man should be," Terri joked.

There were any number of spots we could have patronized where the jukebox played Pavarotti and the cappuccino came with a shot of sambucca. However, I knew where it was that I wanted to go.

I stopped when we came to the Gold Spike, aware there was no more authentic bar in town. The place has been around since 1920, and is as unfashionable as they come. Not only is the wine served in tumblers, but the restroom is reached by running through the kitchen while dodging bullets of hot grease.

We sat at a table near the bar, where a bunch of locals listened nostalgically to Dean Martin soulfully sing, "Everybody Loves Somebody Sometime."

"There's a lesson here. Your mistake was that you asked to go some place simple. That immediately gave Rach the opportunity to head for a dive," Terri bantered, as the waiter approached and took our order.

I sipped my wine when it arrived, and waited for Eric to reveal the reason as to why he'd asked me to come along.

"I really am sorry that I haven't been in touch for a while, but a lot has been going on. I had to fly back to New Orleans, for one thing," he began.

"Well, I wouldn't exactly call that a fate worse than death. The town's a lot of fun," Terri replied.

"Except the reason I went back was because my ex-wife died."

"Oh God, Eric. Please forgive me. I had no idea," Terri said, the color draining from his face. "How awful."

"Don't apologize. There's no way you could have known." He hesitated a moment. "I've told you that I have a daughter, haven't I?"

Terri and I both nodded our heads.

"How old is she?" I asked.

Eric pulled a snapshot from his pocket and placed it on the table.

"That's Lily. She just turned fifteen years old."

I had to hold myself back from gasping out loud as I looked at the photo. A young girl with large brown eyes gazed shyly at the world. Her silky brunette hair hung down around her shoulders like a fine pashmina shawl. But nothing could hide the ugly scars that crawled up along her neck, spitefully covering her throat as if placed there by jealous wraiths. She must have had skin grafts at one time, because the texture of her flesh was rather thick and had an odd patterning to it. Even so, the girl was still exceptionally beautiful.

"My God! What happened to her, Eric?" Terri asked in dismay.

"Shit. This is so hard for me to talk about. It's why I've always considered myself such a lousy father; forget the fact that I was rarely around."

Eric knocked back his scotch and water and ordered another.

"Don't be so hard on yourself. You're one of the nicest people I know," Terri said, covering Eric's hand with his own. "I'm sure whatever happened wasn't your fault."

"That's where you're wrong."

The waiter set a second scotch and water in front of him, and Eric grabbed on to it with the desperation of a drowning man.

"Ellen—that was my wife—she was taking night courses at the time, trying to finish her teaching degree. We were still living together, although I'd already come out. Of course, we were more like roommates by then. Ones who fought a lot and sometimes didn't talk."

Eric stopped and took a long drink of his scotch.

"Anyway, I continued to support them both financially, what with Ellen still getting over the shock. I figured it was the least I could do under the circumstances. That meant I couldn't move out on my own yet."

Terri shook his head sympathetically. "You should have come to me. I had a town house in the French Quarter. I would have given you a place to stay."

Eric massaged his temples with his fingertips, as if trying to rid himself of a headache that refused to go away. "Oh, what the hell. I might as well be honest about it. I was afraid to give up the respectability that marriage gave me. Pretty pathetic, huh?"

"Not at all. Your whole world had been turned upside down at that point," I sympathized, though I still couldn't understand why Eric continued to beat himself up so much.

"All Ellen asked in return was that I watch Lily three

nights a week until she got home from her courses. Naturally, I agreed. Lily was five years old at the time, and I loved being with her. Besides, I didn't know if Ellen was going to ask for sole custody. I wanted to spend all the time that I could with my daughter."

Eric abruptly stopped and stared at the wall, as if he were watching a movie in his head.

"Go on," I gently prodded.

He took a deep breath and jaggedly exhaled, as though his very soul were trying to escape. "I was preparing dinner for Lily one night when the phone rang in the bedroom. It was someone I'd met at the Boy Toy. God knows whatever possessed me to give him my home number. Anyway, we were talking when Lily suddenly burst out in this horrible blood-curdling scream. I swear, I can still hear it to this day. I ran into the kitchen to find that she'd accidentally knocked a pot of boiling water off the stove and had gotten it all over herself.

"Oh Christ," Terri muttered.

Eric angrily shook his head and wiped a few tears from his face. "Jeez, she was just a little kid, you know? Why the hell does something like that have to happen?"

"It was an accident," I replied, not knowing what else to say. "What did you do?"

"I submerged her in cold water as fast as I could and then immediately rushed her to the hospital. But it was already too late. Lily was left with those scars that you see, along with others on her back and chest. That was the final straw for Ellen. She never forgave me. I moved out of the house the very next day."

"But you still saw Lily, didn't you?" Terri asked. "She knew it wasn't your fault."

"Yeah, I saw her, though not as often as I would have liked. Of course, my moving to Europe didn't help. Still, she spent summers with me, and I went back to New Orleans at Christmas each year. I always made it a point to tell Lily how much I loved her, and that she could count on me, no matter what. And for a while, we were fairly close. Then came the teenage years and everything completely changed."

"That's perfectly normal. All kids go through a transition period when they hit puberty," I said, remembering my own nobody-will-ever-understand-me years. "Besides, the two of you have another chance to work things out. I imagine that Lily will be living with you now."

"That's what I thought too," Eric replied, sounding more despondent than ever. "The problem is that Ellen died unexpectedly in a car accident, and her parents have insisted on keeping Lily with them until the end of the school year. They felt that uprooting her before then would only cause more trauma."

"Well, I imagine there are only a few more weeks of school left. Which means that everything's going to work out just fine," Terri remarked, doing his best to sound upbeat.

"Not quite. Lily has run away," Eric revealed.

For a moment, it looked as though he'd literally shrunk inside his clothes, until I realized that his entire body had started to slump.

"She overheard her grandparents discussing a possible upcoming custody battle. They don't feel it's proper for a fifteen-year-old girl to live with her gay father. After all, what kind of role model would I be?"

"What a total pile of crap," Terri impatiently snapped. "That sort of primeval thinking belongs back in the Dark Ages."

"Maybe so. But Lily was apparently upset enough to pack a few things and take off. She even left a note that now we wouldn't have to fight over her. I just can't understand why she hasn't called me yet."

"She has a lot to digest at the moment, what with her mother's death and now this," I replied, though secretly wondering the same thing.

There were times when I'd also wanted to run away during my teen years, as fast and as far as I could. The truth was, I knew someone who'd done just that.

"Have you called the police?" I asked.

"Of course, right away. You know what they told me? Eight hundred and fifty-thousand children are reported missing each year. Of that number, roughly four hundred, fifty-one thousand of them are runaways. The police have to concentrate on those kids that have been abducted. In other words, I was basically told good luck. I feel as if she's fallen into a big black hole and it's up to me to get her out."

"I'm sure you'll hear from her soon," I said consolingly. "When did she leave?"

Eric suddenly looked as though he hadn't slept in weeks. He propped his head in his hands, and his eyes began to flutter.

"Six weeks ago, and not a word since then. I've been racking my brain as to why she wouldn't phone. The only thing I can figure is that Lily must resent me."

He probably wasn't all that far off the mark. She was at the age when girls were more aware of their body image than ever. I glanced at the photo again and could only imagine what Lily had to contend with—the grimaces, hurtful remarks, and taunts. At fifteen, I was fixated on straightening my hair and experimenting with makeup. What must Lily think every time she looked in a mirror?

"Any idea where she could have gone?" Terri inquired, while signaling the waiter for a check.

"Actually, I think she might be right here in San Francisco."

"What makes you say that?" I asked, surprised at his response.

"Because she didn't run away on her own. She left with her pimply faced boyfriend, and San Francisco is where he always said he wanted to go."

"Who is this guy?" I asked, suddenly getting a whole new slant on the situation.

"His name is Randy Edgers. I met him while visiting Lily in New Orleans last year. The kid is a nineteen-year-old high-school dropout who worked in a video store. He's all right, I suppose," Eric said, and then made a face. "Who am I kidding? The kid's a total loser. In fact, that's the one thing Ellen and I both agreed on, and we told Lily so."

"It probably made her want to be with him all the more," I surmised, knowing that's exactly how I would have felt.

"Terrific. Knowing that makes me feel so much better," Eric caustically retorted. "I'm sorry, but it kills me to think Lily feels that's all she's worth. She deserves a hell of a lot more than that."

"She's rebelling, Eric. There's no greater high in the world at that age. This guy's probably telling Lily how much he loves and accepts her. The combination is totally irresistible. Then throw in that she most likely sees him as her knight in shining armor at a time when she's not only grieving but is also confused and afraid. It makes it easier to understand how Lily might choose to pick up and run away."

Like father, like daughter, I was almost tempted to say.

"That's all fine, Rach. But if Eric really thinks they're here, the thing to do is to check every video store in town. After all, that's where this kid worked in New Orleans, so he's probably doing the same thing in San Francisco," Terri interjected, cutting to the chase.

"That's what I *have* been doing," Eric said. "I must have hit every video store in the Bay Area over the past month. I even showed Lily's picture around, but without any luck. I don't know what I'm going to do if I can't find her. She needs a father now more than ever, and I'm not there for her. All I can do is wonder what might have been, had I done things differently. I never should have left New Orleans in the first place."

There it was. The nagging regrets that we all learn to live with; the lingering question of "what if" when it comes to decisions that can't be undone. I pushed down the tears that were beginning to creep up, bringing with them unwanted memories long suppressed.

"That's why I asked you to come tonight, Rachel. I want you to help me."

"What can I do?" I asked, my stomach beginning to churn in a noxious mixture of anxiety and dread.

"You know San Francisco and probably have a better idea of where to search for runaways. Besides, you can always say that you're with law enforcement, and people will listen to you."

"Sure, as long as they don't squint too closely at my badge and see Fish and Wildlife written on it."

"Just spend a day or two going around the city with me, please. That's all I'm asking."

I looked at Eric and knew there was no way I could turn him down; no matter how painful opening up an old wound might prove to be.

"Fine. We'll start tomorrow," I agreed, my body contracting into a tight knot.

I thought again of the number of runaways, and knew that finding Lily could prove to be as difficult as stumbling upon the elusive Lotis blue butterfly.

Terri convinced Eric to spend the night on his couch, fearing he'd be too tired to drive all the way home. I helped get him upstairs and then retired to my own abode.

"Hey chère. You look wiped out. Just how many drinks did you have tonight?"

Santou had kept his word. He'd remained both lucid and awake—enough so that he was concerned about the amount of alcohol *I'd* consumed. We'd agreed that neither of us would go over a certain limit, after an incident we had while living in Georgia.

"I only had one glass of wine. It was just a strange evening, is all."

"How so?" he asked, sitting on the edge of the bathtub as I washed up for bed.

"It seems Eric had been married at one time and has a child."

I glanced at Santou, certain that this was information he already knew.

"Anyway, his former wife recently died in a car crash. Lily, his daughter, was supposed to stay with her grandparents until the end of school and then move in with her dad. At least, that was the plan. Then talk of a custody battle began. Now Lily's run away and Eric has asked for my help. He thinks she might be somewhere here in San Francisco."

"This is a police matter, Rachel. You know that."

"Sure. We're also both aware of exactly what that means. Her name will end up collecting dust in a file along with hundreds of thousands of others."

"So, what does he think you're going to be able to do?"

"I don't really know. My guess is he needs moral support more than anything else. Eric wants me to spend a couple of days going to different neighborhoods with him. He'd like us to talk to as many people as possible, and show her picture around. I agreed."

Santou stood up and kissed me on the back of the neck. "That's because you're a good person, and one hell of a soft touch."

My throat constricted so much that I didn't dare speak any further. It was only as I slid into bed and turned off the light that I felt safe enough to allow a small tear to spill from the corner of my eye.

Big mistake. It opened up a floodgate. Sobs raced in, grabbing hold of my body and taking it on an emotional carnival ride.

"Rachel, what's the matter?" Santou asked in alarm, flicking on the light.

"Turn it off!" I cried out, not yet ready to see or be seen by the world.

Santou doused the light. Then wrapping me in his arms, he rocked me back and forth in the darkness. He waited until my sobs died down and gently kissed my forehead.

"Now tell me what's wrong, chère."

I had no other choice—not unless I wanted him to believe that I was a total madwoman. Still, it was difficult to divulge a matter about which I'd remained silent for so long. It had been years since I'd told anyone. Mainly because there'd always been too many questions, few of which I wanted to answer.

"I had a sister that left home years ago."

"What?" Santou exclaimed, pulling me with him as he sat up in bed. "When was this?"

"Shortly after my father died. Rebecca was sixteen years old at the time, and I was ten."

"Why didn't you ever tell me about it before?"

"Oh, I don't know," I lied, and immediately burst into tears again.

Santou grabbed some tissues, and I wadded them up and blew my nose.

"That's not true," I admitted. "It's because I always felt too guilty to talk about it."

"Why should you feel guilty, chère? I'm sure it wasn't your fault."

"In a way, it was. I could have tried to stop her. Only I didn't," I confessed aloud for the very first time. "Rebecca told me that she planned to run away and made me promise not to tell anyone. It seemed like such an exciting game back then that I kept her secret. I'll never forgive myself for not having warned my mother."

Whoever said confession was good for the soul had no idea what they were talking about. I still felt like crap.

"Did you ever hear from her again?"

I shook my head, and tried to speak over the lump in my throat. "My mother hired someone to search for Rebecca, but she was never found. I don't know if she's alive or dead to this day."

"You were just a kid, chère. You can't hold yourself responsible for your sister's actions."

"But I do. Rebecca's disappearance broke my mother's heart. She was the favorite, the one that was clever and beautiful. I sometimes wonder if I was happy that she left, so I could try to take her place. I think my mother knew it, too, and resented me for it. No matter what I did, it was never quite good enough."

I hated revealing so much, detested feeling this vulnerable. Yet once having started, I now couldn't stop myself.

"I spent my teenage years attempting to prove that I was equally worthwhile. Hell, I've been doing that my entire life. What I finally discovered is that it's fruitless to try and compete with a ghost. Especially one for which I feel so responsible."

Santou pushed a jumble of curls out of my eyes and held me at arm's length.

"Do you know what I see when I look at you, Rachel Porter? Someone who has the gumption to act on what she believes in and is willing to stand up to the world. I see a woman who's strong, courageous, and smart. You've got enough spirit to take on battles that you probably won't win, all because you'd rather go down fighting than to ever give up. The only thing you're guilty of is not appreciating who you really are. So see yourself through my eyes, Rachel, and realize there's no one more beautiful that I could possibly love."

I cried once again. Only this time it was because I knew how lucky I was to have Santou in my life, and just how easy it would be to lose him. I'd learned all too well that the world is an increasingly dangerous place in which things can change in a brief instant.

That's also true of butterflies, I mused. *Only they have one big advantage over us. They get to be born twice.*

I lay awake awhile longer, listening to the rhythmic pattern of Jake's breathing, unwilling to close my eyes and slip into dreamtime. Only when the sound mixed with the mournful lament of a fog horn to become a gentle lullaby, did I grudgingly fall asleep, temporarily leaving this existence.

Nine

I felt sure I'd barely closed my eyes when something jabbed into my side, accompanied by the sound of footsteps shuffling near the bed. But it was a warm breath drifting across the back of my neck that had the hairs rising on my head.

I slowly worked my fingers under the pillow to where a .38 was lodged between the wall and the mattress. Grabbing hold of the gun, I rolled over in one lightning quick move, prepared to face down a bad-ass intruder. Instead I found my landlady inscrutably standing there in the dark, dressed in the loose garb of a tai chi master.

Mei Rose didn't appear to be the least bit fazed by my gun. Rather she kept prodding at me as if I were a chicken being sized up for dinner.

. "What are you doing?" I wailed, pondering how hard it would be to find a new place to live.

"Shh!" Mei Rose hissed like a pissed-off snake. "Be quiet or you wake up Jake. He needs his sleep."

I glanced at the clock: 6 A.M. Or in my world, the crack of dawn, considering that I didn't have to get up for another hour.

"What about me?" I grumbled and lay back down, only to have her fingers poke again into my ribs.

"You don't need so much sleep. Besides, this is the time we go shopping."

121

Terrific. I wondered how much jail time I'd be sentenced to for punching out a senior citizen.

I reluctantly rolled out of bed and splashed some water on my face, deciding that was all the personal hygiene Mei Rose was going to get. Then I followed her downstairs and through the front door, noticing that not even Tony Baloney was up and about at this ungodly hour.

Heading down the hill, we came to Washington Square Park, where a cluster of elderly Asians was already practicing their tai chi. The group looked completely at home, though they were in the heart of North Beach, surrounded by Saint Peter and Paul's Catholic Church, Italian coffeehouses, and social clubs.

The women wore colorful quilted jackets of bright yellows, reds, and pinks, which turned them into a resplendent bouquet of flowers. They gossiped amongst themselves while performing the ancient Chinese exercise in a series of slow, flowing movements. I chuckled, having realized what they reminded me of: an octogenarian group of John Travoltas. Each struck a pose, as though having been caught in a freeze frame of the movie *Saturday Night Fever*.

"*Jo Sun, Nay Ho*," they sang out in greeting to Mei Rose, as we quickly walked by.

She cheerfully waved, but didn't come to a halt.

The smell of freshly baked sourdough bread made my stomach grumble as we passed a bakery, where a worker shoveled loaves in and out of a brick oven. I would have been tempted to stop if it weren't for the anxious clucking of Mei Rose's tongue.

"Hurry, hurry," she urged, moving me along.

"Why? What's the rush?"

"We want to get there before all the best stuff is gone."

Considering the hour, I didn't imagine that would be too big of a problem.

We crossed into Chinatown, and were immediately swept up in a flurry of activity.

Merchants with pushcarts scurried about, wasting no time as they darted in and out of stores selling their wares. Meanwhile, an army of elderly women crowded the streets, each engrossed in shopping for the evening meal. They were as intently focused on their mission as if they were cops pounding a beat.

I dodged an ancient woman that dashed out of Ming Kee's Game Shop with a live bird in tow. Its beak pecked away inside its paper-bag prison, demanding to be released. I peered into the store and spied cages stacked one on top of another, each containing tightly packed fowl. There were roosters, squabs, and silken chickens with long white feathers. Little did they know that their fate was to be tonight's dinner.

Ming Kee's used to butcher the birds for customers right on the spot, cleaning, gutting and taking out the gizzards. However, it created an ungodly mess with feathers littering the streets and blood running into the sewers. The health department finally had to step in and crack down. Now women carried live birds home on the bus, satisfying their urge for freshness by killing the creatures themselves.

Mei Rose chuckled at my apparent fascination. "What? You never knew where your chicken dinner came from before? Maybe you thought chickens were born already packaged and wrapped in plastic at the grocery store."

But I paid little heed, too caught up in all the action going on.

Old men were gathered in Portsmouth Square, where they played games of Chinese checkers. Even so, the loud *clack, clack, clack* of thousands of mah jongg tiles could be heard coming from a nearby alley. Adding to the open-air symphony was the whine of sewing machines, humming like a hive of busy bees—only these workers were women who sat hunched over mounds of garments and pieced them together in darkly sinister factories.

"Come. There'll be other things to look at," Mei Rose prompted, as we cut up to Stockton Street.

Here was where the real Chinatown existed, without tourists, McDonald's, or ticky-tacky souvenir stores. It was here that the locals came to do their shopping twice a day.

I was immediately swallowed up by throngs of pedestrians and pulled along, as if magnetically drawn, toward outdoor bins brimming with bitter melon, litchi nuts and lotus root. The vibrant colors of figs, mangoes, oranges, and durian fruit looked too intense to be real. I stood in awe and watched as Mei Rose jockeyed for position with the rest of the pros, grabbing the freshest produce that she could reach.

Then it was off to the fish market, with its display of snails, conch, and grouper. Had I been alone, I'd have been tempted to liberate all the traumatized turtles and frogs that were piled high in water-filled tubs. As it was, the frogs crawled over and on top of one another like a gang of desperate stowaways crammed inside a ship's hold. They futilely attempted to escape the grasping hands that held them up and roughly prodded and poked at their bellies. The lesson clearly was that it didn't pay to be among the fattest frogs in Chinatown.

Our last stop was a bakery where I joined a pigeon standing on line with the rest of the customers. The bird patiently waited for a few crumbs to fall from the mooncakes and sesame balls that they bought. I eyed the pigeon in silent warning, having become hungry enough to wrestle the bird for the crumbs myself. Mei Rose looked away in embarrassment as my stomach loudly rumbled, pretending not to know me. It was only when we walked outside that she took pity and led me toward a *juk* shop.

We sat at a booth and each ordered a bowl of rice porridge, after which Mei Rose happily chattered on about to-night's meal. Only I wasn't paying attention, my mind having wandered.

"What wrong? You don't feel well?" Mei Rose inquired, unhappy that I hadn't been listening. "Or maybe it's the food." She immediately motioned for the waitress to bring something else.

"No, the porridge is fine," I assured her and proceeded to eat.

"Then what the problem? You let me know. I can always help."

There'd obviously be no peace until I told the woman something.

"Remember Eric from dinner last night?"

"Of course I remember. What you think? That because I'm old, I'm senile?" Mei Rose responded, clearly insulted.

Oy veh.

"Well his fifteen-year-old daughter recently ran away."

I drew the line at telling her that it felt as if my own past had come back to haunt me. Ever since last night I'd found myself staring at every young girl that passed by, wondering if I'd seen her face on a poster as a runaway.

"That no good. Too many problems are entering the house," Mei Rose declared, and seemed to shiver. "There must be bad *chi* coming from Su Lin Fong across the street. We'll have to stop at a shop on Grant and buy small octagonal mirrors to hang in the front windows. That will send the bad *chi* flying back to the Fong house, where it belongs."

Mei Rose was still huffing and puffing about the nerve of Su Lin Fong sending bad *chi* our way when her cell phone rang, playing a poor rendition of the *William Tell* overture.

I finished my porridge while she conversed at breakneck speed in Cantonese, sounding as if she'd taken an Evelyn

Wood course on rapid-fire speaking. Then Mei Rose hung up and shook her head.

"That my niece. She always need help with something. What can I do?" she asked, with a put-upon shrug. "I have to go see her right away. But don't worry. I'll buy mirrors and hang them up later. I think some feng shui might help, too. Everything in your place is facing the wrong way. But that's okay. I take care of that, also. Meanwhile, you carry all the groceries home for me."

I felt like a pack mule as she loaded me up, adding her own bags to those I was already hauling. It's no wonder fast food restaurants have become increasingly popular. Who has time for this sort of thing? To hell with eating healthy. The stress from shopping was just about to kill me. I fumed all the way home, vowing to spend the rest of my life eating nothing but prepared and frozen foods. To make matters worse, no one was there to help carry all the bags upstairs.

I crammed everything into my refrigerator, not in the mood to enter Mei Rose's place and deal with Tony Baloney.

Speaking of having to deal with things, I then placed a quick call to my boss.

"All clear on the western front?" Brad Thomas asked, by way of his usual greeting.

"Everything's fine," I responded. "Just thought I'd fill you in on a few details. I don't know if you've heard, but John Harmon's Jeep was found on a remote dirt road up in Mendocino yesterday."

"That's it? Just his vehicle?"

"Yeah. There was no sign of foul play, according to the police. But then, who knows how well they searched? I have to tell you, I find it troubling that they don't seem to be taking the fact that he's missing very seriously."

"For all you know, they have information that they don't want to give out."

"Such as?" I questioned, unwilling to let him off the hook.

"Such as, it could be the guy's up to his ears in debt and has decided to lay low for a while. Or maybe he's got another woman on the side."

How interesting. Thomas had come up with the same exact reasons as to why Harmon might have disappeared as had Santou. It was enough to make me suspicious about the way a man's mind worked.

"I want you to steer clear of whatever's going on. Let the police handle it. Harmon's not your problem."

"I have no intention of getting involved," I assured Thomas. Not when I had my net set for a big-league butterfly poacher by the name of Horus. "Oh by the way, I'd like to take a few days personal leave."

"This better not have anything to do with Harmon," he again warned. "Nor are you to play vigilante queen by taking off and trying to tackle some other wildlife case on your own."

Jeez, what *was* Thomas, anyway? A mind reader?

"Of course not. It has nothing to do with either of those things," I replied in an indignant tone. "A friend's daughter has run away and he's asked me to help search for her."

"Why, Porter, you should have told me that you'd gotten a P.I. license and were moonlighting on the side. I'd have referred some cases your way," Thomas caustically retorted. "Don't you think *that's* best left to the police as well? Or are you trying to do the job of both the SFPD *and* the Mendocino County Sheriff's Office, as well as your own?"

"Look, I just want to give my friend some moral support. Anything wrong with that?" I questioned, hoping to avoid a fight.

"No, I suppose not," Thomas reluctantly responded. "There shouldn't be a problem, just as long as it's only for a few days and that's *all* you're doing. Besides, it'll give Dan Weymer a chance to handle some of your caseload."

I inwardly groaned, well aware that this was a dig. Weymer was more than just a rookie agent who'd been assigned to our office; he was already nipping away at my heels. Part of the "whatever" generation, he was fast becoming a favorite of Brad Thomas for being more than willing to toe the line. It was no secret that Weymer's goal was upward mobility; the sooner he could fast-track it to the next level, the better. The result was that he had little interest in doing fieldwork and even less in ruffling anyone's feathers, particularly when it came to protecting embattled wildlife. Rather, his focus was one of "What's in it for me?"

"I'll return as soon as I can," I said and hung up, more convinced than ever that I was being put on the back-burner.

However, I had little time to sink into a funk as Terri and Eric walked through the door.

"How are you feeling this morning?" I asked Terri's houseguest.

"My head's better, thanks. Now it's my back that's killing me. That couch upstairs has more lumps in it than a middle-aged queen with cellulite."

"Hey, watch the slurs. I'm feeling very fragile these days." Terri sniffed.

"Oh, please. You know that's not what I meant. How could I? You look absolutely fabulous."

Terri brightened considerably. "For that you get a gourmet breakfast. After all, we're going to need our energy today."

He proceeded to whip up a feast of French toast smothered in a mango and raisin compote, as I pulled out a city map and showed it to Eric. By the time breakfast was through, we'd decided exactly where to begin our search: the Tenderloin district.

"Are you coming along?" I asked Terri, unsure if there was something else he had to do.

"Of course I'm coming. As I recall, Eric asked both of us for help," he chided, letting me know he had no intention of being left behind. Terri glanced at Eric, who nodded at him reassuringly. "While you may be more familiar with San Francisco, I probably have better insight when it comes to the mindset of runaways."

"You're probably right," I concurred, wisely keeping my mouth shut.

Terri was clearly more interested in Eric than I might have imagined. We cleaned up the dishes and then headed downstairs.

"Watch out for the white mop lying outside by the door. He may look harmless, but the pooch has the soul of Genghis Khan," I warned.

True to form, Tony Baloney growled and lunged for our legs as we hurried past. Emitting a couple of yaps to clear his throat, the mutt circled around and around before settling back down, fully satisfied that he'd protected his territory.

We walked toward Washington Square, turning at Mario's Bohemian Cigar Store, a closet-sized café with the best focaccia sandwiches in town. Its outdoor tables were already filled to capacity hosting bohemian wannabes busy arguing politics, intellectual wannabes armed with horn-rimmed glasses and poetry, and artist wannabes furiously drawing away on their sketch pads. Come to think of it, I was also a wannabe. I wanted a jolt of Mario's super-strength industrial caffeine more than anything else in the world. I needed a second wind after my crack-of-dawn shopping excursion with Mei Rose. A couple of shots of espresso and I was raring to go.

We strolled down Columbus until we came to the infamous Condor Club, the first topless bar in America. This was where Carol Doda had descended from the ceiling on a grand piano, displaying her silicon splendors. Two years later, the club also went bottomless, causing a flurry of imitators to spring up along the Strip. The Condor stayed open until the early eighties, when a dancer and her security guard were caught *in flagrante* on top of that same grand piano. It wasn't the act itself that caused a problem, but the hydraulic elevating mechanism which became jammed. The piano unexpectedly rose to the ceiling, killing the security guard and pinning the dancer beneath him for hours. The club closed soon after and eventually reopened as a sports bar. Now there was only an historical bronze plaque outside to recall its former glory days.

"Just think. This is where it all began." Terri sighed nostalgically. "Who would have guessed that expanding a pair of boobs with silicon from thirty-four to forty-four inches would ever set off such a craze? God bless you, Carol Doda." He kissed his fingertips, and gave the plaque a pat.

We opted to save time by cutting over to Powell, and hopped on a cable car with a group of giddy tourists. Shades of Hitchcock's *Vertigo* took over as we climbed up, up, up before plummeting down, down, down toward Market Street. My heart soared with the rancorous clanging of its bell as the car rattled along like a mechanical toy on steel wheels. Standing on the bottom step, I clung to a pole and threw back my head, hoping to catch a whiff of distant sea breeze. We got off at the final stop and took a short walk west, drawing closer to our destination.

The downtown surroundings slowly deteriorated, going from dingy to shabby to downright decrepit, as we entered the Tenderloin. A seedy, drug-infested pit, the district was filled with porn shops, massage parlors, and a dilapidated homeless shelter. Hotel rooms were rented by the hour, serving a "professional" clientele who constantly used the same soiled sheets. Walking the streets were drunks, hookers, and runaways, along with their exploiters.

"What has Lily gone and gotten herself into?" Eric muttered under his breath. "Half of me hopes that I find her here, while the other half doesn't."

I couldn't say that I much blamed him. The Tenderloin boasts the highest rate of rape in the city, and is a dangerous place for a woman of any age. I could only imagine what a teenage girl living on its streets would have to endure.

We headed into the first shop, where Eric pulled out Lily's photograph and showed it around. Though a look of shock passed over each face, there wasn't a hint of recognition.

"Sorry, but we don't know her" was the standard response heard over and over from every store owner, as well as those people who we questioned on the street.

Runaway girls? They're a dime a dozen in this area. Just look around and take your pick.

We knocked on locked doors behind which senior citizens had barricaded themselves, too poor to move anywhere else and too frightened to step outside.

"Trust me. I'd remember that face. I haven't seen it before. Now please go away," each implored.

By the end of the day, Lily's photo bore multiple sets of indifferent greasy fingerprints, and Eric's spirit had hit rock bottom. We'd met with little success, other than to see what we were up against, and the odds weren't encouraging. We decided to pack it in and head back to North Beach until tomorrow morning.

"You know the hardest thing? Imagining that Lily might be out here somewhere. She could be hurting right now, and there's not a damn thing I can do about it," Eric said, his frustration building. "That's why I hate to see the sun go down. I try to stay busy during the day. It's the nighttime that kills me. All I'm left with then are my thoughts and fears. It's gotten so that I can't stand being alone anymore."

"Then you won't be," Terri said, slipping his arm through Eric's. "That's what friends are for. Don't worry about the couch. You can sleep on the bed and I'll borrow a futon from Mei Rose."

"I can't let you do that," Eric demurred.

But Terri firmly insisted. "Oh yes, you can and will. At least until we find Lily. Isn't that right, Rach?"

"Absolutely," I agreed, knowing how helpless Eric must feel. Because of that, I also made a suggestion. "Maybe it's time to check in with the San Francisco police."

Eric swiftly dismissed the idea out of hand. "Ellen's parents already did that. Besides, whatever for? Do you really think the cops out here are going to be any different from those in New Orleans when it comes to runaways?"

I didn't respond. What was the point, when we both already knew the answer?

"All they're going to do is advise me to be patient and wait. And I swear, if I hear that once more I'm going to scream. I don't care what anyone says. I know in my heart that something has happened to Lily. I never realized what it was like to be a father before, but now I know that we're truly connected. Can you understand that, Rachel?"

I nodded, wondering what my sister might look like today, and if she ever regretted having run away.

"I can't sit around wasting time until Lily is found dead somewhere and her name is splattered across a newspaper."

Eric was right. That's when the police would finally kick in and try to track down her killer.

His chest heaved in a silent sob, making his shoulders bob

up and down. That simple movement was enough to cement my determination.

"It's all right, Eric. We'll look until we find her," I promised.

I only hoped that I could keep my word.

Ten

We arrived home to quite a sight. A number of small octagonal mirrors had been hung in every window of the house. They reflected the sunset in a crazy patchwork of light.

"Lordy, Lordy. What's *this* all about? Did Mei Rose finally lose her mind and sell the place to a bunch of carnies while we were out?" Terri questioned, shading his eyes from the blinding glare.

I put on my sunglasses, wondering what Su Lin Fong across the street must be thinking right about now. "It's just this little superstitious thing she has going on at the moment."

"What? More with the *chi*? Like the tree standing in the middle of the hallway isn't enough?" Terri retorted, with a shake of his head.

We headed upstairs, where I could already smell the delicious aroma of a Chinese meal. Opening the door, we found Santou sitting at the table digging into a plateful of steamed fish, white rice, and Chinese broccoli.

"Sorry to start eating without you, but I didn't know when you'd all be home."

"I just hope there's more of that for the rest of us," Terri said, taking a deep whiff.

"There is, though no thanks to Rachel. I had to charm Mei Rose into leaving the remainder of the food in the fridge. She's pretty mad at you, chère. From what I understand, you

135

were supposed to help her with the cooking tonight."

I tried my best to fight the onslaught of guilt, but it was like a tidal wave pulling me under.

"What? You mean it's not enough that I was dragged out of bed at daybreak, and had to schlep all the groceries home like a mule? I'm then expected to rush back after work in order to wash, chop, and prepare an entire meal?"

"Uh-huh," Jake grunted, sticking a forkful of fish in his mouth.

Damn. I hate when I feel like a slug. I'd have turned back around and gone out to eat, if only my stomach hadn't protested.

"Okay, I'll apologize to her later," I agreed, hungrily eyeing the food.

"Oh, I think you're gonna have to do a whole lot better than that," Santou said, with a grin.

"Fine. I'll spend my next free weekend slogging away in the kitchen, pretending to be the Chinese version of Julia Child," I retorted, having no intention of doing any such thing.

"Oh for chrissakes, Rach. Just tell her to give up the ghost already. Now lets zap the food and eat," Terri said, heading for the microwave.

I had to admit, the meal was delicious. I just didn't want to spend the rest of my life cooking.

"So, how'd it go today? Any luck?" Jake asked, as we finished dinner and piled the dishes in the sink.

"Not unless you consider being dissed by a bunch of lowlife pimps in the Tenderloin to be an uplifting experience," Eric glumly reported.

"We seemed to hit a dead end with everyone," I conceded.

"Maybe you just need to go about this differently."

"What? Leave it to the police, like hundreds of thousands

of other parents, while I sit back and let the years roll by? No thanks," Eric sharply retorted.

"Okay, handle it your way. But why don't you tell me a little about your daughter?" Santou suggested.

Eric slowly nodded and pulled out Lily's photo, his fingers gently caressing the image as if it contained a hidden message in Braille.

"She's not a big girl, but small-boned with delicate features like her mother. Her skin is the color of fine porcelain where it isn't scarred." Eric's eyes crinkled, as if picturing her in his mind, and his lips parted in a smile. "When Lily was younger, she liked to say that her eyes were brown as chocolate pudding."

"Where are some of her favorite places to go?" Santou questioned, so seamlessly that one would scarcely realize they were being interrogated.

"To the local ice-cream store. The flavor she loves best is Rocky Road. She's also crazy about videos and movies. I bet she must have watched the film *Cinderella* a hundred times while growing up. Lily liked to pretend she had a fairy godmother who was going to change her into a princess."

"What about TV? Does she watch much of that?" Jake casually inquired.

"Sure. What kid doesn't?"

"Any shows in particular?"

Eric stopped and thought about that for a moment.

"You know, she watches things like *Smallville*, *Friends*, and *The Gilmore Girls*. Oh, and she's a really big fan of the show *Buffy*."

So far, Lily sounded like any other young girl. Eric then listed the things she didn't like, such as gym class, the beach, and going to museums. I continued to listen as every facet of her life was exposed and scrutinized, wondering how my own would hold up under such close examination.

"Does Lily have many friends?" Jake continued to question.

"She tends to be a loner. But then, Lily never quite fit in with the other girls. Her scars always made her feel different."

"What sorts of things did she take with her when she left?"

"Let's see. Some jeans and shirts, along with her favorite pair of sneakers. Oh yeah, and her *Buffy* collection."

"What's a *Buffy* collection?" I asked.

"You know, DVDs of the entire series. What can I say? Teenage girls seem to be into looking hot while pretending to kick demons' asses these day."

Made sense to me. Who said it was only teenage girls that were into such things?

"Now fill me in on her boyfriend," Santou instructed.

"Don't get me started," Eric snapped. "What kind of nineteen-year-old goes after a girl who's only fifteen? I'll tell you. A guy that wants someone he can easily manipulate. Obviously he's intimidated by girls his own age. For the life of me, I don't understand what she sees in the creep. It's not as if Randy is all that good-looking. I mean, he's got this horrid pasty white complexion because he refuses to go out in the sun."

"Maybe he has allergies and needs to take care of his skin," Terri suggested.

"Oh please! Allergies my ass. The kid likes to pretend that he's some sort of freakin' vampire."

Terri's hands flew up in the air like a pair of doves that had been released. "That's it! *Buffy*. Vampires. Now it's all beginning to make sense."

We turned and stared at him, having absolutely no idea what he was talking about.

"Don't you see? If Lily's hanging around with this guy, then where we should be looking is in a vampire's den."

We continued to gape at him in disbelief.

"What? I watch *Buffy*. I know what it is I'm talking about," Terri said, with an indignant sniff.

"Okay then. Explain to me exactly what a vampire's den is," Santou responded.

"All right, so it's not an actual den, but a nightspot that caters to the vampire scene. Remember when I went to SOMA the other night, to look for a job at one of the transvestite clubs?"

I knew of SOMA as the industrial neighborhood south of Market Street. It had become a trendy new hot spot, attracting musicians, artists, and filmmakers to live and work in its warehouse lofts. The result was that chichi clubs and restaurants had begun to spring up.

"Anyway, I passed by this club, Poison, and took a peek inside. We're talking a heavy-duty vampire scene. It was enough to have given Dracula a serious hard-on."

"Then let's go there right now and check it out," Eric eagerly said, beginning to get up from the couch.

But Terri took hold of his arm. "It's only nine o'clock, sugar. The place doesn't start rolling till midnight. You don't want to go too early and take the chance of scaring Lily away, do you?"

"No. Of course not," Eric reluctantly acquiesced.

"Then why don't we go upstairs and watch some TV to pass the time?" Terri suggested.

"Just make sure you stop by here on your way to the club, because Rachel and I are coming along," Santou called out as the two headed for the door.

"You're on," Terri replied, flashing an okay sign with his hand.

I couldn't have been more pleased if Jake had said we were hopping a plane to Paris. But I also didn't want to act too surprised. Instead, I took it in stride.

"Great. So, would you like me to make some tea while we wait?" I knew Jake hated my coffee, considering the primo brew that was available in the local cafés.

"Sounds good. After that, why don't you give me a run-down on what you've been up to for the past few days."

"I'm sure I've already told you. Nothing terribly exciting. Just some work with butterflies, is all," I responded, not wanting to jinx things by revealing too much at this point. Not that there was all that much to reveal. "It's certainly not like the big cases that I worked in the past."

"I hate to say it, chère, but you've got a bad attitude."

"What do you mean?" I shot back, instantly on the defensive.

"For chrissakes, listen to yourself. You're being negative just because you're not dealing with a grizzly or some other carnivorous man-eater. It's clear that you don't put much stock in the value of bugs."

"That's not true," I responded, unwilling to admit that Jake was correct.

"Let me give you a little biology lesson, chère. Butterflies are the most important pollinator of crops right after bees. In fact, you could say they're a bellwether for what's happening on this earth. Try thinking of them as the above-ground equivalent of canaries in the mineshaft. The amazing thing is people see them as just these pretty little things. But butterflies have one hell of a tough life. For instance, did you know that only one one thousandth of their eggs survive?"

I shook my head in surprise, having never heard Santou speak like this before.

"In a sense, they're rather like a Greek tragedy. Butterflies have this short, brilliant flight, only to die, as their wings become torn and tattered. I'll bet you also didn't know that the Greek word for them is *psyche*, the same as the word for 'soul.'"

I looked at Santou in astonishment. My God. The man sounded like a poet. "Where did you learn all this?"

"Oh, there are lots of things I know that would surprise you," he joked.

I decided to reveal a bit of what I was working on, since Jake seemed to care so much about butterflies.

"Remember I told you that a consultant for Fish and Wildlife has been missing ever since he went up to Mendocino? Well, I discovered more about the butterfly that he was sent to find. It's a species called the Lotis blue."

"Sure. I've heard of it."

I shot Jake a skeptical glance, certain he had to be putting me on.

Santou chuckled, seeming amused by my reaction. "I used to catch bugs as a kid, chère. Or didn't you know little boys did that sort of thing?"

"Very funny," I retorted.

"I had a pretty good butterfly collection at one time. Even back then, getting hold of a Lotis blue was tantamount to finding the Holy Grail, particularly for a museum. Come to think of it, I can name two museums here in the States that boasted specimens, only to have them mysteriously disappear. That's how desirable that particular butterfly has always been. From what I hear, there are only a handful of Lotis blue specimens in the entire world, probably making it the ultimate butterfly to possess."

"Who'd be most interested in getting hold of one? A museum, or a private individual?"

"Both, I would imagine. There are some pretty hard-core collectors out there. I remember reading somewhere that one in ten Japanese men is a serious butterfly hunter. Maybe that's an angle to consider while investigating the disappearance of that consultant. You're absolutely certain he was searching for the Lotis blue?"

"Yes. Fish and Wildlife is on the verge of declaring it extinct."

"Okay then, stop and think. How much would an extinct butterfly be worth to an avid collector? You'd know better than most people. It's possible your consultant stumbled across something that he wasn't supposed to find."

I wondered. Trepler had said he'd kill anyone that ever tried to take his specimen. The question was, would he be willing to commit murder to get another?

"So what do you think now, chère? Do smaller species deserve just as much protection as those that are larger?"

"When you're right, you're right," I admitted and gave him a kiss.

Santou never ceased to amaze me. But there were other matters that I had to focus on at the moment. I poured the tea and took my cup into the bedroom, wondering, What does one wear to a vampire club, anyway?

I nixed a blue skirt as too fancy, a gray sweater as too drab, and a red blouse as just plain asking for trouble. For all I knew, it was the equivalent of waving a red flag at a bull. Except in this case it probably meant "Come closer. I want you to suck my blood."

I finally settled upon what usually seemed right for just about any occasion: a basic little black dress.

Santou outdid me by pulling a purple silk shirt out of the closet. I watched as he slipped it over his chest, his arms gliding through the billowy sleeves, as the collar fell gently around his neck. Then he stepped into a pair of black pants that always fit him just right.

It's funny how quickly we learn to take those that we love for granted, certain we know all of their whims and quirks.

However, this was a man that I hadn't seen before. The outfit emphasized Santou's brooding nature, turning him into part poet, part pirate, part seducer. Terrific. I'd probably have to beat off every vampiress in the club with a stick.

"Ready, chère?" Jake asked, his smile indicating that he was pleased by my reaction.

"Uh-huh. I'm just not letting you out of my sight tonight."

"That's the idea," he said, teasingly running his fingers over my breasts.

Terri and Eric knocked on our door at the stroke of midnight. I opened it to find Gomez and Morticia Addams standing there.

Terri was a knockout, garbed in a formfitting full-length burgundy satin dress that would have given Marilyn Monroe a run for her money. He'd accessorized with a long black wig, a rhinestone necklace shaped like a spider, and enough white makeup to have been voted Queen of the Ghouls.

Eric looked equally stylish in a black shirt and suit topped off with a Zorro style cape.

"What did the two of you do? Rob a costume warehouse?" I asked with a twinge of envy.

"It wasn't necessary. We just raided Terri's closet," Eric dryly responded.

Now I knew why Terri had lugged four enormous suitcases to San Francisco with him.

"It appears that we're all dressed to kill, and ready to paint the town red. So let's go mingle with the creatures of the night," Terri dramatically exclaimed, as we headed out for the club.

Grungy and dirty by day, SOMA resembled nothing less than a carnival at night, its barren industrial architecture fading into the background. I barely noticed the lot filled with Ryder vans, the elevated rail of the BART train, or the noise coming from the adjacent freeway. Instead, I focused on all the neon signs, along with the array of stretch limos and glamorous models.

"Over here," Terri directed, steering us away from the bright lights toward an ominous-looking alley.

We approached a plain metal door where the word POISON was written in letters that appeared to be dripping with blood.

"Nice touch," Santou wryly noted.

The door opened onto a hallway where gargoyles leered at us from their perches on the wall. One seemed to come alive, only to transform into a gatekeeper materializing from out of the darkness. He waved Eric and Terri inside, while using his body as a barricade to prevent Santou and I from following.

"Sorry, but this is a private party. No mundanes allowed."

"Would you mind interpreting that for me?" I asked Terri, who hovered nearby.

"He means no non-fabulous night people, though I'd rate you two as pretty glamorous, myself."

Santou stepped back and gave me the once-over. "Terri's right, chère. You look terrific."

"Thank you. And you're hot, hot, hot as well," I replied with a mischievous grin.

"That settles it. We're in," Santou announced, and flashed his FBI badge.

Open sesame!

Our burly gatekeeper stepped back and allowed us to pass.

We followed the hall to where a set of steps led down into a subterranean room. The lights were dim, giving the place a *Night of the Living Dead* effect that perfectly set the mood. Though it was nowhere near Halloween, one would have been hard-pressed to think otherwise, what with all the vampires, ghouls, and witches roaming about. The place was creepy yet sensually hypnotic at the same time, complete with the drone of Goth music thumping away in the background.

"Every night must be a full moon in this place," I commented, looking around.

"No wonder I'm feeling so frisky. I'll go get us some drinks," Terri said, and headed for the bar.

As for Santou, his eyes were glued to a cocktail waitress dressed in a black bustier, black bikini panties, black garter belt, black fishnet stockings and heels. I particularly liked the black bat that was tattooed on her belly. She turned, as though aware that Jake's eyes were upon her, and seductively sauntered over.

"I'd be happy to get whatever you'd like. By the way, I love your shirt," she said, sliding a tapered black fingernail enticingly down his chest.

"Isn't the fabric wonderful? But let me tell you, it was hell washing out the blood stains from the last woman who touched him like that," I warned with a sweet-as-angel-cake smile.

She curled her painted black lips, exposing a set of fangs, and then swiveled on her black stiletto heels and left.

"That wasn't very nice. Weren't you being just a bit territorial?" Jake asked, wafting between surprise and amusement.

"Damn straight," I replied.

A man with devil horns attached to his forehead strolled by and turned to leer at me. Contact lenses made his eyes appear deep demon red, as though he'd been feasting on blood and was now filled to the brim. Speaking of which, Terri reappeared carrying three goblets in hand. Santou and I immediately released him of his burden.

"Mmm. Dee-lish," he declared, taking a sip of the dark red liquid.

"What is it?" I asked, hoping Terri hadn't made a pact with the devil to remain eternally young.

"It's called a Blood Bath. I think it's three parts red wine, one part Chambord liqueur, and a splash of cranberry juice, with a maraschino cherry on top. The bartender says it's the cocktail of choice among vampires in the know. It's supposed to symbolize the blood coursing through our veins."

I took a taste. Not bad.

Santou promptly downed his drink and then proceeded to polish off mine.

"Where's Eric?" Terri asked after a while.

I'd been so busy taking in the scene that I hadn't kept an eye on him.

"I don't know," I admitted, and started looking around.

"Maybe he found Lily," Terri hopefully suggested.

"I don't think so. But there's definitely trouble brewing ahead," Santou said, gesturing toward the bar.

All I saw was a hot, young thing wearing a skimpy red corset.

"There's going to be trouble, all right, if you go anywhere near her," I advised.

"No, not there. Over there."

I followed where Jake's finger pointed. Eric was heatedly pushing his way through the crowd, his target a waiter who looked as though all the blood had been drained out of him.

"Oh, shit. I bet that's the boyfriend," Jake said, and quickly began to make his way toward them.

I followed close behind.

Eric lunged as the waiter turned to run, dropping his tray of drinks on the floor. The liquid oozed across the tiles, causing people to slip and slide, so that I had to bob and weave my way around them.

We reached the pair just as Eric's hands clamped onto Randy Edgers's throat.

"Where's Lily?" he angrily demanded, throttling the sun-challenged waiter.

"Hey, man. I don't know what the hell you're talking about. But for chrissakes, you're killing me!" he wailed.

It took us both to pry him off Edgers.

"You're right. I *will* kill you if you don't tell me where my daughter is, right now," Eric growled.

"You're out of your gourd. I already said I don't know. Lily didn't come to San Francisco with me." Randy gestured toward Santou and myself. "But this couple overheard enough to testify that you threatened my life, and I damn well intend to press charges. I hope you enjoy spending time in jail with the rest of the fags."

"Did someone make a threat? Because I didn't hear anything. How about you, chère?" Santou asked, turning to me.

"Not a word. Why? Did something happen?" I blithely responded.

"Oh, I get it. The three of you are in cahoots, right?" Randy spat, dislodging a loose fang.

"It's better than that. I'm an FBI agent and I don't like guys who run away with underage girls. So if I were you, I'd spill everything you know. That is, unless you'd prefer I take you into headquarters for questioning."

Randy's complexion turned from ghostly pale to a ghastly shade of white.

"I don't believe you," he replied, doing his best to present a brave front.

It was the quiver in his voice that gave him away.

Jake pulled out his badge and shoved it in the kid's face.

"Believe me now?"

Randy Edgers silently nodded.

"All right. Then let's start again. Did Lily come to San Francisco with you?"

"Yeah, okay. She did. So what?"

"Why, you son of a bitch," Eric growled, and moved in to grab Edgers again.

This time Terri held him back. "Eric, let him talk. All that matters right now is that we find Lily."

"Hear that? This is your chance to make good, Randy. Tell us where she is, and you won't be charged with kidnapping," Santou bluffed, hoping Edgers would fall for his line.

"Kidnapping? Who are you kidding? She came with me of her own free will. Lily didn't feel like hanging around for some lousy custody hearing. Why should she, when I was offering her something a whole lot better?"

"Yeah, you're quite the stud. So, where is she now?" I demanded.

"And why should I tell you?" Randy pugnaciously retorted, thrusting out his chin.

"Because otherwise, I promise that your life will become a holy living hell," Jake informed him.

With that, we proceeded to form a tight circle around Vampire Boy. Edgers looked at each of us, and must have realized that we weren't kidding.

"All right, you win," he crumbled. "It's not as if I give a shit, anyway. We broke up nearly a month ago. Last I heard, she'd moved in with some dude down around Santa Cruz."

"What's this guy's name?" Santou skeptically questioned.

"How the hell should I know? It's not like she sent me a housewarming invitation," Edgers snapped. His eyes darted around, as if searching for an escape route. "Believe me, if I knew, I'd tell you. I don't need this kind of trouble."

"That better be true," Eric seethed. "Otherwise, you'll be seeing a lot more of me, and the next visit won't be so pleasant."

"Ooh. I'm really scared of some candy-ass queer who can't even face me without bringing all of his friends," Randy sneered.

"You little bastard," Eric swore, and took a jab at him.

Randy doubled over, clutching his stomach, only to butt Eric with his head and send him crashing to the floor.

"That's enough already," Santou said, placing himself between the two. "I'll check out the information and be back in touch with you."

"Yeah, you do that," Randy scoffed, and began to walk away. "Meanwhile, you'll be hearing from my lawyer."

"Are you all right?" Terri asked, helping Eric to his feet.

"I'm fine. I just want to find Lily and be done with this."

"Well, you're one step closer than you were before," Santou consoled. "But right now, I think we should all head home. We're not going to learn anything more tonight."

"That's fine with me. I can't stand being in the same room with that creep," Eric muttered.

"You three go ahead. I'm going to stay and hang out for awhile," Terri informed us.

I shot him a questioning glance.

"I fit in better than the rest of you, which makes it easier to shmooze. Maybe I can pick up some additional information," he explained.

"Thanks, Terri. I appreciate that," Eric said and gave him a hug. "I'll wait up for you."

"Don't be silly. Go to bed. You never know. I might get lucky."

I noticed that Eric looked slightly crestfallen, and wondered if Terri had any idea that his friend was beginning to fall for him.

Eric went straight upstairs once we got home, and Santou and I prepared for bed. It was as I walked out of the bathroom that I caught Jake reaching for his vials of painkillers.

"I don't think that's a wise idea. You've already had a couple of drinks tonight."

"You know, chère. I'm really getting tired of your mother act. Why don't you give it a rest?" Santou snidely retorted.

The words hit their mark as intended.

"And here I thought I was simply acting like someone who cared," I snapped back.

"Well maybe that's not what I need right now. Did you ever stop to think that you have absolutely no idea of what I'm dealing with?"

"Yes, I do," I automatically responded.

"No, you sure as hell don't!" Santou lashed out in frustration. "You have no goddamn concept at all. You've never been stuck behind a desk, unable to go out in the field and do what it is you love. But that's exactly what I'm facing for the rest of my career. You want to know how that makes me feel? Completely impotent, angry, and useless!"

That's when I knew what the pills and booze were really about—Santou was attempting to put a lid on his fear.

"You'll be back in the field again. You just need time to heal, is all. You push yourself too hard, Jake," I gently told him.

"And how much time do I give it?" he demanded, his pent-up rage turning to bitter tears. "What if things never get any better? What if this is as good as it gets?"

I threw my arms around Santou, wanting more than anything to protect him. For the first time, I began to understand what Jake was really going through. I knew, because a brand-new pain now lodged itself in the pit of my stomach, where it settled in like a clenched fist.

"I swear things will get better. I know they will," I pledged, my own eyes starting to well up.

"Don't make promises you can't keep, chère."

"Please, just make an appointment to see a physical therapist. You've got nothing to lose, and it might actually help. One more thing. Let's go for a consultation with another doctor and talk about the drugs that you're on."

Santou simply looked at me, breaking my heart.

"I'll abide by whatever the consensus turns out to be," I promised.

He wordlessly nodded in agreement. For better or worse, our fates were entwined. That much I knew for certain. We'd become each other's soldier and all the king's men. Except that, unlike Humpty Dumpty, we were putting each other back together again.

I held Jake tight throughout the night and listened as he slept, determined to do whatever I could to help him.

Eleven

I awoke to the scent of eggs and bacon floating in the air. It was a relief after the dream I'd just been having. No, it wasn't my usual nightmare of the controlled delivery gone awry. This one was even more disturbing.

I'd dreamt that needles were slowly being thrust into my body, one at a time. But truly terrifying was the chorus of screams all around me. I'd turned my head to discover that I wasn't alone, but one in a group of women with long, dagger-thin needles inserted in their arms, legs, and abdomens; even their eyes. That's when I realized that we'd all been pinned alive.

Their anguished shrieks continued to echo in my ears even now. I ran my hands along my body to make absolutely certain that I'd actually been dreaming. At this rate, maybe *I* was the one who needed to be taking tranquilizers.

I took another deep whiff of the scent wafting in from the kitchen. Terri must already be up cooking breakfast. That is, if he ever bothered to go to sleep last night.

I rolled over to give Santou a good-morning kiss, but he wasn't there. I quickly got up and threw on a robe. A shower could wait. I followed my nose.

The figure in the kitchen wasn't that of Mei Rose. And if it was Terri, he was looking mighty good these days. A tall, lanky man stood facing the stove, dressed in nothing but a pair of briefs and a shirt. Though I tried to sneak up behind, the sound of my bare feet padding on the floor gave me away.

Santou turned around and my heart began to flutter. His tousled hair hung low over his eyes and he flashed a lopsided smile, as his arm reached out and grabbed me around the waist.

"Come here, woman."

His mouth tasted of bacon as it explored mine, leaving me slightly breathless. If he hadn't had a hot frying pan in his other hand, I would have been tempted to whip up something even more tantalizing in the kitchen.

"You do know this is exactly what every woman dreams of, don't you?"

"What's that?" Jake asked.

"A man with a tight ass who not only can cook but also knows how to kiss like that," I said with a grin.

"In that case, I guess it's good a thing I'm already spoken for."

"You've got that right," I agreed, conveying that I didn't like to share.

I set the table and we sat down to eat breakfast.

"You do know that kid was lying through his fangs last night, don't you?" Santou remarked between bites of toast.

"You mean about Lily being in Santa Cruz? I suspected as much. Only Eric was so desperate for the least little clue that I couldn't bring myself to say anything."

"Good thinking, chère. I'm sure he's gonna want to hot-foot it down there and begin searching for her right away. Don't say anything to discourage him. Eric's too emotionally involved to be of any help here. Meanwhile, I'll see what I can dig up, and share whatever I learn with you."

I didn't say a word, too astounded to speak. I was hoping

that Santou wouldn't change his mind and rescind the offer. This was the first time he'd ever included me in on a potential case, and it felt as if our relationship had just taken a giant leap forward. As a reward, I let Jake have the last slice of bacon.

We both dressed and Santou left for work, after which I threw the dishes in the sink and went upstairs to check in with Eric and Terri.

The door swung open before I'd even finished knocking. Eric stood there, fully dressed and wide awake.

"I can't believe Lily's been in Santa Cruz this entire time. For God's sake, it's just an hour south of where I live and work. She must know that. I pulled out a map last night and marked some areas where we can begin our search. In fact, I'm good to go whenever you're ready."

"I'm sorry Eric, but my boss called this morning. I'm afraid I have to go back to work today," I lied.

Eric's expression went from hopeful to despondent in less than a second.

"But I'll break away as soon as I can and join you. Just keep in touch. Will Terri be going along?"

"No. Something came up for him as well," Eric replied, gloomily.

I felt so guilty that I nearly broke down and told him the truth. Fortunately, a shred of common sense prevailed.

"It might be better if you're down there on your own, anyway. At least for a while. Then Lily won't think that some sort of posse is after her. But don't worry, Eric. I promise that I'll continue to help."

"Okay. So then, I'll see you in a few days. Right?"

His chin quivered and I gave him a reassuring hug.

"In a few days," I repeated, all the while knowing it was a big, fat lie.

"In that case, I won't hang around, but will just take off. Would you let Terri know, when he wakes up, that I'll give him a call?"

"Will do."

I watched as he walked downstairs, all the while wondering why Terri was suddenly so busy. I was about to leave, myself, when he called out to me from behind the bedroom door.

"Rach, are you still here?"

"Yes."

"Good. Don't go yet. I need your feedback on something. I just didn't want Eric to see. I wasn't sure how he'd feel about it."

I did a double-take as a vamp walked out. Terri was dolled up in a skintight black gown with a plunging neckline, stiletto heels, and a long black wig. The cherry on his sundae was that he also wore full vampire makeup, turning him into the undead, spitting image of Elvira, "Mistress of the Dark."

For chrissakes, Ter, what's going on?" I asked, beginning to wonder just what had taken place at the club last night after I'd left.

Chalk it up to having seen one too many vampire films, but I walked over and began to inspect his neck.

"What are you doing?" Terri asked, fidgeting under my touch.

"Checking for fang marks. I can't imagine any other reason why you'd be dressed like this."

"Why else do you think? I got a job, of course. Okay, so it's not quite what I was looking for, but I hear the tips are good. And I might be able to help find Lily. The only problem are these miserable fangs." Terri opened his mouth and bared his teeth.

Holy canines, Batman! They certainly looked sharp.

"The damn things are killing me. Not only that, but I've

got to lose a few pounds, or this dress is going to rip straight across my butt the first time I bend down."

"Are you really sure you want to hang out with a crowd that dresses up as vampires every night?"

"Look, Rach. My only other option is to ask people whether they want paper or plastic as I'm bagging their groceries. It's not like there's a large pool of employment out there for me. To tell you the truth, my main concern is all this heavy white makeup. It's going to play havoc with my pores. Besides, as I said before, I really want to help Eric. I like the guy a lot."

"I believe the feeling is mutual."

"You do?" He blinked in surprise.

"Absolutely."

"Who knows? Maybe I won't die alone, after all." Terri smiled and began to blush beneath his makeup. "Now let me wash this stuff off my face before it adheres to my skin permanently."

I left Terri to his cleanse, rinse, and moisturizing routine. While I wasn't about to rush into work, neither did I want to waste any time. With that in mind, I trotted back downstairs and placed a call to my new ace informant.

"Yeah?" Aikens barked into the phone.

"Have you got any news for me yet?" I queried, skipping all pleasantries.

"Oh, it's you. I don't have time for this right now," Mitch growled, sounding harried. "A new batch of larvae just hatched, and thanks to you, I've got my hands full."

"Make time," I told him. "What have you found out?"

"Whadda ya kidding me? For chrissakes, it's only been a coupla days. I haven't come up with anything yet."

"Don't screw with me, Mitch," I warned. "Or I'll pull your stay-out-of-jail card. Remember, I still have that tape recording, and there's no telling what I might find the next time I drop by your house. Come to think of it, I really didn't take all that good a look around."

"All right, already. I get the message. There's a guy that used to be a top gun in the butterfly trade at one time. I'm trying to track him down. He should be able to help you out."

"Where is he?" I asked, eager to get things rolling.

"That's the problem. I don't know."

"You're not earning any Brownie points this way, Aikens. Stop jerking me around."

"I'm not. I swear it! Look, this guy doesn't exactly hang out a shingle to advertise where he lives. I mean, he used to be famous for sneaking into national parks. I'm talking about places like the Grand Canyon. That's where he'd dig up rare *indra* larvae, raise 'em, and sell the specimens for big bucks. This man is my hero. He was so good at collecting that he almost became a butterfly himself while out in the field. We're talking a real pro. He'd wear one set of clothes on the climb down into the Canyon, another while he was digging, and then change into a third set for the trip back up, just so he wouldn't be recognized by anyone who'd seen him earlier. Now *that's* keeping a low profile."

"All right then. What's his name?"

"Brother Tom, or Tim, or Charles, or something."

"You're telling me that this guy's your idol, and you don't even know who he is?" I scoffed. "What's with the 'brother' stuff, anyway?"

"You know. *Brother.* Like a Franciscan friar."

"Yeah, right. First there's a guy called Horus, and now some sort of Franciscan friar that's involved in the plot. What kind of idiot do you take me for, Aikens? I'm afraid you just blew it. You can plan on seeing me later today."

"But, but . . ." Mitch sputtered into the phone, as I hung up.

Let him stew on that for a couple of hours. My guess was he'd know a whole lot more by the time this afternoon rolled around. Even so I was feeling antsy, wanting to do something right now, but not sure exactly what. The phone rang and I quickly picked it up, certain that Mitch must have already caved.

"Hey, chère. I've got some information for you."

Wow, that was fast work. No doubt about it: Santou was good at his job.

"I managed to get Edgers's home address. You might want to pay him an unannounced visit. Maybe you can ferret out what's really going on.

"Thanks for the tip, Jake. There's nothing I'd love to do more."

"Now, how did I know that?" Santou replied, with a smile in his voice. "You can thank me properly tonight."

"That's the second thing on my 'to-do' list," I teased. "Take an extra vitamin for energy. I'll see you later on."

I grabbed my bag and rushed outside, only to be blindsided by a piercing ray of light. I felt as if I were a bug and a giant magnifying glass were being focused on me.

I used my hand to shield my eyes and looked around. Wouldn't you know? Su Lin Fong had set up her own line of *chi* defense. An octagonal mirror had been hung in every window of *her* house, all aimed directly at Mei Rose's residence.

Just great. The street had been turned into a spiritual battle zone, in what could very well be called the War of the Looking Glasses. Even Tony Baloney seemed to have become a victim. The pooch lay with his head buried in the sheepskin rug, where a low, continual growl could be heard. I almost felt bad when the mutt didn't attempt to make a lunge for me.

I hopped in my Ford and beelined it down to SOMA. My sister kept popping into my mind, no matter where I went these days. Truth be told, she and Lily were beginning to blur more and more. Half the time I wondered if it was really Rebecca for whom I was searching.

The rest of the time I pondered if my sister had secretly hoped to be found. If so, why hadn't the P.I. hired by my mother been able to uncover the least little clue as to her whereabouts? But then, with 451,000 runaways a year, how much of a chance had there actually ever been?

I used to run to the front door each time the bell rang, convinced the police would be standing there with my sister in tow. Looking back on it now, my hopes seemed incredibly naïve. Who'd I been kidding? Only myself.

I'd gone so far as to set up a makeshift memorial in our shared bedroom, complete with Rebecca's photo, Bruce Springsteen's *Born To Run* album, and her favorite teddy bear. I'd light a cranberry-scented candle every night and make a wish with all my might that she'd come home soon. After all these years, I still found myself waiting.

SOMA looked completely different during the day. Gone were the limos and stylish models. They were replaced by beat-up vans and angst-riddled post-punkers doing their best to appear churlish while walking along the street. By daylight, the barren neighborhood existed mainly as an outlet for an off-ramp from the freeway.

I drove by the Brain Wash Café, a place where lonely souls could congregate to post messages in cyberspace while washing and drying their clothes and sheets. Those with other interests hung out at the Crypt, which had a full array of S&M toys for sale.

Ohmigod, there was a parking space! I squeezed my vehicle into a spot that was a bit too small, pushing those in front and back out of the way. Then I wandered down the street searching for Randy Edgers's building. I finally found the concrete structure, which resembled a bunker more than anything else. Edgers's name was on buzzer 410, just as Santou had said it would be.

I rang, but received no answer. Call me a cockeyed optimist. I kept right on ringing.

"What the hell do you want?" a voice finally wailed, made even more screechy by the cheap intercom.

"It's Rachel Porter. We met last night."

"Sorry, babe, but I'm way too tired to party right now. Why don't we hook up later on?"

"I'm the woman who was with Lily's father at the club."

That produced a long pause. I broke the silence by buzzing some more.

"Oh, shit. What are you bothering me for?"

"We need to talk."

"Look, I don't care who you are. This isn't a good time. Now you'd better get outta here."

"I'm not going anywhere. Just so you know, Lily's father isn't with me. I came alone. If you're smart, you'll let me in."

"What are you, nuts? If I'm smart, I won't," came his snappy retort. "I'm going back to bed now. You can talk to me in my dreams."

So be it. I decided to see how well he could snooze with my finger glued to the doorbell. I held it down, creating one continuous nerve-jangling ring. It took less than a minute to produce the desired effect.

"You bitch! I swear to God, that's it. I'm calling the cops," threatened the frazzled voice crackling through the squawk box.

"Go ahead. In case you've forgotten, my friend is with the FBI, and I'm law enforcement as well."

"Oh man. This is total bullshit," Edgers groused. "All right. Come up and let's get this thing over with."

Those were my sentiments exactly.

The metal door buzzed open and I hoofed it up four long flights of stairs. Edgers stood waiting at the entrance to his space. To say he looked like death warmed over would have been paying the kid an undeserved compliment. He wore only a pair of dirty boxer shorts that were on the verge of falling off his scrawny hips. It provided me with way too good a look at his sunken chest, stooped shoulders, and skinny legs. He would have made mighty sparse pickings, even for a desperate vampire.

Edgers stepped aside and I brushed past him to enter a room as dark as a cave. Tattered brown curtains hung over the windows, keeping any light from coming through. I only hoped the scattered mounds on the floor weren't the remains of anything animal or human. I did my best to skirt around them just in case. A couple of heat lamps were shining in one corner. Otherwise, I wouldn't have been able to see anything at all in his den.

The moment of truth arrived as I grabbed hold of the filthy brown material and pulled it aside, allowing the sun to come pouring in.

"What the hell are you trying to do? Blind me?" Randy grumbled, covering his eyes.

Maybe he was part vampire, after all. Edgers's complexion was sickly white even without makeup. The light revealed a face that was badly pitted with acne.

"For chrissakes, I didn't get to bed until four o'clock this morning. This is like the middle of the night for me," he complained.

"Maybe you should get on a better schedule," I suggested, glancing around—not that there was much to look at.

Most dungeons were furnished better than this place. There was no sofa, no table, not even a bed. Maybe the lack of furniture was to showcase the one and only object that Edgers had spent his money on: a large black lacquered coffin with its lid flung open.

I walked over and peered inside to spy a thin layer of

foam rubber that had been crudely cut to fit. However, even this make-do mattress was in the process of deteriorating. Small pieces of hardened yellow foam lay scattered about like stale bread crumbs, caught in the folds of a stained sheet thrown on top.

It was then I spotted a few other items in the room. One was an aquarium containing a number of small, fuzzy mice, all huddled together like shell-shocked victims. Hmm. Dracula's manservant, Renfield, had taken to eating bugs. Maybe Edgers was surviving on rodents.

But what really aroused my interest was a much larger glass tank that sat positioned near the sun lamps. A cardboard box with a hole at one end had been placed inside, while crumpled newspapers and wood chips lined the floor.

I reached in and *tap, tap, tapped* on the box top. A moment later, a large lizard's head popped out. Then the creature, itself, appeared.

A venomous reptile, the Gila monster was about eighteen inches long with a blunt face, powerful jaws, four short legs, and a stout body. Its black skin was beautifully mottled with an intricate design of spots and pink bars. Small beadlike scales covered its back like some expensive, *tres chic* accessory. The only things this creature had that a Kate Spade handbag lacked were a forked tongue and very sharp claws.

One thing I knew to be true was that when a Gila monster bit you, it damn well didn't like to let go. The other was that Edgers needed a state permit to own one.

"Nice pet you've got there," I commented.

"Who, Lucifer? Yeah, I like him. He used to scare the shit out of Lily, though," Edgers related with a chuckle.

"Maybe that's why she left you," I said, taking full advantage of the opening.

Randy simply shrugged at my suggestion.

"Okay then, what do you think happened?"

"What are you? Some kind of shrink? I already filled you in on everything last night."

I seriously doubted that.

"You know what I find hard to believe? That Lily would have run off with another guy. After all, she left home to be with you, right?"

"Yeah, well there's no accounting for some women's taste," Edgers replied, hitching up his boxer shorts.

They immediately fell back down, like a pair of low-slung hip-huggers, as Randy made his way across the wooden floor. I wondered if he had some lizard in him, as well. His bare feet were parched and cracked, and his toenails were long and yellow.

I watched in silence as Edgers reached into the small aquarium and picked a fuzzy mouse up by its tail. Then he walked in my direction, with the terrified mouse squirming and wriggling in the air.

What's he going to try to do? Scare me? I wondered in amusement.

My only regret was that Edgers didn't also have a tail, so that I could dangle him in midair and see how he liked it.

But any feelings of humor instantly vanished as Edgers suddenly bent down and, with a quick snap of his wrist, slammed the rodent's head against the floor. After that, he continued to carry the dazed mouse toward me.

I said nothing, too angry to speak, as Edgers laid the tiny creature at my feet. He picked up a pair of utensils near the cage. One was a snake stick, the other a forceps. Edgers opened the aquarium top and deftly thrust the stick behind the lizard's neck, pinning it in place. Then he retrieved the still breathing mouse and, with the forceps, shoved it inside Lucifer's mouth.

My stomach twisted at the first sickening gnash of bones

that were crunched beneath its powerful jaws. Then my nausea swiftly turned to rage.

"Maybe the problem is you weren't man enough for her. Could that have been it, Randy?"

What do you know? Edgers *did* have some blood in him, after all. A hint of color rose in his cheeks as his skin flushed.

"I guess that's why she took off with someone else. Because you weren't able to fully satisfy her."

Randy's jaw visibly tightened, as if he were holding back words that were burning to come out.

"But hey, it's not your fault if you couldn't please her. Some men just have performance problems, is all," I continued on, purposely doing what I could to needle him.

Edgers clenched his fists, making me wonder if he was going to take a swing at me. However, he remained stoically silent, so I decided to try a different tactic.

"You know what I really think?" I asked, sidling up close to him. "Lily must have done something to piss you off, and you probably made her pay for it. I'm even beginning to wonder if Lily might be lying dead somewhere."

"For chrissakes, what the hell's wrong with you? I didn't do a damn thing to her!" Randy exploded. "That bitch left *me*. *I'm* the injured party here."

"All right, I believe you," I tried to appease him. "But Lily's not in Santa Cruz, is she?"

Edgers glared at me, keeping his lips tightly closed.

Maybe it was the mouse. Or perhaps it was thoughts of Rebecca. But the next thing I knew, I had Edgers up against the wall.

"I'll ask one more time. Is she in Santa Cruz, or not?"

I added a little incentive by slamming my palm under Randy's chin and smacking his head hard against the plaster.

"Okay, okay! You're right. She's not. Last I heard, she was hanging out with some old tattoo nut in the Haight."

"That's not good enough," I warned, beginning to apply pressure to his trachea with my forearm. "I need an address."

"I don't have one," Randy blurted, gasping for air.

"Gee, that's too bad," I responded, refusing to let up until Edgers began to gag and squirm just like the mouse that he'd fed to Lucifer.

"But I know the name of his store. It's a place called Big Daddy's Body Shop," Edgers managed to sputter, his face turning red as a blood clot.

I loosened my grip and he stumbled away.

"You crazy bitch! What were you trying to do? Kill me?"

"No. I just wanted to stun you a bit like you did to that mouse. You're lucky there's nothing around here to feed you to, otherwise it would be way too tempting. Tell me something, though. I'm curious. If Lily left, why did you cover for her last night? Why not tell her father where she went?"

He tenderly rubbed his throat. "Because I hate fags even more than I do her," Randy sneered. "Why should I help him? Let him find Lily on his own."

Edgers was one lowlife, miserable slimeball. Lucifer blinked at me as if in agreement.

"One other thing, Randy. You'd better be telling the truth, or I'll be back to take that lizard away from you."

"What the hell are you talking about?" Edgers croaked, still massaging his throat. "That's private property. You can't do that."

"Sure I can. It's illegal to buy Gila monsters taken from the wild. And I'm willing to bet you don't have a permit to prove that Lucifer was purchased from a legitimate breeder."

With that I strolled across the floor, and walked out the door, slamming it hard behind me.

Twelve

I'd heard about Haight Ashbury as a kid. How could I not have? It had been glorified in songs and movies. There was also all the paraphernalia once thought to be so cool—leather vests, peace signs, water pipes, black-light posters, incense, and assorted psychedelia. That was one reason I hadn't quite known what to expect when I'd first landed in San Francisco. Just one quick stroll through the Haight had been enough to discover that it was now a glorified walk through a Disneyfied world of hippiedom.

I parked my Ford on Cole Street and got out. Once again, I was not disappointed. Teens with long hair and tie-dyed shirts wandered about smoking doobies, just as their predecessors had done nearly forty years ago. However, since then a few other things had changed.

Who would have dreamt there'd be a Gap, a Banana Republic, and a Ben & Jerry's near the corner of Haight and Ashbury—once the heart of the anti-establishment rebellion? But that was nothing compared to all the souvenir shops blatantly packaging and hawking the counter-culture experience.

It was impossible to walk past a store window without being bombarded by countless images of may-he-party-on Jerry Garcia. The Grateful Dead had become so successful that they were now looked upon as deities in the land of crass commercialism. The only things more numerous than the Jerry Garcia T-shirts and posters were all the panhandlers and Charles Manson look-alikes roaming the streets. I passed one man who so resembled the former Pied Piper of misfits that he actually gave me the creeps.

"How about some spare change for a condom so that I don't breed?" was his clever panhandling line.

I figured he had a point, and gave him a dollar.

The Haight is also a mecca for used clothing. Vintage stores beckoned to me with their array of cast-off garments at rip-off prices. But it was the Piedmont that really lassoed my attention. Decorating its window were micro miniskirts, long vinyl gloves, faux fur bikinis, and fabulous feather boas. There were even gold metal bras with the words SLUT and BITCH spelled out on them in rhinestones. The store was every drag queen's dream, reminiscent of La Cage Aux Folles on acid. I made a mental note to tell Terri all about it.

A little farther down the block stood a sandwich board in the middle of the sidewalk announcing a list of daily piercing specials. Sunday was for ear rims, while Monday was for nostrils. Either service could be had for the price of twenty bucks. Tuesday's specialty was tongue piercing, and Wednesday's bargain was for eyebrows. On Thursday you could have a ring put in your navel for only thirty dollars. Friday was considered prime time, being the lead-in to the weekend—or the perfect occasion to kick back and have your nipples pierced. Last but not least was Saturday, also known as date night. What could be more fun as a couple than to have someone pierce your lips?

I looked up at the awning and my suspicions were confirmed. I'd arrived at Big Daddy's Body Shop. Opening the door, I walked inside.

Bzzzzzzz!

By the sound of things, I'd either entered a crazed dentist's office or stumbled into a giant beehive. I followed where the noise led.

Sitting behind the counter was a tattoo artist wearing what appeared to be a miniature blowtorch attached to his arm. The machine was held in place with straps of Velcro. Next to him was a man who was naked from the waist up. Talk about your living, breathing work of art. The guy was a human canvas—one that looked as though he should have been locked behind bars.

His pumped-up muscles were engraved with a network of cobwebs, their gossamer filament littered with skulls. Perforation marks encircled a thick, beefy neck, along with instructions that read CUT HERE. Just for fun, hot and cold faucets had been tattooed over both nipples. However, the illustrated man didn't end there. My eyes traveled down his chest, and I took a deep breath as they came to rest on his washboard abs. A gruesome graveyard covered every bit of flesh, with a different name chiseled on each of the headstones.

The man stared straight ahead, as if in a trance, while the inking gun screamed in glee. So intense was its buzz that I could have sworn the electrical current passed from the needle straight into me. A whisper of a smile flitted across Mr. Canvas's lips, as though the pain were sheer ecstasy.

I tore my attention away from the tattooed Frankenstein and focused on the artist responsible for his illustrations.

The first thing I noticed was the size of the man's hands. They were massive, with fingers long and tapered. I realized where I'd seen similar ones before—on Michelangelo's sculpture of David. I could only assume that this must be Big Daddy.

He wore his hair tightly pulled back in a ponytail, further emphasizing the fact he was going bald. As for his nose, it was regal and aquiline, showcasing a profile that should have been on a coin. A beard covering the lower half of his face was so thick and full that it looked like a mask. But the deep-set eyes were the key to the man, himself. They never once wavered from their work.

I watched in fascination as another illustration now began to take life. A black panther started to slither down Mr. Canvas's arm, one sleek limb at a time. The feline looked so realistic that its supple muscles fairly rippled beneath the hide.

Big Daddy constantly dabbed at the man's arm with a sponge as his needle worked like a sewing machine, piercing the skin at 2,200 times per minute. He finally acknowledged me with the hint of a nod, though he still didn't bother to speak.

I decided to pass the time by looking around his shop. The room itself was interesting, with pillars all about. One had a sign posted on its surface, and I wandered over to read what it said. What I hadn't expected was a history lesson. But that's exactly what I got.

I learned that Egyptians had once used double pillars as symbols of protection at their entrance gates. One pillar had been designated *Tat*, denoting strength, the other *Tattu*, meaning "to establish." However, *Tattu* had a second interesting significance—as a gateway to the region where the mortal soul is blended with an immortal spirit.

"Can I help you?"

The deep, melodious voice took me by surprise. It wasn't at all what I'd expected as I turned to find Big Daddy. There was no question but that he definitely lived up to his name. The man was tall enough to make me feel small standing beside him.

"Are you interested in having a tattoo done?" he inquired, as I continued to study him. "There are any number of interesting patterns to choose from. Or, if you like, one can be custom-designed. However, my specialty is freehand technique, which is what most of my customers seem to prefer."

I should have expected the question, but it caught me off guard. There were any number of reasons why I'd never considered a tattoo before, though one in particular stood out above all the others. It had to do with my grandmother's history. She'd received a tattoo as a young woman. However, it hadn't been by choice. She'd been a prisoner in a concentration camp.

Even now, I recalled the engraved numbers on her withered skin. I used to take hold of her forearm and run my fingers over them. She would push my hand away and pull her sleeve down, saying there were some things in this world too horrible for any child to know about. It wasn't until later that I'd learned what the numbers had meant.

I shivered, amazed that such a memory could be conjured so easily when least expected. Then I carefully shut it back inside the secret drawer where it was kept.

"Or perhaps that's not what you're here for," Big Daddy remarked, apparently noticing my reaction.

"Actually, I'm looking for a teenage girl and was told that you might know her."

Big Daddy flicked his ponytail back with a brush of his hand and nodded, as if he knew exactly what I was talking about.

"Which one?"

Which one?

I stared at the man, momentarily speechless. It wasn't just his words that astounded me. I felt myself being reeled in by his eyes, the sensation that of being softly cocooned.

"Her name is Lily Holt," I replied, determinedly breaking the spell.

Big Daddy furrowed his brow, and appeared to frown through his blanket of facial hair. "Sorry, but the name doesn't ring a bell."

Either Big Daddy was lying, or Lily had cleverly changed her identity.

"If you don't mind, I'd like to backtrack a minute. Would you please explain what you meant by 'which one'?" I asked, never taking my eyes off him.

Big Daddy held my gaze, and returned it in kind. "First, I have a question of my own. Exactly who are you?"

"Rachel Porter, a special agent with the U.S. Fish and Wildlife Service."

Big Daddy looked at me oddly and then broke into a grin. "I can't say that I get many of your ilk in here. But if I might make a suggestion, I think your tattoo should be that of a lioness."

"Why's that?"

"Partly due to your personality, and partially because of that hair thing you've got going."

It took every ounce of self-control to keep my hands from flying up and brushing back my mane.

"Anyway, the name's Carl Simmons. But my friends call me Big Daddy."

"Nice to meet you, Mr. Simmons," I said, purposely ignoring Big Daddy's chuckle. "Now will you tell me what you meant?"

Big Daddy's eyes flickered in amusement. "I have a better idea. Why don't you explain why a Fish and Wildlife agent is searching for a missing girl? Perhaps I'm wrong, but I don't believe that's within your agency's purview."

"She's the daughter of a friend that I'm trying to help," I answered, feeling more than slightly annoyed. "Now it's your turn."

"Suffice it to say that I'm known for harboring runaways. I provide a safe haven for a few kids at a time until they're able to make it on their own."

"And why would you do that?" I skeptically questioned.

There was something about Big Daddy that just didn't sit right with me.

"I'm afraid that's a long story for which there's no time right now. I have an appointment arriving shortly. But let me give you a piece of advice. You shouldn't be so afraid of getting a tattoo. Think of it this way. It's the only form of art that you'll take with you to the grave."

He smiled, and his teeth morphed into a queue of stained white shrouds lined up in an impenetrable forest. Then the door opened behind him.

I caught sight of a man who didn't seem to belong in a tattoo shop. If I had to guess, he looked rather like an accountant. His pin-striped shirt was neatly tucked into a pair of dark pleated pants, which were clean and freshly pressed. A slim briefcase was lodged under one arm. It was held in place by fingers whose nails were polished and manicured. I quickly hid my own badly bitten cuticles.

He looked to be about thirty years old, with a baby face and body that was fit and trim. His blond hair hung soft as silk. The color was that of immature wheat, and held a slight wave to it. I could tell he'd tried to eradicate the little bit of curl there was by applying gel and severely parting his hair to one side. In fact, the man appeared so precise as to border on being terminally rigid. Or perhaps it was my own problem when it came to things that were too orderly.

He caught my eye and smiled while walking toward us in stiff-legged fashion.

"You'll have to excuse me now," Big Daddy said by way of dismissal, while turning to greet his visitor.

He warmly wrapped his arms around the man's slender form. "Spencer, it's good to see you again. Did you bring those sketches as promised?"

I wended my way toward the door, lingering long enough to watch as Spencer removed a sketch pad from his briefcase and began to flip through the pages. I subtly maneuvered around until I was able to catch a glimpse of some of the drawings. A pair of wings and a flash of blue immediately caught my eye, sending my heart into overdrive and temporarily banishing all thoughts of Lily.

Perhaps I was on the verge of being obsessed, but I'd have been willing to bet that those sketches I'd seen were of the Lotis blue butterfly.

Thirteen

I planted myself at a café within view of the tattoo shop, purposely choosing a window seat. If I'd felt uneasy while speaking to Big Daddy before, a five-alarm fire was now raging inside my head.

Charles Manson had lived in the Haight back in sixty-seven, during the "Summer of Love." In fact, his house was only a few blocks away. The Haight had proven to be the perfect spot from which to recruit his notorious "Family"— a ragtag bunch of naïve runaways. Either I was beginning to imagine things, or the parallels between Manson and Big Daddy were becoming frighteningly similar. Even so, how did the Lotis blue butterfly fit into it all?

I waited until Spencer left Big Daddy's Body Shop and then quickly walked out and followed him. I caught up just as he was about to get into his vehicle. The car was as clean and understated as its owner—a navy blue Ford Galaxy.

"Excuse me. Could I speak to you for a minute?"

Spencer turned and flashed a bright smile as he caught sight of me.

"Why, hello. Weren't you in Carl's tattoo shop a short while ago?"

I nodded and returned his smile with one of my own.

"This is so strange, because I was just thinking of you. I wondered who you were and was sorry that you'd left. Since then, I've been trying to imagine what it is that you do. It's a game I like to play sometimes."

I found myself both flustered and flattered by his sweet, open candor.

"I'll be more than happy to tell you. My name is Rachel Porter, and I'm a special agent with the U.S. Fish and Wildlife Service."

"Pleased to meet you, Rachel. I'm Spencer Barnes."

We shook hands, and I became acutely aware of the fine network of veins just below the surface of his skin.

"Wow. A Fish and Wildlife agent, huh? I used to think about doing something like that."

"Really? Why didn't you?"

"I eventually decided to become an artist, instead. I like to imagine that the subjects I draw live on forever in some way. I don't believe you can say the same thing about those animals that you come across. But then, I probably have some sort of Ponce de Leon complex," he remarked, with an easy laugh.

"Don't we all?" I genially responded, thinking of the facial moisturizer on which I'd just spent fifty bucks.

"Then I guess we have something in common," Spencer jovially responded.

"Listen, I caught a glimpse of your drawings back at the tattoo shop and thought they were wonderful. Can I buy you a cup of coffee?" I offered.

Spencer checked his watch. "Sure. Why not? I'd like that," he pleasantly agreed.

I purposely led the way to a café on the next block, not wanting Big Daddy to see us together, going so far as to sit at a table in the back of the room.

"I hate to seem pushy, but would you mind showing me your drawings? I'd love to get a better look at them," I said, after our coffee had been served.

Gee, I'm sorry. But I gave all the sketches to Carl. Those pieces were specifically commissioned for tattoos."

Damn. I tried my best to hide my disappointment.

"I couldn't help but notice that some of them were of butterflies," I casually remarked.

"Oh sure. It's a very popular design among women. I do those all the time," he offered.

"Yes, but there was something unusual that struck me about them. They seemed to be of one butterfly in particular."

"What are you saying? That they looked exactly alike?" Spencer asked, sounding a bit hurt.

"No, of course not," I hastily added, not wanting to insult him. "What I meant is they appeared to be all the same *variety* of butterfly. One that I believe is called the Lotis blue."

"It sounds as if you think that butterfly is pretty special," Spencer observed.

"The Lotis blue is extremely rare. In fact, a lot of people would love to get hold of one."

"You mean there's actually a market for that sort of thing?" Spencer asked in surprise.

"Damn straight. You'd be amazed at the prices some people are willing to pay for a butterfly that's so collectible."

Spencer blushed and became oddly quiet.

"Did I say something to upset you?" I finally asked, breaking the silence.

He wrinkled his nose and made a grimace. "You'll probably think I'm just being silly, but I don't understand why people have to swear so much. Especially an attractive woman like yourself. I find it very unbecoming. Besides, you seem much too nice a person for that sort of thing."

"I'm sorry if I offended you," I said taken aback, and not sure how else to respond.

"That's all right. People slip up sometimes. But we're still friends, aren't we?"

"Of course," I agreed, wondering if perhaps I did curse too much.

"Good," Spencer replied, and took a sip of his coffee. "You know, it's funny you should mention butterflies. There's a story about them that I loved as a boy. Would you like to hear it?"

I nodded, beginning to think that Spencer was still rather childlike in some ways.

"Okay. Two caterpillars were crawling through the grass when they spotted a butterfly flitting above them. One bug was fascinated, while the other was frightened, knowing he'd rather stay on the ground, where it was safe and he had plenty of food. But the first caterpillar didn't care about such things. He yearned to have wings and fly. That bug wanted it so much that he finally changed into what he dreamt of becoming. However the second caterpillar stubbornly clung to what was familiar, never daring to imagine a better life. My mother said the lesson was that only those who know their true inner selves can soar like a butterfly. Isn't that beautiful?"

He smiled and I realized what an angelic face Spencer had.

"Yes, it is," I agreed, finding him strangely fascinating. "By the way, there's something I'm curious about. Carl mentioned that he takes in runaways. Do you happen to know how he got involved with that?"

"I'm not really certain, though I know there's a story there somewhere. I've just never heard the whole thing."

"Does he actually help them?"

"Oh yes," Spencer responded, nodding eagerly. "He truly cares for the kids in every way. He gives them food and shelter, as well as ministering to their souls."

His words struck a nerve. I was growing increasingly concerned that Manson was Big Daddy's role model.

"But why does he do it?"

"You really need to ask Carl that yourself. It's his story to tell."

Maybe so. But I suspected Spencer knew more than he was willing to say.

"I'll be honest. I went to see Carl because I'm searching for a young girl."

"I wondered what you were doing at his shop. You don't seem like the type to get a tattoo," Spencer responded.

"Perhaps you've run into her during one of your visits. The girl's name is Lily Holt," I continued, refusing to let the subject drop.

Spencer gazed off into space, and then slowly shook his head. "Sorry, but I don't remember having ever met a Lily."

"It's possible she's using an assumed name."

"That's true. Perhaps she created a whole new identity. Describe her to me," Spencer suggested, beginning to sound intrigued.

Damn! This process would be so much easier if only I'd asked Eric for a photo.

"She's fifteen years old, about five feet three inches tall, and has long brunette hair. But what sets her apart are the scars covering her throat and neck."

He looked at me quizzically.

"She was in an accident as a child."

Spencer's eyes softened, and my hopes began to soar. Could it be that he'd actually seen her? I held my breath, waiting for him to say the magic words.

Instead, he leaned in toward me and his fingers lightly touched my throat. They began to trace a jagged scar that ran across the width of my neck. It was a constant reminder of a case that had nearly cost me my life.

"You're scarred too," he murmured.

I surprised myself by not pulling away. Rather, I allowed

his fingers to continue along their path, finding his touch oddly soothing.

"Nobody gets out of this life unscathed," I remarked as he reached its end.

He nodded, and it felt as if a bond had been established between us.

Only then did I notice the small scar etched into Spencer's own temple. However, rather than mar his angelic looks, it made him all the more real and accessible. I decided to try and appeal to him once again.

"Listen, if you can't tell me how Carl got involved with runaways, then at least explain why it is that your drawings were of the Lotis blue."

Spencer's sweet smile was as guileless as a cherub's. "Honestly, I thought I was just drawing pretty blue butterflies. I must have seen a picture of them somewhere."

I had little choice but to believe he was telling the truth. Photos of blue butterflies aren't all that uncommon.

We finished our coffee and walked back to his car. Once there, Spencer pulled a scrap of paper from his briefcase and jotted down a note.

"Here. This is my phone number. Feel free to call me any time."

I slipped the piece of paper into a pocket, and gave him my business card in return.

"Thanks," Spencer said.

He placed his briefcase on the passenger seat next to some blue feathers that were trimmed and notched. Then he slid in behind the wheel.

"I really enjoyed our talk. We should do it again soon."

I nodded in agreement and watched as he drove off. Then I went in search of my own vehicle.

Unlocking the door, I climbed inside the Explorer and

pulled out my cell phone. It was time to give Mitch Aikens a buzz.

There was no answer. Big surprise. The little weasel was probably dodging me.

That was all right. I didn't really feel like driving out to Daly City today, anyway. Besides, it wasn't as if Aikens was going to be able to hide all of his butterflies overnight. I began to head home, knowing that the matter could easily wait until tomorrow.

I parked in Mei Rose's driveway and walked over to where Tony Baloney was snoozing up a storm. He must have been knocked out by the sun's rays bouncing off all the mirrors across the street. I leaned down to make sure he was all right. The dog growled at me even in his sleep.

I sprinted upstairs and entered my apartment. Or maybe it really wasn't, since nothing looked the least bit familiar. It took a moment before I realized why. Every piece of furniture had been carefully rearranged. Could Terri actually have been all that bored today? Then I knew what must have happened: Mei Rose had vowed to feng shui the place.

I walked over to the windows and closed the blinds in an attempt to block the glare from pouring in. However, Su Lin Fong's battery of octagonal mirrors continued to do their job. It was difficult to tell which of the two women was ahead in the *chi* war at this point. Either way, I counted Tony Baloney and myself among their casualties.

I grabbed a soda and ran upstairs to check in with Terri. He greeted me by immediately plucking the can from my hand.

"Why are you drinking that crap? It'll rot your teeth and it's loaded with calories. Here. Have some of this, instead," he insisted, and replaced my soda with a cup he held in his hand.

I took a sip and wondered if Terri was trying to poison me.

"My God, what is this stuff? It tastes perfectly awful."

"It's tea that Mei Rose gave me," Terri revealed. "She said I should brew some every day and it would help keep me young and beautiful."

"And you believed her? You've got to be kidding. Have you taken a good look at Mei Rose lately?" I asked him.

Terri stared at me for a moment, and then slowly nodded his head.

"I see your point," he said, and dumped the tea into the sink.

Something looked different in his place as well. It must have been the huge stack of books that was piled on the floor. I bent down to see what Terri was reading.

The Quotable Vampire. I, Vampire. Vampire Ourselves. Plus every book Anne Rice had ever written. Last, but not least, was that all time favorite classic, *Dracula*, by Bram Stoker.

I was beginning to think Terri was getting a little too wrapped up in his new job. My suspicions were confirmed as I followed him into the bedroom. Posed next to his bed was a life-sized cut-out of Elvira.

"Don't you think this is carrying it a bit far?" I queried, throwing an arm around her shoulder.

"Not at all. She's my new idol," Terri responded.

Oy veh. Maybe incorporating Christina Aguilera into his act hadn't been such a bad idea after all. I decided to try and lead him in that direction.

"Listen, I found a great clothing store in the Haight that I know you're going to love. They carry everything from sequined hot pants to Lurex metallic tights, and a full array of garter belts. There are even sunglasses with dancing flamingos on their frames."

"Terrific. I've been trying to think of a quirky new garment line that Sophie and I can have some fun with. Maybe the store has a Web site featuring their designs. I'll get Sophie to log on and copy some of their patterns. God knows, I'm itching to get out of the doggy yarmulke business."

"What are you trying to do? Get yourself embroiled in another lawsuit?" I questioned.

"Don't be ridiculous, Rach. Companies do it all the time. What do you think goes on with those gowns the celebs wear to the Academy Awards? Some designer lends Gwyneth a six-thousand-dollar dress, and two days later Aunt Sadie can buy the same exact *schmatte* for a hundred twenty-five bucks at the local discount store. Besides, how else am I going to make the big bucks for my face-lift?"

Terri paused long enough to lick his finger and rub a smudge of dirt off my cheek.

"Don't worry, Rach. There's a face-lift in it for you too, once we hit the big time. Always remember: beauty may be only skin deep, but that's what everyone sees."

Lily Holt's image wafted into my mind, and a flurry of shivers flew up my spine.

I actually made dinner for Santou that evening. Okay, at least I boiled spaghetti and threw a jar of sauce in a pot. Even better, Jake didn't seem to mind.

"Just the two of us eating alone tonight? What's up?" he asked, sitting down to my one-course meal.

"Terri's starting his new job and wants to fit into his gown. As for Mei Rose, she's still stewing about the other night when I didn't make it home in time to cook dinner."

"Those wild, wacky kids of ours," Santou joked. "So did you pay a visit to Edgers today?"

"Absolutely."

"How'd it go?"

"It took some coaxing, but he finally admitted that Lily

never went to Santa Cruz. According to Randy, she's still here in San Francisco. She's supposedly living with a tattoo artist in the Haight who takes in runaways."

Jake arched his eyebrows. "That sounds pretty strange to me."

"No kidding."

"What's the guy's name?"

"Carl Simmons. He owns a place called Big Daddy's Body Shop."

"I guess we should be happy he doesn't call it Big Daddy's Body *Farm*," Jake morbidly joked.

"That's kind of what I was thinking," I admitted. "I keep getting these images of Charles Manson and his Family. Crazy, huh?"

Santou shrugged. "Not necessarily. Who knows in this town?"

"Anyway, I went by the shop and spoke with him. Simmons denies ever knowing anyone by the name of Lily Holt. I figure he's either lying, Lily is using a pseudonym, or Edgers is doing everything he can to steer us away from her."

Jake pulled a piece of garlic bread from its heat-and-eat foil sack. "I'll check Simmons out tomorrow and see if this guy has any kind of record. Then we'll take it from there."

If this was teamwork, I was all for it.

I went to bed that night with thoughts of runaways and lunatics dancing in my head. But when I finally fell asleep, it was butterflies of which I dreamt.

My mother was alive, looking young and beautiful in a way I'd never seen before. Rebecca was there too, sitting by my side. Wildflowers grew in multitudes so thick that we couldn't feel the ground beneath us. Then their petals sprouted wings and flew up toward the sun.

I threw back my head and searched the sky, entranced to

find the petals had turned into colorful butterflies. The beating of their wings kept rhythm with my heart, as they multiplied, filling the heavens like miniature pieces of art.

When I finally looked down again, I found that my mother and sister were gone, and two butterflies were perched in their place. I remained perfectly still, not daring to move, fervently hoping they'd stay. But no sooner had I wished it than they unfurled their wings and took flight.

I ran after them as long as I could, until they disappeared from sight. A sob rose in my throat and I started to cry. Only my tears turned to silken threads that wrapped themselves around me from my feet up to my head.

I lay inside my chrysalis not knowing what to expect. Then a whisper tickled my ear, and my mother repeated a rhyme that she'd always said when kissing me good night.

> *Don't be afraid when I die,*
> *For my soul will become a butterfly.*

More than anything, I prayed that she was right.

Fourteen

Santou was already gone by the time I woke in the morning. Either he was getting better at quietly rolling out of bed, or I was sleeping the sleep of the dead.

I showered, dressed and ate a Pop Tart, after which I searched for my cell phone. It was only because I wanted to check messages that the damn thing was nowhere to be found. Most likely, it was playing hide-and-seek in my Ford.

My plan of attack was to drive over to Mitch Aikens's and catch him off guard. I figured he'd probably still be asleep and so wouldn't expect me. With that in mind, I grabbed my bag and headed downstairs.

Tony Baloney was clearly feeling much better today. He nearly bit off a chunk of my leg as I walked out the door.

"Better luck next time, sweetie!" I called back to the pooch, feeling pretty frisky myself.

Then I climbed into my Explorer. What do you know? There was my cell phone sitting on the passenger seat, as if it had been waiting for me all along. I promptly dialed in my code. Sure enough, Aikens had left one message yesterday afternoon at four o'clock.

"You can stop pinning my balls to the wall. I finally found Horus. Only we need to straighten out a few things between us before I hand over any information. This is good stuff and it ain't gonna come cheap."

Funny what one little phone call can do. I was suddenly riding a high that I hadn't felt since moving to this town. It was as if my luck had abruptly turned around. Maybe this butterfly gig would prove to be a pretty decent case after all. As for Aikens's demands, I'd handle him in my own way.

I felt so good that I stopped at Mario's, grabbed a latte, and was traveling along Highway 101 in no time. Well, maybe that was overstating it a bit. True, I was on 101. However, I was stuck in bumper-to-bumper traffic. My pulse raced faster than the cars in front of me until I thought I'd nearly lose my mind.

The only way I managed to keep my cool was by playing Spencer's game. I tried to imagine who Horus might be. Not that it really mattered. Butcher, baker, or candlestick maker, this butterfly poacher would be hanging up his net for good.

I finally reached the exit and sped down the off ramp, not wanting to lose one more second. Pressing pedal to metal, I zoomed through Daly City and made it to Mitch Aikens's place in five minutes flat.

I jumped out of my Ford and rushed up the walkway, nearly knocking over the ornamental gnomes in my haste. Then my finger locked onto the bell where it steadfastly remained until somebody finally decided to open the door.

What I hadn't expected was for Ma Aikens to be standing there with a pair of eyes that looked like two pieces of raw sushi. But then, she didn't seem to think I looked too hot either. One glimpse of me and she began to sob hysterically.

"Oh, you poor girl. I'm so sorry. The two of you made such a lovely couple."

"What are you talking about?" I asked suspiciously. "Is something wrong?"

"Mitch is gone," Ma Aikens lamented.

Damn! I should have known he'd make a run for it. He was probably halfway to the Mexican border by now.

"Where'd he go?" I questioned, grabbing hold of her bony shoulders.

"Up there." She pointed skyward while blowing her nose into a wad of wet tissue.

"You mean, he took a plane somewhere?"

Ma Aikens began to sob even harder than before, her hand grasping at the air as if trying to catch a ghost.

"No, you don't understand. Mitch would never have left me. For chrissakes, I couldn't even get him to move out of the house. I guess there's no way to break the news, other than to just come out and say it. Poor Mitch is dead," she revealed between quivering lips.

For a moment, I wondered if this was a setup that Mitch had concocted. Then I took another look at the woman. Her eyes were nearly swollen shut, and she swayed unsteadily on her feet. Either Ma Aikens was telling the truth, or giving one hell of an Academy Award–winning performance.

"I can't believe it," I muttered half to myself, finding it hard to accept.

She waved me in, and we walked past the suit of armor. I was tempted to lift the face guard and check to see if Aikens was hiding inside.

"What happened?" I asked, imagining he'd probably had a heart attack.

"It was a terrible accident. Terrible, just terrible," she moaned, taking a seat at the kitchen table and burying her head in her hands.

I brushed some cat hair off the kettle, filled it with water, and turned on a burner.

"Now tell me everything from the beginning," I instructed, after placing a cup of instant coffee before her.

Ma Aikens took a sip. "Is this my Maxwell House? It tastes pretty damn good."

"The accident?" I reminded her, as she stirred in two spoonfuls of sugar.

"Yeah, just give me a minute," Ma Aikens said, and lit up a cigarette. "All I know is Mitch got a phone call late yesterday afternoon, and took off right afterwards. But he distinctly told me that he'd be home for dinner. Otherwise, I'd never have cooked four pork chops. I can't eat that many by myself. In fact, two are still sitting in the fridge. It looks like I'll be eating leftovers tonight."

"What happened then?" I asked, trying to keep her on track.

"What happened? What happened is that he never came back. I figured he either hooked up with you, or some other girl. Nothing personal," she quickly added. "You were his favorite, of course. But you know how men are. You gotta keep 'em on a short leash, or they tend to stray. Anyway, I didn't think much of it until the crack of dawn when the police called. Some hiker stumbled upon poor Mitch's body early this morning."

"Where was he?"

"On San Bruno Mountain. He must have been chasing a butterfly and lost his footing, because he was found at the bottom of a cliff."

"Did the police say if it was an accident?" I inquired, trying to frame my question in the most delicate possible way.

Evidently, it wasn't delicate enough, because Ma Aikens looked at me with a stricken expression. "Why? Are you suggesting that it might have been suicide?"

"No, of course not," I quickly backpedaled.

"Because my Mitch would never do any such thing. Not with everything he had going for him. Maybe you don't realize it, but my son made lots of money. He probably didn't tell you because he was afraid you were a gold digger."

Now she was sounding more like a prospective mother-in-law. What I didn't tell *her* was that the whole scenario sounded rather implausible. Butterflies rarely flit around late on cloudy afternoons, which is exactly what yesterday's weather was—cold, damp, and foggy. Mitch would have known that better than most anyone.

"On top of everything else, what am I supposed to do with all his damn butterflies now?" Ma Aikens moaned, as if having just remembered them. "Mitch loved those things, but I'm certainly not going to spend my life taking care of the little buggers."

"Don't worry. I'll see to it they get a good home," I assured her. "In fact, why don't I go check on them right now?"

"That's very sweet of you, dear," she said, having played me perfectly. "Just pour me another cup of coffee first, will ya?"

I did, and then made my way toward Mitch's room.

It looked exactly as it had the other day, only Snowball was now curled up in Aikens's decrepit chair. The feline had ripped open the seat and pulled out some stuffing to make himself a cozy nest. He purred in satisfaction as I ran my hand over his knotted fur. In fact, the cat was so content that he didn't even attempt to follow me into the next room.

My pulse raced as I entered and closed the door behind me. This was what I loved best—snooping around in a place where I wasn't supposed to be. There was no question but that Mitch wouldn't have approved of my being in here alone. Just knowing it was taboo made me feel all tingly. Hmm. I wondered what that said about my psyche?

I didn't waste a minute, but immediately began to poke through things. Jeez. What a god-awful mess. And this was the cleanest room in the house. Mitch had been sloppy enough to make even *me* look orderly. Boxes, containers, and vials were strewn about everywhere.

I now noticed a few items that I had overlooked on my first visit. Primarily that Aikens liked to raise caterpillars in a variety of ice-cream containers. Whadda ya know? We'd had something in common, after all. When it came to name brands, Mitch had also been an equal-opportunity ice cream eater.

A pile of empty cartons formed a large mound in one corner of the floor. There was Baskin-Robbins No Fat Strawberry, Ben & Jerry's Chunky Monkey, and Breyer's Grand Light Cookie Dough, along with quarts of pistachio, piña colada, chocolate chip mint, and Double Rainbow's Cable Car Cashew. I began to rummage through the hoard with my foot, curious what other flavors he'd purchased.

Whoa, hold on there a second. My shoe knocked against something that didn't sound like a hollow container. I waded deeper into the heap and began to toss ice-cream cartons aside, only to realize they'd been used as a clever subterfuge. Hidden beneath were large plastic boxes exactly like those in which my mother used to store our seasonal clothes. I pulled them out and deftly popped their lids open one by one.

Lo and behold, each held a wide variety of butterflies from around the world. Best of all, every glassine envelope had been neatly labeled.

There were owl butterflies from South America. Their spots were camouflaged as startled eyes that looked surprised to find themselves in such a predicament. Scarlet swallowtails from the Philippines appeared regal as elegant widows. Each of their jet-black wings was streaked with long daubs of scarlet, as if they'd bloodied themselves in mourning. Numerous gray-brown markings transformed white peacocks into a cornucopia of windowpanes. I had to look twice to make sure they weren't actually ornaments composed of Tiffany glass. Meanwhile, brown-and-white paper kites seemed so perfect as not to be real, but rather the result of beautiful origami creations.

I flipped past malachites, painted ladies, zebra longwings, and Gulf fritillaries. There were even question marks, a butterfly that loves to feast on rotting fruit, carrion, and dung.

As interesting as all this was, these butterflies were also perfectly legal. In other words, they weren't what I was looking for. Damn it! Could Mitch have been telling the truth all along? Had he really been on the up and up, and only occasionally strayed into illegal territory?

Chomp, chomp, chomp.

The endless chewing of larvae in the background told me that my suspicions hadn't been wrong.

What a pushover. Don't be such a chump, they seemed to say.

"Are you all right in there?" Ma Aikens called from the other side of the door.

I was so absorbed in my thoughts that she nearly scared the life out of me.

"Everything's fine. It just takes time to feed them," I responded, noticing there was still food enough left to last the caterpillars the rest of the day.

"I'd come in and help. But to tell you the truth, those damn things give me the willies. I'm beginning to think that maybe we should just chuck 'em all."

"Absolutely not!" I responded, a bit too emphatically.

That was enough to make Ma Aikens crack open the door and peek inside.

"Why? Are they worth a lot of money?" she asked suspiciously. "Because I hope you don't plan to sell them behind my back and cut me out of my fair share."

Why, the wily old witch. Her son wasn't even buried yet, and she was already counting the cash.

"I don't believe they should be sold at all," I coolly retorted. "Instead, they should be raised and kept in Mitch's memory."

That seemed to temporarily appease her.

I guess you really did care for him," she relented. "What the hell. I wouldn't know what to do with them, anyway. Mitch never included me in on his business. How about you? Did he tell you anything?"

"Nothing at all," I answered honestly.

"Well the faster this mess gets cleaned up, the quicker I can rent out these rooms. I'm on a fixed income, you know. You wouldn't happen to be looking for a place to live, would you?" she asked wistfully.

I shook my head.

"All right then," she sighed. "I'll let you get back to your work. Do you think you can get them all out by today?"

"I'll certainly try," I replied.

I waited until the door was firmly shut and then began to look around some more. However, so much crap filled the room that it was difficult to focus. I decided to tackle the problem by starting at one end and working my way to the other.

I tore through boxes filled with computer paper, large garbage bags, light bulbs, and electrical cords. Dozens of cheap plastic wine glasses were packed alongside defunct computer games. There were buckets of dried-out paint, cartons filled with ancient vacuum-cleaner parts, and a sack containing nothing but suntan lotion. Mitch must have found all this stuff in abandoned storage units and planned to auction it off one day on eBay.

I was about ready to call it quits, when I spotted a grimy tarp haphazardly flung under one of the counters. Grabbing hold of a corner, I dragged it toward me. My adrenaline shot into orbit at the sight of a fireproof box just begging to be opened. I tried to lift the lid. Naturally, it was locked.

Okay. Now where would Mitch have stashed the key? Hopefully not on his keychain, or I was out of luck. My only other option was to take the damn thing home with me.

I reached in and dragged the box out, relieved to find it was light enough to be portable. That's when my fingers brushed up against something that was metal with notched edges.

Good old Mitch. Dead or alive, you had to love the guy. He'd thoughtfully taped the key onto the back of the safe. I pulled it off and unlocked the lid.

More butterflies.

My heart sank, unsure of what I'd been hoping to find. I absently thumbed through the glassine envelopes, my mind roaming to other matters.

Had Aikens really lost his footing on San Bruno Mountain? How would I ever track Horus down now? And who'd be the one to sift through *my* things when *I* died?

I'd already flipped through half the specimens when I forced myself to slow down.

What are you doing? It's not as if you're a butterfly expert and have any idea what you're looking at, a little voice chided.

Mini-me was right. I needed to remain focused on my work. With that in mind, I started at the front again, and this time carefully checked the labels.

Holy mother of Joseph, Abraham, and Moses. I studied sticker after sticker, wondering if I was actually reading them right. If so, I'd hit the mother lode. Hidden inside were Lange's metalmarks, Myrtle's silverspots, El Segundo blues, and San Bruno elfins, among a slew of others—each and every one of them endangered. Aikens had clearly been a much larger dealer than I'd realized. It made me all the more skeptical regarding his so-called accident.

I quickly locked the safe back up and carried it out, closing the door behind me. Could Aikens possibly have been murdered for the very specimens that I held in my hands?

And if so, why hadn't his killer been here by now to get them?

Snowball mewed, and I gave the cat a distracted pat before starting down the hallway. Two steps later, I stopped dead in my tracks. What, had I completely lost my mind? I'd just nonchalantly strolled right past Mitch's computer.

I darted back in and turned it on, after which I moved Snowball and his mutilated chair out of the way. Then I listened for Ma Aikens as the PC hummed to life. She was busy yacking up a storm on the phone. However, it wouldn't take long before she'd once again grow curious as to what I was doing. I needed to examine the info on his hard drive and leave as soon as possible.

My fingers nervously tapped the desktop, waiting for the screen to light up. The next instant, it turned black and a small box appeared in the upper left hand corner. Damn. Wouldn't you know? Aikens had a lock on his computer that required a password.

No way in hell are you giving up now, Mini-me commanded, verbally kicking my ass.

Okay. I'd done this before. It wasn't impossible. After all, what were codes for if not to be broken? I became more determined than ever to discover what Mitch had been hiding.

I promptly began to type in catchwords that I thought he might have used, such as *Snowball*, *Red Elf*, and *Sally*. But each time I received the same response.

PASSWORD DENIED. PASSWORD DENIED. PASSWORD DENIED.

Damn it!
Come on. Stop and think! Mini-me reprimanded.
Perhaps Aikens had been more esoteric than I'd realized. I placed my bet and took a long shot by entering the scientific names for different varieties of butterflies.

Papilio.

PASSWORD DENIED.

Lycaenids.

PASSWORD DENIED.

Euphilotes.
Bingo and glory hallelujah! Aikens's screen lit up as
bright as a Christmas tree, and I immediately set to work unlocking its secrets.

I'd have been in luck if I'd wanted to know what was being
bought and sold on eBay. However, not a sliver of information
was to be found concerning the butterfly trade. I shut down the
computer, feeling totally defeated. I'd come so close to finding
another piece of the puzzle only to have it all snatched away. It
was enough to make me kick a pile of Mitch's dirty clothes in
frustration. That's when I realized there was still one last place
left to look: the beat-up desk on which the computer sat.

Pulling out drawers, I began to rummage around. There
was no question but that Aikens had had a knack for collecting junk. I slogged through even more of it now. But it
wasn't until I'd emptied the very bottom drawer that I found
something worthwhile. A pile of letters lay hidden beneath a
pile of crap. I removed them, opened the first envelope and
began to read the contents.

Goosebumps instantly broke out on my arms.

Dear Mitchell,

*I received your parcel last night. What a wonderful
surprise! Not only did you send everything I requested,
but they arrived in excellent condition. I'm particu-*

larly grateful for your gift of two pair of Euphydryas editha bayensis. *How could you have known that I wanted those?*

However, please keep in mind that I'm most interested in receiving rare Lycaenids. *What can I say? I have a special weakness when it comes to little blue butterflies. I can't help but go gaga over these precious beauties.*

A smiley face was drawn at the end of this sentence.

I'm fascinated by their mind-boggling complexity and have made it my goal to collect every single rare subspecies. Robert Frost certainly was correct when he described them as "sky flakes." They truly are gifts from heaven. I'm amazed that ordinary people don't appreciate them more, but are drawn to the flashier specimens.

A sad face followed that line.

Anyway, many thanks, and I'll try to throw some clients your way.

I caught sight of the closing and my heart began to pound.

Your friend,
Horus

That lying son of a bitch. Mitch had known how to get in touch with him all along.

I quickly moved on to the next letter, which likewise proved to be from the mysterious dealer. Enclosed was a price list as well as an inventory of specimens for sale. Horus made certain to note that protected and rare butterflies were also available. Individual prices would be given upon specific request.

I collect, sell, and accept only the most perfect material, he noted with pride.

The only thing missing was a clue as to Horus's real identity. Still, I was struck by the absolute meticulousness of his handwriting. It made my own penmanship look like a childish scribble. Of equal interest was that he'd chosen to correspond in longhand rather than by e-mail. Why hadn't he at least typed his letters on a computer? It made me all the more curious about the man.

The rest of the mail contained inquiries from foreign collectors interested in obtaining highly prized and endangered California butterflies. That is, until I came to the very last letter. Every sentence had been boldly underlined. But it was the apparent rage with which pen slashed through paper that made my blood run cold. The lines cut so deep, I would have sworn its author had used a knife as his writing instrument.

I distinctly warned you never to send any specimens that were less than perfect. How dare you try to pawn off inferior-quality butterflies on me! Just who do you think it is you're dealing with? I've told you time and again that breeders must always raise their stock with the fastidiousness of a surgeon. By not doing so, it demonstrates just how irresponsible and stupid you really can be. I'm beginning to think that I've wasted my valuable time on you.

You've also betrayed my trust. How could you disclose the exact location of a colony of Oregon silverspots to other collectors after I distinctly instructed otherwise? Now they'll go in, overcollect and wipe them out, hurting my sales.

Aikens had clearly made a very big boo-boo. Even I knew the importance of not divulging a rare species' location—

not when they're as highly prized as De Beers diamonds. The smart dealer keeps his mouth shut and sells only a few at a time, that way maintaining a high market price.

The diatribe continued, reminding me of the letters that the Unabomber had sent to the *New York Times*. I flipped to the final page and again caught sight of Horus's signature. Stuffing all the letters in my purse, I pulled out my cell phone and placed a call to Dr. Mark Davis.

"Do you have news about John Harmon?" he immediately inquired.

"Not yet," I admitted. "I'm handling another situation at the moment. Remember the collector on San Bruno Mountain you originally called me about?"

"You mean the idiot that was running around catching protected butterflies?"

"Yeah, that guy. His name was Mitch Aikens. Anyway, he died yesterday. The problem is he was hand-raising an enormous number of eggs, larvae, and caterpillars at his home. There are also some butterflies that have just hatched. I was wondering if you'd be willing to take them."

I held my breath, unsure what I'd do if he said no.

"You're really in a bind?"

"I'm afraid so."

"Are there any rare ones among the lot?" Davis asked.

I could hear the eagerness in his voice, although it was carefully modulated to sound noncommittal. Apparently, even this guy had been bitten by the collecting bug.

"There very well could be. I just don't know for certain."

"All right," Davis agreed with pretended reluctance. "I suppose I could help you out and make room for them."

I gave him the address.

"You can tell Mrs. Aikens that I'll be by later on today," he said.

"Wait, I have one more question before you go. Have you ever heard of a dealer by the name of Horus?"

The moment of prickly silence that followed provided a sufficient answer.

"I've heard the name before," Davis reluctantly admitted in a guarded tone. "However, I don't know of anyone who's ever met the man, or if he actually even exists. Why do you ask?"

I wasn't about to reveal that I had correspondence from the guy in my hot little hand.

"I've been told that Horus is a big-league dealer specializing in rare and endangered butterflies. I'm trying to track him down."

"Good luck," Davis responded with a cynical snort. "Do you know his real name, by any chance?"

"No," I admitted.

"Okay then. How about where he lives?"

I bit my lip to keep from sniping back with a snappy retort.

"I thought not. You probably don't even have the slightest clue as to the type of person for whom you should be looking."

Davis, himself, was beginning to remind me a bit of Horus. Both men were egotistical and clearly liked to feel superior. That was fine, as long as it worked in my favor. I decided to pump Davis for all the information I could get.

"I have an idea. Why don't you fill me in, since you're such an authority on the subject," I goaded.

"All right," Davis agreed, sounding genuinely pleased. "Your compulsive collector tends to be a white male that's unmarried, has a need for control, and loves to possess things. Butterflies are the perfect choice because they're small and easy to dominate. What makes it all the more titillating is the additional power of life and death that he holds over them."

I was fascinated, having never heard it put this way before.

"In fact, it's a lot like big-game hunting in that respect. Your obsessed collector isn't so much interested in purchasing butterflies as he is in the ritual of the hunt, itself. The excitement comes with the capture of an elusive species, then the long drive home, and finally the spreading and pinning of their wings. After that, the object is his to possess forever, rather like a trophy head."

The description was enough to give me the creeps. This was a different kind of poacher than I'd ever hunted before.

"Thanks for your help," I acknowledged. Now all I had to do was to find the guy.

I hung up, prepared to leave, when a rusty old garbage can caught my eye. Inside were a few crumpled pieces of rubbish.

I've learned never to walk away without examining every possible item as a potential clue. With that in mind, I turned the can upside down, adding its contents to the rest of the trash on Aikens's floor. Then I began to poke through it.

There were the usual bills, mostly final notices demanding payment. I wondered if Ma Aikens knew that her electricity was about to be turned off. Nothing else proved to be of much interest—except for an empty envelope. It bore no return address, so I checked the postmark. Mendocino.

Bzzzzz!

It felt as if I'd just been zapped with a cattle prod. Mendocino was rapidly turning into my ground zero. First, Harmon had disappeared from the area. Then I'd learned it was the only spot on earth in which the Lotis blue could be found. Now came the discovery that Aikens had been corresponding with someone from the town. It was as if a guardian angel weren't hovering over my shoulder, but shouting directly into my ear.

Then a second thought hit me. Was it possible that Trepler

might actually be Horus? There was only one way to find out. I grabbed the fireproof box, scooted down the hall, and out the front door, hurrying toward my vehicle. I was already in the Ford by the time Ma Aikens caught up.

"Hold on there one minute, missy! Just where do you think you're going?" she demanded.

Damn! She must have somehow discovered I'd absconded with the butterflies. I tucked the fireproof box further beneath the seat with my heel.

"I'm late for an appointment, and have to rush. But Dr. Mark Davis will stop by to collect the butterflies this afternoon. He's a professor at Stanford University, so you know they'll receive good care."

Ma Aikens seemed to forget what she'd been about to say, the news apparently taking her by surprise.

"I swear, if that doesn't beat all," she proclaimed, her face beginning to beam with pride. "Mitch always claimed he knew enough about butterflies to teach in one of those big fancy schools. It looks like he was right. I guess, in a sense, he's kinda going there now."

I took off after promising to see her again soon and drove north, heading across the Golden Gate Bridge.

Fifteen

I didn't bother to check my speedometer. Instead I careened past every car on the road, blatantly breaking the speed limit before sharply turning onto Route 128. I had no choice but to slam on my brakes and slow down after that. Boughs of gnarled oaks formed an arbor overhead as the road abruptly rose and then dropped beneath my tires. It threw me from side-to-side like a roller-coaster ride on a set of spine-tingling, hairpin curves. Both my stomach and the Explorer chug, chug, chugged back uphill, accompanied by a flock of birds screeching in glee while catching updrafts like feathered mini-gliders.

Soon I entered the dark passage of redwoods with its menacing sense of gloom. It was as if I were Gretel, and the woods, the Wicked Witch. I hurried through the ominous corridor as fast as I could, nearly flying until the coastal road appeared. The next five miles were spent navigating a harrowing ribbon of cliffhanging switchbacks. I could have used a hefty martini by the time I reached Mendocino, but instead made tracks directly to Trepler's house.

His shiny kick-ass Lexus announced that he was home. I paid no heed to the chickens who once again warned me to leave him alone. Instead, I took a deep breath, prepared myself for a hostile reception, and knocked on the door. I wasn't disappointed, as Trepler hurled it open and stared at me as though I were a large piece of dirt that needed to be swept onto the road.

"You're one helluva brazen bitch, aren't you?" he observed, spitting out each word as though it left a bad taste in his mouth. "Otherwise, you'd never have the nerve to show your face here again."

Trepler paused, and his eyes slowly brightened like two gas flames springing to life. "Oh, wait a minute. I get it now. The government toady must want some more information."

He broke into a malicious grin, his teeth as uneven as misaligned kernels of corn.

"Of course, that's it. Why else would you come back to see some evil, perverse lepidopterist who sticks pins into insects for fun, and probably rips the wings off grasshoppers just for the hell of it? I'll let you in on a little secret. I also like to club baby seals in my spare time."

I calmly looked at the man, waiting until he'd finished his rant.

"So, what is it that you need to know now, huh? How to tell the difference between a butterfly and a moth? Because that's how bright a bulb each and every one of you special agents seems to be. Face it. You don't know your ass from your elbow, never mind being able to distinguish one butterfly from another. What a piss-ass lot of pathetic, puny losers you all are."

"All right! Enough already," I retorted, beginning to lose my patience. "You know damn well I wouldn't be here unless it were important."

Trepler stared at me from under a pair of drooping eyelids. "You've got guts. I'll give you that much. But I've got nothing to tell you."

I placed my foot against the door, in case he tried to close it on me. Trepler took note, and shook his head in exasperation.

"So exactly what is it that you want?" he asked curtly.

"A butterfly dealer died yesterday on San Bruno Mountain, near Daly City."

"Big loss," Trepler sniped. Is that something I'm supposed to care about? Most dealers are a bunch of slime bags, anyway."

"You mean, unlike collectors?" I asked, curious to hear his response.

"You damn well better believe it. We're talking two completely different animals. Butterflies are nothing more than dollar signs to most dealers."

"As opposed to you, for whom they equate into a fancy new Lexus," I couldn't help but jab. "Correct me if I'm wrong, but didn't you say that car was a bonus? I believe it was for helping to clear the way on a project that will essentially destroy a vulnerable butterfly's habitat."

Trepler glared at me in annoyance. "Why don't you just get to the point and tell me why it is that you're here?"

"The butterfly dealer I told you about? His death was deemed an accident. However, I suspect that actually he was murdered. The same goes for Harmon, the Fish and Wildlife consultant, whose car was found on a remote road up here. The police don't seem to think that amounts to much either, but I'm convinced his disappearance also involved foul play."

"Well, hip hip hooray. Aren't you quite the little detective," Trepler dryly commented. "But you still haven't answered my question. What is it you want from me?"

"There's another butterfly dealer whose name keeps popping up. I'd like to talk to him. I have reason to believe that he lives in the area."

I paused, hoping Trepler would respond. But his face maintained an expression of pained irritability.

"Perhaps you can tell me where I can find him. The man goes by the name of Horus."

It was as if I'd just said the word *Beelzebub*, causing Trepler to twitch involuntarily.

"Then you *do* know him." I pounced, as if having already received my answer.

But Trepler shook his head. "You don't know what it is that you're talking about. No such person exists. You're chasing after a ghost."

However, his face was now drawn and his complexion had turned unnaturally pale.

"What do you mean?" I asked, not believing a word.

Trepler's eyes darted from side to side, as if checking for something that wasn't there. My heart began to sink, realizing that he probably wasn't Horus.

"Go ask around town. You'll eventually figure it out for yourself."

Trepler ended our conversation by once again slamming the door in my face.

I walked down the driveway, past the chickens, who this time clucked *We told you so, we told you so.*

Getting in my Ford, I left Portuguese Flats and headed back into the heart of Mendocino. I drove past bed-and-breakfast places and little knickknack stores, all seemingly possessed by Laura Ashley, with their pretty pastel paint jobs and wooden filigree flouncing around windows, porches, and doorways.

I parked my vehicle on Main Street and followed Trepler's advice, going in and out of shops to ask if anyone knew of a resident by the name of Horus. The reaction was always the same. People looked at me as though I'd lost my freakin' mind.

I finally gave up, bought a sandwich, and decided to eat along the bluffs. I followed a path that continued to wind for miles around the cliffs, feeling as if I'd walked into a painting.

The wind rippled through long grass that tickled my legs, each of the blades glistening with dew. I tried to carefully tip-toe through bright yellow daffodils and baby blue flowers, their colors as luscious as a Monet painting, but there was no way not to squish a few. Even the sky appeared dreamlike, having been kissed by the passing mist. A steel gray fog bank rolled off in the distance, making the scene all the more intense.

It's in these waters that gray whales trek to Baja, California, each February. They migrate back to the Bering Sea with their newborn calves in the spring, traveling a distance of twelve thousand miles round trip. I scanned the horizon now, hoping to spy a whale spout, but none was in sight. Sidling closer to the edge of the cliff, I glanced down at the small strip of beach below.

Coarse sand was strewn with long strands of kelp and littered with pieces of driftwood. Logs the size of mastodon bones were buffeted about in the turbulent waves. Powerful swells had carved blowholes and grottoes into lichen-streaked cliffs as easily as if they'd been made of Play Doh. A batch of scummy foam bobbed about in a tide pool, where it was held captive, unable to escape.

Mendocino had the appearance of a prim and proper New England town. Yet I had no doubt that a layer of violence simmered beneath the surface, just waiting to erupt. As if on cue, a wave crashed against the headland with such force that a fine cloud of spindrift shot into the air. It rained down upon me, leaving a salty taste in my mouth.

Glancing up, I caught sight of a gull frantically flapping its wings, unable to make any headway against the breeze. The hoarse bark of a seal out at sea caught my ear. The creature sounded in distress and I leaned forward a bit more, wanting to see if I could spot it.

"That's where it was wrecked."

A voice like the rumbling of rocks caught me by surprise and I jerked in reaction. The next thing I knew, I lost my balance on the slippery edge. The situation quickly worsened as stones and soil began to crumble and give way beneath me. My heart lurched into my throat, knowing that I'd never survive such a fall. But there was nothing I could do to steady myself. Instead, I flung my arms out wide, as if hoping to fly, while mentally preparing to tumble. I knew I'd most likely land on the rocks below and drown, as my legs started to slide out from under me.

I cried out, angry as hell at the turn of events and scared to death all at once. Rather than fall, however, I was plucked from the jaws of death by what could only have been an angel. A pair of strong hands grabbed onto my outstretched arm and pulled me back in the nick of time.

I was so shaken to the core that my breath came in jagged spurts. I turned to thank my rescuer, only to be further surprised. Standing before me was the homeless man whom I'd seen striding along the cliffs just a few days ago.

"You need to be more careful, miss. Didn't you read the signs back there?" he asked, looking concerned.

His voice churned and reverberated in the air as he bent down to pick up his walking stick.

"No. I guess I must have missed them," I replied, taking a giant step back from the edge, still afraid that my quivering legs might buckle beneath me.

"Well these cliffs are pretty hazardous. You saw that for yourself. Lots of the rims are unstable. We've also got what are called sleeper waves around here. They crash real high onto the rocks, much more than normal waves do. People tend to get in trouble when they turn their backs while standing too close to the edge. You never know what can happen.

The ocean might just reach up and grab hold of you," he advised with a straight face.

"I'll remember that," I said, and meant it. "Thanks for saving my life back there."

The man nodded, and I noticed that strips of gaffers' tape covered threadbare spots on his pants and jacket, though his dreadlocks appeared to have been freshly shampooed. They glistened sleek as strings of licorice in contrast to his skin, which looked to be permanently chapped and reddened by the weather.

"I could really use some company after such a close call. Would you mind sitting with me for a while?" I asked, and motioned to a nearby bench.

The man remained standing for a moment, as if unsure what to do. Then he finally sat down. I joined him, remembering the sandwich that I'd shoved into my purse. Pulling it out, I offered him half. He accepted and we chewed together in what seemed like perfect syncopation.

"I'm Rachel Porter," I volunteered, hoping to break the silence.

"People call me Big Sam."

I furtively glanced at the man, wondering if he was an old white hippie from the sixties who'd once visited Jamaica, smoked too much ganja weed, grown an awesome set of dreadlocks, and never mentally returned. However, that didn't seem like an appropriate question, so I decided to follow up on something he'd said before my near fall.

"You mentioned a wreck of some kind. What were you talking about?"

"The *Frolic*, of course."

I shot him a questioning look, still not understanding what he meant.

"That's how the town came to be back in 1850. The *Frolic*

was a schooner loaded with cargo from China. It crashed on the rocks and shifting sandbars in that water. A salvage crew was sent to retrieve whatever bolts of silk and chinaware they could," Big Sam explained. "Instead they discovered something far more valuable—a huge redwood forest. This was during the Gold Rush, when San Francisco needed lots of building material. J. B. Ford, the schooner's owner, also happened to be a lumberman. When he heard about the redwoods, old J. B. rushed out here from Maine as fast as a train would carry him and established Mendocino as a logging town."

"So that's why the place looks like a New England village," I replied, realizing it now made sense.

Big Sam nodded. "Ford set up a sawmill on these headlands. Only it was quite a trick trying to get the lumber onto those boats and transport it out, what with all the dog holes around here." He chuckled, as if having witnessed the scene himself.

"What are dog holes?" I asked, never having heard the term before.

"They're the rocky inlets and shallow harbors all along this coastline. They earned the name because schooners couldn't dock safely. The inlets are only large enough for a dog to come in, turn around, and go back out. That's why they had to design chutes and slides that extended out to sea from the cliffs. Those wooden pilings that you see lying all over the beach? They're the remains of an old cargo loading system. Mendocino was quite the place back then. In fact, it was known as the original skid row."

I took another look at Big Sam, and wondered if he was putting me on. "What do you mean? That there were a lot of down-and-out folks living here then?"

Big Sam finished the sandwich, pulled a tissue from his pocket, and fastidiously wiped each finger.

"What I mean is that the poor came to Mendocino looking for work. They ended up sleeping alongside the skids that were used to haul big tree trunks down to the sawmill. That's how Skid Row first got its name."

I was beginning to wonder if Big Sam might have been a history professor at one time. How else could he have known so much about the town? I was toying with that idea when a brainstorm hit me. This was the perfect person to ask about Horus.

"I'm trying to find a man who lives around here. Maybe you can help me."

Big Sam shrugged. "Could be. I know lots of people in the area. What's his name?"

"Horus," I said, hoping he wouldn't let me down.

Big Sam looked at me with eyes as tempestuous as the sea. Then he turned and pointed toward town. My eyes skipped from building to building as I tried to follow the direction of his finger, unsure of where it led.

"Over there. Don't you see it?" he scolded.

I looked again, and realized he was directing my attention to the large winged figure holding a sickle. So much for my fantasy that Big Sam was a brilliant academic gone astray. I should have known a homeless man wandering the bluffs wouldn't be completely lucid.

"That's Horus," he emphatically stated. "Why are you interested? What do you do for a living?"

"I'm a U.S. Fish and Wildlife agent."

"So you protect all the animals?"

"Uh-huh," I responded, my thoughts focused on how I would ever find Horus.

"Even little blue butterflies?"

I tried to take a breath, but all the oxygen in the air had mysteriously disappeared.

"What do you know about them?" I asked in a scratchy

whisper, barely daring to hope that Big Sam held the magical key to their existence.

"Just that I see them around sometimes."

"Where?" I excitedly questioned, my heart starting to race out of control.

"Everywhere. On the headlands. Fluttering over the waves. Sometimes even flying around in my dreams."

Damn! Once again, my eagerness had played me for a fool. Blue butterflies were probably the equivalent of pink elephants to him—the West Coast version of a psychotic hallucination. Even so, I decided to try one last question.

"Can you tell me who owns the property outside of town that used to be the old Baker place? I think it was called the Sanctuary at one time."

"Sure. That belongs to the brother now."

The brother? What the hell did he mean? Was Big Sam referring to his own brother? A fraternal brother? Or a soul brother of some kind?

"What sort of brother are you talking about?" I asked, hoping to straighten out the confusion.

But Big Sam seemed to have become as impatient with me as I had with him.

"I'm not gonna to keep answering these dumb questions if you can't understand a single thing I say," he grumbled, his mood changing as drastically as the current around the coastline. "I don't have time to waste. Just leave me alone!" he warned.

Then he got up and rambled away.

I watched as Big Sam followed the trail around the bluffs in the late afternoon light until he disappeared from sight.

I sat for a while longer, listening to the waves crash against the rocks, watching as the dimming light made a final stab at the sky, its pink fingers reaching so deep inside the clouds that it filled them with blood. The sun slowly sank into the Pacific, turning the water a muted lavender. Cormorants made a last dive for dinner, popping back up to the surface with the exuberance of bobbing floats. That's when I saw what could have been whales. Only the shapes revealed themselves to be massive gray rocks that melted and disappeared in the darkness, and I knew it was time to go home.

I made my way back to the Ford, buckled on my seat belt, and headed out of Mendocino, leaving its ghosts and secrets behind. What had been a challenge in daylight now proved to be downright harrowing as I maneuvered as best I could along the coast road. Fog billowed toward me from across the Pacific, silent as a pale river, moving stealthily as a cat on the prowl—and I, its unwitting prey. I tried to make good time but couldn't see where the road ended and the cliffs began, everything having become shrouded in a ghostly mist. As if that weren't enough, it now began to rain, so that my vision became obscured. Angry drops beat furiously against the windshield with the cumulative force of a thousand tiny fists.

I breathed a sigh of relief as I turned off Highway 1 and entered the redwood corridor, only to experience fear of a different kind. I'd never before known that darkness could have so many different layers, ranging from murky twilight to impenetrable blackness. However, one thing about the night remains eternally true: The darkness is filled with unseen things that exist solely to taunt you.

The looming trees surrounding me were no gentle giants, but threatening ogres watching my every move. They joined forces with the fog, which threw itself against my windshield, as determined as a voracious animal. A sharp cry pierced the silence, setting the night on edge. It was the howl of a wraith savagely wailing to get in. I let my mind wander, hoping to escape the ghastly sound, only to have it meander back to the old Baker property.

I wondered, could the "brother" who now owned the Sanctuary possibly be the same Franciscan brother that Aikens had told me about? Did such a person really exist?

I was so deep in thought that I nearly jumped straight through the roof as my cell phone rang.

"Chère, where in the hell are you?" Santou demanded, sounding perturbed.

Then I remembered: This trip had been so spur of the moment that I hadn't told anyone.

"Sorry, Jake. I drove up to Mendocino early today on a hunch, only it didn't pan out. I'm on my way back home right now."

"Next time let me know when you take off like that, chère," he reprimanded. "For chrissake, it's bad enough you don't have any backup. But what if you disappeared like that consultant of yours, and nobody knew where you'd gone? What then?"

Harmon flit through my mind, and I knew in my gut the man hadn't run off. The only explanation was that he was dead.

"I didn't mean to worry you, Jake. I'll let you know where I am from now on. Okay?"

I didn't bother to add that Harmon had managed to vanish without a trace, even though people had known exactly where he was at the time.

"All right," Santou gruffly responded. "I'd appreciate that."

I no longer took offense at his chiding over my comings and goings, aware that he'd grown increasingly anxious ever since his accident.

"Anyway, there's another reason I called. I dug up some information on Carl Simmons that I think you'll find interesting."

"Really? What is it?" I asked, trying to maintain my focus on the road.

"The guy's got one helluva diverse background. He was caught dealing in illegal butterflies during the late seventies, right after a number of them were placed on the endangered species list. You probably wouldn't have heard about it. He received only a minor slap on the wrist back then."

"Naturally. Not that it would be any different today," I cynically retorted, aware that people still didn't take the idea of poaching butterflies very seriously.

"I discovered something else equally fascinating that should intrigue you. Big Daddy Simmons was a Franciscan brother at one time."

"Holy shit," I uttered, totally floored.

"Believe it or not, it gets even better than that," Jake confided. "A complaint was once lodged against him by a runaway. Somewhere there's a police report."

"What!" I exclaimed, nearly driving off the road. "What was the charge?"

"That's a tidbit I haven't been able to uncover yet."

I had little time to digest the news, as a pair of bright lights appeared in my rearview mirror from out of nowhere. They swiftly grew in size from burning cigarettes to twin flashlights to two large headlights rapidly bearing down on me.

"I've got to go, Jake. I'll call you back in a few minutes."

"Why? What's going on, chère?"

I hung up rather than answer, needing to fully focus on the situation. Whoever was behind the wheel was either drunk, rushing to a hospital, or possibly both. In either case, it made the road all the more dangerous.

I angled as far to the right as I could, hoping the speed demon would simply pass by. But that wasn't the vehicle's intent. Instead it drew close, its brights flooding my side and rearview mirrors as if purposely attempting to blind me. Then there was a forceful bump against my fender, and I was thrown forward onto the steering wheel. Its hard edge angrily bit into my stomach.

Great. Wouldn't you know I'd get some joker on my tail that wanted to play? Normally, I'd have been happy to take him on, and leave the sucker in my dust. But I didn't know the road and visibility was near nil, giving my opponent the homeboy advantage.

Another powerful thump announced the initial fender bender had been no mistake. I was left with little choice but to speed up and try to outrun my assailant. Flooring the Ford, I cursed Trepler, Horus, and the impervious night, as well as the maniac driving behind me. But that did nothing to stop the twists and turns that gleefully jumped into sight, surprising me at the last possible moment. I gripped the steering wheel tight, as though that would help me stay on the road. But the bends and curves continued to playfully swerve while I struggled to maintain control. *Nyah, nyah, nyah, nyah, nyah,* they seemed to taunt, like a gang of rowdy bullies running wild in a schoolyard.

The rain came down harder as I jerked the steering wheel, causing my tires to skid across the blacktop. All I could hope was that a logging truck didn't approach from the opposite direction. The very thought made my stomach churn. It felt as though I'd been swallowed whole by a video game over which I had no control. Rather, I was being held captive by some hyperactive kid who was in charge of the joystick. Still, the apparent danger would have been worthwhile if only I could have lost the bastard who was tailing me. But his headlights continued to burn a hole through the night, like a couple of lit sticks of dynamite.

I wasn't sure how much longer I could continue at this pace without flying off the pavement. As it turned out, it wasn't something I had time to worry about. I received one last hard bump, and then the demon vehicle screamed in delight as it pulled alongside me.

I glanced over to where the dark van hovered on my left, dwarfing my own SUV by comparison. The monster made good use of its bulk, careening into my side in a blatant attempt to push me off the road.

"You son of a bitch," I muttered, and held on with all my might.

My stubbornness only seemed to make the van and its driver all the more determined. The vehicle veered into the far lane, and then came swerving back full force, causing metal to slam against metal. A nauseating squeal resounded in the air, and I realized it was the terrifying screech of my tires. The next thing I knew, I was helplessly spinning out of control, as though on a madcap carnival ride. I instantly lost my sense of direction, unable to tell which side of the road I was on, or if I was on it at all. Then my teeth slammed together and every bone in my body rattled. There was no longer any question but that my tires had left pavement and were now skidding across hard ground.

There were trees all around, coming at me from everywhere, as my Ford straightened out. I felt like a Keystone cop, frantically steering as best I could while trying to dodge Douglas firs and redwoods soaring high into the firmament. My vehicle couldn't find any traction although I slammed on the brakes. At the same time, a wall of massive tree trunks appeared in front of me in my headlights. I gripped the steering wheel while pushing back against the seat and pressing down hard on the brakes, certain my foot would shoot straight through the floor at any minute.

My tires finally gripped and the Ford jerked to an abrupt halt, flinging my body forward with the ease of a rag doll.

Smack!

My forehead struck sharply against the steering wheel and, for a moment, I temporarily forgot where I was. Then a bright light came from behind to embrace me.

Oh, shit! Could it be I was dead and these were the welcoming rays beckoning me into the great beyond?

I blinked several times before slowly realizing they were highbeams bouncing off my windshield. The stream of light refracted into a large spider web in the night, bringing the nightmare back home.

I remained perfectly still, but for my right hand which reached for the gun in my purse. I'd damn well defend myself should my attacker try to finish me off. However, he was either satisfied with the damage done, or wrongly fingered me for dead. The mysterious van peeled out, leaving me alone in the dark.

Sixteen

Santou had accused me for years of having a hard head. He must have been correct. My sole injury appeared to be a painful bump on the forehead that was accompanied by one hell of a massive headache. A few assorted bruises also throbbed, making their existence known. But other than that, I seemed to be fine—all except for my hands, which wouldn't stop shaking. Equally disturbing was that my vehicle was now firmly stuck in a grove of redwoods.

I located my cell phone. The next challenge was to control my trembling fingers long enough to punch in the correct number and ring Santou.

"What's going on, Rachel? I tried to call back, but you didn't answer."

"Sorry about cutting you off before, but I was involved in an accident with another vehicle," I admitted.

"Are you all right?" he quickly asked.

I heard the concern in his voice, and didn't want to make matters any worse than absolutely necessary.

"It's just this damn road, what with the rain and it being dark," I hedged. "I guess we were both going a little too fast. Anyway, I ended up driving off the blacktop and into the woods. I'm afraid I'm going to have to be towed out."

"How about the other vehicle? What's the damage there?"

"The driver was fine. He already took off."

There was a pause, and I instinctively knew what was about to come next.

"In other words, it was a hit and run."

"You could say that. He probably didn't have any insurance."

"Just tell me this, was it a deliberate crash or simply an accident?"

"It's a lousy night out, Jake, and the fog is thick as hell," I replied, giving my version of the truth.

I couldn't be sure if Santou bought my excuse. But at least he stopped grilling me for now.

"You're breaking up. I can barely hear you. Give me your location as best you can," he said, kicking into rescue mode.

I was tempted to say *the highway from hell*, but managed to control myself.

"I'm stuck somewhere in Navarro Redwood State Park along Highway 128, not far off the coast road," I shouted, supplying what information I could.

"Can you open the door and get out?" Santou yelled back.

"Let me try."

I lifted the handle, but the door wouldn't budge. Shifting my weight, I kicked the panel hard with my foot. It creaked open just enough for me to squeeze through.

"Okay, got it," I answered.

"Fine. Now see if you can walk."

I suddenly became nervous. What if I were wrong and really had been injured? I gingerly placed one foot on the ground, followed by the other, and slowly began to move.

"I'm all right," I told him, choosing not to mention the fact that my right leg was sore.

My philosophy has always been, whatever doesn't kill you makes you stronger. Otherwise known as *Dear Lord, please keep me far away from all doctors*.

"Great. Now find a flashlight and make your way back to

the road, while I call a towing service. Just sit tight and wait once you get there."

I did as instructed, grabbing a flashlight from under the front seat. Then, turning it on, I tried to ignore the crones, ghosts, and goblins lurking behind each tree, all waiting to pounce on me. I continued to walk as the darkness transformed every shadow and shape into something terrifying.

For chrissakes, buck up, Porter. You've got a gun. Besides, you deal with lunatics and pissed-off poachers all the time.

That was true. However, those were physical things over which I had a certain degree of control. It was the unseen that scared the hell out of me.

The fog played hide-and-seek, sending me first one way and then another, as I tried to get my bearings in the thick mist. It was the sound of a passing vehicle that finally steered me in the right direction.

Oh, please, don't let that be the tow truck passing by, I prayed.

I hurried toward the rumble of wheels, attempting to ignore the pain in my leg, only to arrive too late. I had little choice but to sit in a pile of dead evergreen needles by the side of the road and wait. If it had been the tow truck, it would eventually return this way.

With time to kill, I mulled over the information that Santou had uncovered. Carl Simmons had to be the Franciscan brother that Mitch Aikens had told me about. I pictured Big Daddy in my mind again, and found it hard to believe he'd ever been a man of the cloth. But apparently, it was true.

Aikens had also boasted that Simmons used to be a big-time butterfly dealer. He'd idolized the man for having successfully poached butterflies in wildlife refuges and national parks. If Simmons were capable of those incarnations, there seemed no reason to believe that he wasn't also Horus.

It was then that a pair of flashing yellow lights cut through

the darkness and a tow truck came into view. I signaled back
with my flashlight in a make-do version of Morse Code. I'd
have thrown myself in front of the truck if need be, in order
to gain its attention. Fortunately, that wasn't necessary. The
tow truck stopped and a bloated version of Rocky Balboa
jumped out.

"It's lucky your husband caught me when he did. I was
just about to shut down for the night," he said in place of
hello.

The word "husband" didn't sound half bad, and I didn't
bother to correct him. Instead, I led Rocky through the redwoods to where my Explorer sat sulking. He checked it out
and then attached a cable under the back end.

"Okay, climb inside your vehicle and let's see if we can
get this thing started," he instructed.

The Ford hemmed and hawed a few times, then coughed,
spit, and farted. Rocky lifted the hood and began to talk to
himself; or, perhaps he was communicating with my vehicle.

"Try it again," he directed.

I did, and this time the engine kicked over, purring like a
large, contented cat.

"All right. What say we haul ass out of here," Rocky suggested. "Stay in your vehicle, and try not to hit anything."

He walked to his truck, flipped on a switch, and the winch
began to reel my Ford back toward the road like a large
metal fish. My Explorer and I eventually made it onto Highway 128 in one piece.

Aside from a couple of dented fenders, a beat-up hood,
two discombobulated doors, one broken headlight, and numerous nicks and bumps, my vehicle was in pretty good
shape, everything considered. Best of all, AAA was footing
the bill.

I gave the guy a twenty for his trouble and set off again,
this time keeping watch for any menacing vans skulking

along the road. I knew I was free and clear as I peeled onto
Highway 101 and headed for home. Only there was some-
place else that I first had to go. I turned off my cell phone, so
as not to be disturbed, and drove over the Golden Gate
Bridge, making my way straight to the Haight.

The street scene was an ongoing party, as usual—one in
which the show never stopped. It was a blast from the past,
complete with bellbottoms, buckskin, and love beads. The
district could have made a fortune had they only charged
admission.

I parked my Ford next to a guy sleeping on a tattered pais-
ley couch in the middle of the sidewalk. Then I hot-footed it
to Big Daddy's Body Shop. The place was locked up tight.
No problem. I dialed a San Francisco operator and got Carl
Simmons's home address. Surprise, surprise. He lived a couple blocks from the old Manson house.

Ashbury Street was quiet in comparison to the carnival taking place below. The only foot traffic were local residents and
those hard-core fans paying homage at the former dwelling of
the Grateful Dead. A few had taped tattered scraps of paper
onto its walls, each of which contained a heartfelt message.

My life is meaningless without your music. Your fan in
life and death forever, Janice.

Others stood and reverently pressed their palms against
the front door, as if hoping to absorb its psychic energy.

I continued up the street. Some local Dead Head was obviously doing all right. An old turquoise Thunderbird, in
primo condition, sat parked nearby.

I finally came to Simmons's address, a run-down two-
story structure. Blue and lavender paint peeled off the Victorian house in strips, like layers on an onion, giving the place
a tie-dyed effect.

I climbed the rickety stairs and found Carl Simmons's name listed on the second-floor buzzer. Someone was clearly home. *Jefferson Airplane*'s music blared onto the street exhorting passersby that they'd better find somebody to love.

I pressed the bell, purposely keeping my finger planted on it.

"Is that you, Sherry?" a voice finally called out from above.

"No. It's Rachel Porter," I shouted back, attempting to be heard above the music.

Big Daddy poked his head out the window and looked at me in surprise. I waved, and flashed a pleasant smile, hoping the bastard would come to the door.

"I'll be right there," he responded, after a moment's hesitation.

Oh, goody.

Grace Slick was advising Alice about popping a couple of pills to change her size when the music abruptly stopped in mid-chorus. A minute later, heavy footsteps could be heard bounding down the stairs, and Carl Simmons opened the door. He must have just hopped out of the shower, because his hair was wet and his skin smelled of deodorant soap.

"This is a surprise," Big Daddy said, tucking in his shirttail. "Most clients don't stop by to see me at home."

"You forget. I'm not a customer," I genially responded. "I'm here because we need to talk. Do you mind if I come in?"

Simmons appeared somewhat reticent as he looked at me and shrugged.

"I don't suppose this could wait until tomorrow. I'd prefer if you came by the shop."

"Why? Do you have company?" I pointedly inquired.

"Would it matter?" Simmons responded.

"Not one little bit."

He stepped aside and let me in.

I followed him upstairs, noticing that both the steps and banister were also badly in need of a paint job. I could only imagine the condition of his flat. However, I was in for quite a surprise—as Simmons opened the door and I entered what might easily have been a museum. I'd never have suspected the man to be such a connoisseur of art.

Masks and paintings hung on every inch of wall space, giving the place a sophisticated feel. There were animal masks from Mexico, tribal faces of Africa, and primitive artwork from Bali. The remainder of his living room was taken up with an impressive collection of CDs and books. Simmons's taste in music ran the gamut from Bach to Billie Holiday to the Doobie Brothers and Fat Bastard. His reading material was equally eclectic. I caught sight of volumes of Shakespeare and Homer's *Odyssey*, as well as William Burroughs's *Naked Lunch*.

This was plainly a man who read the classics rather than merely scanned the Cliff Notes. It was also the apartment of a pack rat with clutter spread all about. I smiled, having realized of whom he reminded me. Simmons was the upscale, "lite" version of Mitch Aikens—which made me wonder just how he made all of his money.

"So, to what do I owe this pleasure?" Big Daddy asked, getting straight to the point.

I decided I might as well be equally direct.

"I hear you're involved in the butterfly trade," I said, hoping to catch him off balance.

"I no longer am, although I used to be," Simmons responded, his demeanor remaining cucumber cool. "However, that was in a past life. Or are you going to try and retroactively throw me in jail for some hyped-up, bullshit offense?"

The guy was already beginning to piss me off.

"Past life, huh? That's funny, because your name only recently came up in connection with the trade."

"Stranger things have happened. You must have spoken to someone who was fondly remembering the good old days."

"Perhaps. The odd thing is the person who mentioned you died under suspicious circumstances, just yesterday. Any thoughts on that?"

Simmons remained silent, not giving anything away.

"I'm not about to let up until I get to the bottom of this. Maybe you should consider telling me what you know before things get any more out of control," I advised.

"Sorry, but I have no idea what you're talking about. I stopped dealing in butterflies years ago after realizing that I wasn't cut out for the business."

Now he'd really whet my interest.

"Care to elaborate?" I suggested.

Big Daddy motioned for me to take a seat, while lowering his own bulk onto a velvet-covered sofa. I planted myself in a Biedermeyer chair. There seemed no question but that the butterfly trade had been very, very good to the man. Simmons apparently managed to stomach it long enough to obtain a number of beautiful possessions.

"Butterflies are beyond a passion for the true collector. They're an absolute obsession, making everything else in life secondary," he explained. "It's what's known in the trade as the 'sickness.' Marriages are destroyed, jobs are lost. Some collectors grow so fixated that they spend their last dime on a rare butterfly and become financially ruined. Think of it as the equivalent of acquiring high-end art, such as a Van Gogh or a Rembrandt painting. If you have the money, are good at collecting, and know when to sell, then the endeavor can be incredibly lucrative. If not, you tend to end up in deep shit."

"That's all very interesting, but you still haven't told me why *you* got out of the trade," I persisted.

Big Daddy cracked his knuckles one at a time and grimaced, as if putting off something distasteful.

"Look, I got out of the business when I finally realized what it was doing to me. At first the whole thing was amazingly alluring. You have no idea how seductive it is to get caught up and lose yourself in so much beauty. It's like a great sexual thrill. But then I became greedy. I didn't want just one of each species. I craved every single specimen. It got to the point where I'd go into an area and collect all the larvae I could. Then I'd rip out the remaining food plants so that no one else would be able to find them. Why? Because I knew that would help protect my investment and drive the market price up. I'd have done anything to ensure that I had the very last specimen. Then I'd turn around and sell it for mucho bucks."

Simmons was right. Anyone who would push a species to the brink of extinction for ego gratification and profit *was* gripped by a sickness. I would have gladly slapped Big Daddy behind bars right now if only that were possible. Instead, I tried hard not to show my disgust.

"The problem began when I started to identify more with the butterflies than I did with my clients. I became so good at finding rare specimens, that I actually began to think like one while out in the field." Big Daddy sadly grunted and shook his head. "That's when I knew I had to make amends for my actions. So I joined the Franciscan order. I presume you already know about that?"

I nodded, not wanting to interrupt Simmons while he was on a roll. Big Daddy folded his hands across his stomach, and stretched out his arms and legs. It made him look more like Paul Bunyan than Friar Tuck.

"I felt it was the ultimate penance I could pay for my role in disrupting the order of nature. What better way to redress such wrongs than devote a few years of my life to St. Francis of Assisi?"

"Maybe so. But I also happen to know that you didn't totally clean up your act."

"What do you mean by that?" Simmons coldly responded.

"Oh, come on. What about the complaint that was lodged against you by a runaway girl? Or don't you count that on your list of transgressions?"

Big Daddy's face turned beet red. "It was a boy, not a girl," he blurted out, and then realized what he'd said. "Look, that complaint came after I'd left the Franciscan order, and the accuser wasn't a runaway, but my foster son. He was angry at the time and it was his way of getting back at me. The charges were investigated and dropped. You can check it out if you like."

This was the first I'd heard that Simmons had a child.

"Why would he do something like that? What was your foster son so mad about?" I asked, figuring where there was that kind of smoke, there had to be one hell of a large fire.

"His mother had recently died and he was upset. He felt that I was in some way responsible."

Oh, boy. Simmons was turning out to be an even murkier character than I had anticipated.

"Was he right?" I questioned, not really expecting an answer.

Simmons took a deep breath and slowly exhaled, bringing his hands to his lips as if in prayer.

"Do you believe in God?"

"I believe in a higher power," I cautiously replied, not sure where this was heading. I'd dealt with religious zealots before, and had learned to be wary.

"There's an excerpt from *The Canticle of the Creatures*

by St. Francis that's touched my life in a way I'd have never imagined. It's taught me to view those tragedies that befall us in a positive light. St. Francis was right. I've been through the fire, and it's made me all that much stronger."

I gripped my purse tighter, not knowing what to expect, ready to go for my gun if necessary as Simmons began to quote from the canticle.

> *"Praise be to You my Lord*
> *For Brother Fire*
> *Through him You enlighten the night*
> *And he is fair and merry*
> *And vital and strong."*

Big Daddy smiled, and I wondered what he was talking about.

"I came to the Bay Area after leaving the Franciscan order. I was going through a meltdown at the time, wondering if I'd done the right thing, questioning if I should have stayed. I received my answer one day while driving along Highway 101. An accident occurred, and a car caught on fire. I pulled off the road and ran over to help. I managed to rescue the child, but couldn't reach the mother. The poor woman perished in the flames. I found out later that the boy had no other family, and so he became my foster son. After all, we had a bond. We'd both been branded by the fire.

"Then you were also burned?" I queried.

"All the way down my arms, chest, and back. I decided that if people were going to gawk, they might as well stare at something good. So I went to a tattoo parlor and had my scars covered over. I was so blown away by the results that I became a tattoo artist, myself," Simmons explained. "Now I'm the instrument through which people express themselves, whether it be tattooing symbolic wings on a woman's back so that she can soar, or helping others who have been scarred. It's how I turned the flames into a positive experience. Care to view the results?"

I nodded, finding I'd become morbidly curious.

Big Daddy unbuttoned his shirt and slid an arm free. Slinking down his shoulder was a jaguar with a multitude of spots. Every whisker was intricately detailed, as well as the coarse nap of the cat's fur. It took a moment before I realized that the texture was actually scar tissue. Simmons next opened the front of his shirt to display a Noah's Ark filled with a multitude of animals. There were monkeys, giraffes, and lions, along with sheep, cows, and goats. Each was so realistic that I was tempted to run my fingers over them.

Big Daddy grinned in delight at my response. "This is my way of telling a story without talking to you."

He then turned and bared his back to reveal the Grim Reaper. The skeleton stared menacingly at me, his bony frame wrapped in a deep purple robe. Engraved in its folds was what I took to be another quote from *The Canticle of the Creatures*.

> *Praise be to You my Lord*
> *For our Sister Bodily Death*
> *From whom no living man can flee*

Each letter was misshapen and squiggly, having been tattooed on a canvas of scars with a pattern like that of chicken skin.

"I like to think of life as a series of doors. Death is simply the last one we pass through," Big Daddy intoned, while turning and dropping his shirt to the floor.

I gasped aloud, feeling as though the very breath had been ripped from my body. Simmons's right arm was totally covered in butterflies.

Big Daddy stared at me in surprise. "What's the matter? Don't you like butterflies? Most women do. You'd be amazed at the number who specifically request them for tattoos."

But the image conjured something far different for me—a childhood memory that had remained locked away until this very moment. I remembered it now, as surely as I remembered sneaking barefoot from my bedroom and eavesdropping on a conversation that was meant to be private. I'd never told anyone before, though it had shaken me to the core and tainted my adolescent nightmares. However, I now found myself compelled to share it with Big Daddy.

"My grandmother once told a story about the concentration camp in which she was held prisoner," I began. "She snuck into the children's barracks one day, curious to see how they lived. What she discovered preyed upon her for the rest of her life. The walls inside were covered with hundreds and hundreds of butterflies. The children had carved them into the wooden planks using their fingernails, pebbles, and whatever else they could find. My grandmother stood there transfixed by the sight, when something even more amazing happened. She swore that all those butterflies suddenly came alive, filling the room with the sound of their beating wings," I revealed.

"From then on, the butterflies haunted her dreams every night. She felt the children must have known they were going to die, and dealt with it by imagining they'd leave their bodies and become beautiful butterflies. My grandmother was never able to look at butterflies the same way again after that."

Tears sprang up in Big Daddy's eyes and he nodded, as if understanding all too well what the children had meant.

"We're keepers of the images that define us, whether they be tattooed on our bodies, seared on our souls, or burned into our minds. I wear them on my skin. You wear yours inside. But butterflies have many different meanings. Come. I want to show you something."

Big Daddy walked across the floor, opened an antique desk drawer and pulled out a handful of Polaroids. I headed over to join him, only to pass an open door along the way. I nonchalantly glanced inside and immediately came to a dead stop, unable to believe my eyes.

Hanging on the walls were charcoal portraits of teenage girls exactly like those I'd seen in Mendocino, right down to their haunted expressions. However, one in particular stood out from the rest, prompting me to step inside for a closer inspection. There was no question but that the drawing bore an uncanny resemblance to Lily. All except for one thing. The girl in this portrait had no scars on her neck.

Every nerve in my body quivered as Big Daddy entered the room and came to stand close beside me.

"Who's that?" I asked, never removing my eyes from the drawing.

"A girl by the name of Buffy Xander. Why do you ask?"

Buffy. Of course. The TV character that Lily so idolized.

"Her real name is Lily Holt."

Simmons folded his arms across his chest so that the tattoos merged together on his body. "Ahh, yes. The runaway that you've been trying to find. I remember now."

Right, I caustically thought. *As if he'd ever forgotten.*

"In that case, it seems you were correct. Buffy, or Lily as you call her, *is* a runaway," Big Daddy matter-of-factly informed me.

"Is she staying here with you?" I curtly asked, not in the mood for games.

A case of the willies began to set in as the portrait stared back at me with knowing eyes.

"She was," Simmons acknowledged.

"What do you mean, 'was'? Where is she now?" I impatiently questioned.

"She's gone." Simmons walked up to the drawing and caressed the girl's face with his hands. "It's strange. She must have caught wind that you were looking for her, because she left only yesterday."

The son of a bitch. Big Daddy had probably been the one to tip her off. I studied the man, watching to see if he nervously shifted his weight, or if his eyes darted back and forth—any little physical movement to reveal that he was lying.

"Evidently, Lily has an uncanny sense of timing," I dryly commented. "Who are these other girls?" I motioned to the remaining portraits.

"They're some of the teenage runaways that I've tried to help over the years."

My hands grew clammy, wondering if the man standing next to me might possibly be a psychopath. I thought again of Charles Manson and his propensity for malleable young girls. Then I glanced back at the portraits and realized there wasn't a teenage boy among the lot.

"Are any runaways staying with you now?" I casually inquired, careful to keep my tone neutral.

"Not at the moment. They leave when they're ready to move on. Hopefully some return to their families and try to make a go of it. God knows, I do what I can to make them realize that it's the right thing to do."

I'd pretty much had it with Big Daddy's righteous line of bullshit.

"If you really believe that, why not just contact the police immediately rather than play guru to a bunch of confused and lonely kids?" I verbally attacked.

"As you pointed out, I don't even know their real names," Simmons fired back. "Besides, I might be resigning them to hellish situations from which they'd only run away again, and what good would that do? At least by offering them sanctuary, I help to keep a few kids off the street, or possibly even worse."

Sanctuary. The word set off a firestorm in my brain. "Then it's true. You own the old Baker place, don't you?"

"Yes," Simmons warily answered.

"Did you also do these drawings of the girls?" I asked, no longer able to fend off a growing feeling of dread.

"No. They were done by a friend of mine. I'm afraid I don't have that kind of talent," Big Daddy wistfully responded.

I stared again at Lily's portrait, and this time discerned a lascivious smile about her lips that no fifteen-year-old girl should have had. But there was something else about the picture that bothered me even more.

"Why are there no scars on this drawing?" I questioned.

"Aah, you noticed," Big Daddy replied with a smile. "That's the artist's vision. It's a statement of sorts. He likes to idealize all the girls, and show how they'd look without any physical deformities."

All the girls? Jeepers creepers grew eight legs and came alive, crawling up my backbone and embedding itself deep inside my body. I glanced down, caught sight of the photos in Simmons's hands, and grabbed the pile.

Each snapshot was that of a teenage girl posing coyly for the camera. One flaunted spiky green hair and wore a wooden cross around her neck. Another brandished ladybug earrings and a little pink camisole top. Still a third girl had a bunch of cheap bangle bracelets dangling on her arm. She stood next to a young Madonna look-alike who boasted a ring on each finger and one in her nose.

I was barely able to contain myself by the time I'd finished flipping through the more than two dozen snapshots. The fact that Big Daddy had reminded me of Charles Manson now began to seem like child's play. My eyes remained glued to the photos, trying to bend my mind around what it was that I saw. The similarities contained in each image were definitely unnerving. All of the girls had two distinct characteristics in common: a Lotis blue butterfly tattoo and a physical scar.

"Just what in the hell is going on here?" I demanded, my hands shaking in a lethal combination of confusion, anger, and fear.

"I'm afraid I don't know what you're talking about," Big Daddy coldly responded.

"I thought you were out of the butterfly trade," I countered, still unable to put exactly what I was feeling into words.

"I am," Simmons fumed, as if insulted that I would doubt him.

"Then tell me why all these girls have been branded with a Lotis blue butterfly," I retorted, frustrated that so many unexplained coincidences were piling up.

Big Daddy arched a surprised eyebrow. "Well, well. It seems you know your butterflies."

"What I want are answers," I furiously replied.

Simmons gave me one of his understanding nods, and I was sorely tempted to smack the man.

"Being that you know about the Lotis blue, you must also be aware of its history. Fascinating, isn't it?"

"Go on," I warned, clenching my hands.

"It's somewhat like a fairy tale, don't you think? A pretty little butterfly vanishes for years at a time only to miraculously reappear one day, even more enchanting and desirable than ever. The girls that stay here always love that story and beg me to tell it to them often. Especially those with scars. It seems to give them a feeling of hope. It's like those children in the concentration camp that you were telling me about. They seem to find themselves drawn to a creature that disappears inside its cocoon for a while and then emerges, no longer an ugly caterpillar but rather like the proverbial phoenix rising from the ashes."

I found myself stymied, unable to come back with a snappy response. Simmons's tale was sugary sweet on the surface. But my gut kept telling me that something was horribly wrong.

"Perhaps life will change for these girls as well," Big Daddy continued. "They like to dream that they'll fall asleep and wake up one day to discover they're no longer flawed, but have turned into beautiful butterflies."

"Except that never happens, does it?" I retorted, finally finding the right words. "Instead they spend their lives on a fruitless search, yearning for the impossible, only to end up feeling all the more empty and worthless. Even worse, they no longer have the love and support of their families to fall back on. Explain to me how that helps them in the long run."

This time, it was Big Daddy who was at a loss for words.

"If you really care about the girls, you'll let me take these photos," I told him.

"Why? What do you plan to do with them?" Simmons asked, beginning to look alarmed.

"I intend to hand them over to the police. Some of their families are probably frantically searching for them. If so, they'll be able to narrow their pursuit to here in San Francisco."

"But those are the only mementos I have," Big Daddy protested and tried to retrieve them.

I quickly pulled the photos out of his reach.

"No they're not. You've still got the drawings," I reminded him, matching the charcoals to a number of the snapshots in my hand.

I turned to leave, waiting until I'd reached the front door to nail Big Daddy with my final question.

"One last thing. Who is Horus?"

Let's see him spread his wings and fly away from this one, I thought, aware that I was probably looking at the crafty butterfly dealer, himself.

Simmons's complexion grew ashen, and he swayed ever so slightly. My heart quickened, knowing that all I had to do was to tighten my net.

"Where did you hear that name?" he asked, sounding strangely out of breath.

"From the man who died shortly after telling me about you," I revealed. "It seems someone called Horus is an important dealer in the butterfly trade. As a matter of fact, he lives in Northern California. My guess is in either San Francisco or Mendocino—or possibly both."

Big Daddy nervously licked his lips, and another thought hit me. Could it be that Simmons had located an existent colony of Lotis blues and was siphoning them off, one at a time, to collectors?

"I take it you've been up to Mendocino then?" Big Daddy inquired, in a strained voice.

I nodded, choosing not to give too much information away; hoping that the man would trip up and hang himself.

"Then you've already seen Horus," Simmons replied in barely a whisper.

My mind flew into action, trying to figure out who he was talking about. Did he mean Trepler? Or the homeless man on the headlands? How could Simmons possibly have known whom I'd met with anyway?

"Oh yeah? All right then, so who is he?" I asked, not supplying any names.

Simmons steadily held my gaze. "The winged statue holding the sickle."

Great. First there'd been Big Sam. Now Simmons was

acting delusional. Had everybody in Northern California dropped one too many tabs of acid?

"Don't screw with me, Carl. Not about this. I've already been handed that pile of crap. I may not yet know who Horus is, but I'm damn well certain there's a lot more to it than that."

"You're right," Big Daddy replied, his stare turning a bit too intense for my liking. "The statue involves a myth dealing with innocence and sin that leads to punishment in the netherworld. From that comes purification and rebirth, just like the butterflies, which are born twice."

Okay. It was just about time to call in the men with the nets and straitjackets. Not for nothing was San Francisco known as America's number-one destination for lunatics and freaks. Nurse Ratched would have had a field day with this guy.

I didn't turn my back on the man as I edged closer to the door. Reaching behind, I placed my hand on the knob.

"If you were cognizant of Egyptian mythology, you'd already know the winged figure is Horus," Big Daddy continued. "He's the God of Time, though there are those of us who prefer to call him the Angel of Death."

Big Daddy was turning out to be one more raging loony tune—or else, he was a damn good actor working hard to get me off his trail. In either case, it was clear that I'd get no more out of him right now.

"I'll be in touch," I advised, not waiting until he pulled out his Jason hockey mask and put it on.

Then I scurried out into the night.

It wasn't until I was driving home that something else clicked in my mind. Simmons had never asked the name of the dealer that had betrayed him. Perhaps it was because he already knew.

The other thing eating at me was that Lily had been so

close by all this time. I felt in a race against the clock, though I wasn't sure why. All I knew was that it was imperative that I find her quickly—particularly if Simmons were half as dangerous as I feared.

The girl's image sprang to mind, her brown eyes filling with terror. Was it possible that Lily had tried to leave against Simmons's wishes, and he was now holding her captive somewhere? If so, my visit might make Big Daddy paranoid enough to go over the edge. I grew nauseous at the thought of what could possibly happen to Rebecca.

Rebecca.

The name resonated inside me like a musical chord, and I realized what had just happened. Lily and Rebecca were starting to become one. A wave of dizziness swept over me as I broke into a cold sweat.

For chrissake, Porter. Take a few deep breaths and stop freaking out, Mini-me chided. *Otherwise, you won't be of much good to anyone.*

Maybe so, but one thing was becoming increasingly clear. I had to find Lily. Otherwise, Rebecca would never be able to rest—and neither would I.

Seventeen

The *chi* mirrors on both sides of the street had called it quits for the night. They'd long been asleep by the time I pulled into the driveway. This had proven to be one incredibly frustrating day. I'd have gladly woven a silken cocoon, crawled inside, and folded myself up like a piece of origami until I'd shed my skin and morphed into someone wiser, smarter, and much more clever. For I was beginning to fear that I'd never find Lily alive.

Tony Baloney's sheepskin rug lay on the ground looking sad and forlorn, having apparently been tossed from its basket and left outside. I carried it in with me so that the fog wouldn't sneak up in the dark and spirit the rug away.

I placed it in front of Mei Rose's door and skirted around the potted palm in the middle of the floor, hoping my landlady was correct and that it kept all the bad ghosts at bay. Then grabbing hold of the banister I dragged myself upstairs, trying hard to believe there was still hope for Lily, not wanting to think that I might have failed her.

I opened the door to find both Santou and Terri waiting for me inside.

"I thought you were coming straight home. Where in the hell have you been?" Santou anxiously questioned.

"Well, I was towed out of the woods for starters," I began.

"We know that much, Rach. For God sakes, Jake's been

trying to get hold of you. Only you haven't answered your damn phone. We finally had to call the tow truck driver in order to learn you'd been found and that everything was all right," Terri scolded.

Oy veh. Now I knew things were bad. Even Terri was pissed at me.

"What did you do? Turn your cell phone off on purpose?" Santou accused.

There seemed no way out, but to tell the truth. "Yes, okay. I'm guilty as charged. But there's a good reason for it."

"There'd better be," Terri advised. "Do you know how worried we've been?"

"I went to see Simmons and didn't want the phone to ring and disturb our conversation."

"See? I told you that's what happened," Jake said to Terri, his anger turning to excitement. "All right. So, what did you learn?"

I pulled Big Daddy's photos from my purse, and spread them out before us like playing cards.

Santou let loose a low whistle. "Unbelievable. Don't tell me. These are some of the runaways that Simmons has taken under his wing."

"You've got it," I confirmed.

"Ohmigod, and look! Every single one of them has a scar," Terri added in astonishment.

Santou and I exchanged a wary glance without a word.

"There's just one problem," Jake commented after closely scrutinizing each snapshot.

"What's that?"

"There's no picture of Lily here."

"You're right, there isn't. However, Simmons had some charcoal portraits at his place, one of which had to be her," I revealed.

"Do you really think it was Lily?" Terri questioned.

I nodded. "Simmons said it was a girl by the name of Buffy Xander. I figure that's a pseudonym, if ever there was one."

"Good work, chère," Jake confirmed with a grin.

"This is incredible!" Terri exclaimed. "Wait until Eric hears that you found her."

"Not so fast. She's not there anymore," I disclosed. "Simmons says Lily found out we were searching for her and skedaddled from his place yesterday."

"What? You've got to be kidding me," Terri cried in dismay.

So keen was his disappointment that I felt even worse than before. I wondered if I could have somehow handled my initial meeting with Big Daddy a bit better. Had I tipped my hand too soon? Was I partially responsible for Lily's latest vanishing act?

"What's your take on the situation, chère?"

"I think Simmons is involved in her disappearance," I replied, still keeping my worst fears to myself.

"Well, this is just great. So what do we do now?" Terri glumly inquired. "And what am I supposed to tell Eric?"

Each question fell like a ton of guilt on my soul.

For God's sake, not every crisis in life is instantly solved and tied up with a nice, neat bow! I nearly screamed.

Instead I took a deep breath, wanting no more than to curl up, close my eyes, and drift off into the Land of Nod, a place guaranteed to be filled with sweet dreams. Only I knew that wasn't likely to happen. Rather, I'd be plagued by visions of Rebecca, Lily, and the courier who'd been mistakenly killed as me.

"Listen, I just discovered that Simmons also has a house in Mendocino. I've got to catch a few hours' sleep. But after that, I plan to drive up there and search his place," I revealed.

"And what do you expect to find? Lily sitting outside holding up a sign that says, 'Here I am. Help me'?" Santou scoffed. "Don't be crazy. Simmons isn't that stupid. He's not going to make it easy. The best thing is to set up a stakeout and watch his every move. He'll lead you to her, sooner or later."

Later was exactly what I didn't want, fearing it could prove to be fatal.

"I'll take the first watch," Terri immediately volunteered. "Just tell me what to do. Should I go and sit outside his house?"

I glanced at the clock. It was already past midnight. Something else was wrong. Terri wasn't dressed up as Elvira.

"Aren't you supposed to be working at the club tonight?" I asked.

Terri twirled a lock of his curly blonde wig and slowly rolled his eyes. "I didn't get a chance to tell you yet. I was fired, Rach."

"But you were only there one night. What happened?"

"I insulted some poor excuse for a werewolf, and he complained to the manager. Do you believe it? But it just so happens I was right. His costume smelled and looked like a ratty old bath mat. For chrissakes, it was stinking up the place." Terri dismissed the incident with a wave of his hand. "It doesn't matter anyway, because I came up with a fabulous new idea. I'm going to offer a gay-vampire walking tour of San Francisco. Just think about it. Can you imagine? I plan to hire hot tour guides that look like Tom Cruise and Brad Pitt."

Actually, the idea didn't sound half bad.

"Just tell me where this Big Daddy bad-ass lives, and I'll take off like a bat in flight," Terri enthusiastically offered.

He was so eager to help that I didn't have the heart to refuse him.

"All right, but on one condition only: that I come with you."

"Absolutely no way!"

A passerby would have thought that *I'd* been the offending party draped in a mildewed bath mat, based on his reaction.

Terri took one look at my expression and quickly tempered his response.

"This is really important to me, Rach. I care about Eric and the best way I can show it is to help bring his daughter back. Let me at least do one watch on my own so that it doesn't look like I'm always tagging along just keeping you company. Besides, this Big Daddy guy knows who you are, while he's never seen my face. He won't be suspicious if I'm the one playing lookout."

"Terri's right about that, chère," Santou agreed. "If Simmons gets a whiff of what's going on, chances are that you'll never find Lily."

"What do you say, Rach? Please?" Terri pleaded.

I was so exhausted that I probably would have been of little use to him, anyway.

"Okay," I agreed. "Take my Explorer. You can keep watch inside the vehicle."

I gave him the keys, along with explicit directions to Big Daddy's place.

"And bring your cell phone along," Santou instructed.

"Don't worry. Unlike Rach, I'll actually turn mine on," he teased.

"Very funny. Simmons should be easy to spot. He's about six feet five inches tall, has a long brown beard, a ponytail, and is balding in front. He tends to wear jeans and a black leather jacket. Also, his apartment is on the second floor and faces the street," I told Terri.

"Park on the opposite side and halfway down the block so that you're not too obvious, but have an unobstructed view of both his window and the front door," Jake added. "And buy yourself a cup of coffee so that you stay awake."

"Hey, you're talking to someone who's always worked nights," Terri breezily retorted.

"And call me if Simmons leaves the building," I continued, not wanting to forget anything.

"Okay. What should I do if that happens?"

"Follow him and I'll meet you wherever he ends up."

I just hoped it wasn't in Mendocino.

"Now you're absolutely certain that you want to do this?" I questioned, trying hard not to sound overly concerned.

"You know, you're really going to have to learn to delegate better, Rach. Otherwise, how will you ever handle things when you're finally promoted and made a boss?" Terri lectured, while heading for the door.

Right. Like there was a chance in hell of *that* ever happening.

"I'll grab a cab and join you as soon as I get some sleep," I responded, following him to the top of the stairs.

Then I flew to the window and watched Terri drive off, feeling nervous as a mother hen.

"Don't worry. He'll be fine," Santou assured me, as we undressed and got into bed.

Jake not only hogged all the covers but instantly fell asleep, annoying the hell out of me. I fully intend to hook up with an insomniac in my next life; someone who'll be thoughtful enough to stay awake and keep me company.

I eventually dozed off, but it wasn't to the gentle Land of Nod. Rather, Mister Softee's music began to play in my head. I'd started to slip into my usual nightmare when a jarring sensation jerked me awake.

I lay perfectly still, unsure of what was going on, as a creaking sound slithered its way across the floor. Then the ground undulated in waves and the house began to shake, rattle, and roll. A second later, the furniture joined in, accompanied by the windows, which shimmied and shook, adding a tremulous vibrato to the growing musical encore.

I tried to roll over and wake Santou, only to discover that I was no longer in my bed. Instead, I'd been netted, labeled, and pinned like a large butterfly to the wall. There I remained, unable to do anything at all as an earthquake roared into full force, ripping my world apart.

I opened my mouth and screamed as loud as I could, though I feared it wouldn't do any good. This might very well be a dream. But what if I woke and it still didn't end? Then I'd never again be safe but trapped inside my fears, forever the victim, always a target.

The quake slowly subsided, along with my shriek, until it was a mere tremor. Finally, even that diminished as I felt Santou's breath tickle my ear, and his hand jostled my shoulder.

"Hey chère, you're having a bad nightmare. Snap out of it," he said, gently shaking me awake.

I sat bolt upright, propelled by the pounding of my heart. Turning on the light, I checked my palms for pinmarks. None were there. Then I glanced around the room, wanting to make certain that everything was in its proper place.

"What were you dreaming about? It sounded as if one helluva knock-down, drag-out fight was going on," Santou quipped, brushing a lock of hair from my face.

I looked at him and knew I could tell Jake just about anything.

"Sometimes I get frightened, is all."

"Frightened of what?" he asked, his profile icy-white in the moonlight.

I wrapped my arms around my knees and hugged them tight, trying to think of how best to explain it.

"It's like when a closet door has been left ajar and the

room is dark. Anything could be lurking inside. The same goes for having to check under the bed or behind the shower curtain at night. That's what I sometimes have to do with my mind. I can never get rid of this small, nagging fear that's in my head. It becomes worse when I go to bed. Sometimes I dream I can hear the house settling. I'll wake up, walk to the window, and look outside."

"And what do you see?" Santou questioned, beginning to stroke my hair.

I shivered, envisioning it even now. "A face staring back at me. Only it's no bogeyman, but a person who appears to be perfectly normal. Someone I'd probably never think to look at twice. That's what truly frightens me. The idea of being fooled; of not recognizing who the really dangerous monsters are until it's too late."

"Those are nothing but shadows in your mind," Santou consoled, pressing his lips to my forehead. "You're just thinking about Simmons and Lily."

And Rebecca, I reflected, still beating myself up over her disappearance.

"You're right. I'm afraid that I'm missing something. There's got to be another piece to this puzzle that's been overlooked."

"I'll let you in on a secret, chère."

I gazed at him and held my breath.

"I'm just as scared as you are most of the time."

"Yeah, right," I scoffed.

"It's true," Santou confessed, with an embarrassed laugh. "Why else do you think I got hooked on all those pills? Everybody's afraid of something in this world. The trick is to learn to put our demons to rest."

Easier said than done, I thought. My demons had a twenty-four-hour field day inside me.

"Speaking of which, we should try to catch some shut-

eye. Otherwise, we'll have to get up before you know it,"
Santou advised, slipping his knees in behind mine.

Lily, Rebecca, and Simmons must have agreed. They finally lay down and went to sleep, allowing me to drift off
once more, this time into a blessed state of dreamlessness.

Eighteen

Jake kissed me on the cheek as I nestled deeper into the pillow.

"I'm out of here, chère. I've gotta get to work. Listen, is it all right if I take those pictures of the girls with me?"

"Sure. Go ahead," I mumbled, barely aware of his footsteps as they crossed the bedroom threshold and went out the front door.

I stretched and pulled the covers over my head, trying to block the light from Su Lin Fong's mirrors, while lazily wondering what photos he'd been talking about. Then I remembered. The images came flooding back in minute detail, complete with bangle bracelets, scars and butterflies. They were of Simmons's band of runaway girls; those without anchors to the world. Teenagers that wouldn't be missed.

That's when I thought of something else. I hadn't heard from Terri all night. Everything must have remained quiet on the Haight Ashbury front, otherwise he'd certainly have called by now.

I quickly jumped out of bed, showered and dressed, and then dialed his cell phone.

Ring! Ring! Ring!

"Enough already. Just answer the damn thing," I grumbled, curious as to why he was taking so long.

I finally got my wish, though it wasn't the response I had expected.

"Hello?" Terri croaked.

The realization hit us both at the same time.

"Oh, my God! I'm so sorry, Rach. I must have fallen asleep."

My legs grew weak, and the room tilted ever so slightly around me.

"Don't move. Don't get out of the Explorer. Don't do anything. Just stay where you are," I tersely instructed and hung up.

I grabbed a few things and ran downstairs past Tony Baloney, all the while cursing myself for having let Terri take on such a weighty responsibility.

Calm down. Maybe everything's all right. For all you know, Simmons is still fast asleep.

But my gut told me something far different.

You let him get away, you fool. Now you'll never find Lily!

I flung myself in front of the first cab that came by, bringing it to a screeching halt. Then I jumped inside and prodded the driver to race like a maniac. I remained perched on the edge of the seat, ready to throttle him should he even try to slow down.

What a surprise. I finally caught a glimpse of the Haight as something other than a nonstop party. Of course, it was also seven-thirty in the morning. I guess even Grateful Dead fans and wannabe hippies eventually need their sleep.

The cabdriver breathed a sigh of relief as I leaped out at the corner of Haight and Ashbury and rushed up the street. Terri waved to me from the Ford but I passed him by, my sights set on the blue and lavender Victorian house.

I rang Simmons's buzzer again and again, without any luck. I became desperate enough to pick up a couple of pebbles and chuck them at his front window. However, there was still no response. I finally had no choice but to concede that the man wasn't home.

I turned to leave, only to find Terri standing behind me, his face scrunched up and streaked with tears.

"Oh, God! I don't know what to say, except that I'm so sorry. I feel absolutely sick about this. How could I have let it happen? What's wrong with me, anyway? I'm a total dimwit. A pathetic loser!" he groaned.

Any anger I felt instantly vanished, knowing perfectly well the same thing could have happened to me.

"Don't say that. It's going to be all right," I told Terri, and gave him a hug.

He broke into a sob, crying so hard that I pulled a ragged tissue from my bag and helped blot his tears.

"Listen, for all we know, Simmons left early this morning and went straight to his store." I tried to console him, though I didn't really believe it.

"Well then, what are we waiting for?" Terri asked, using the last of the soggy tissue to blow his nose. "Let's get going."

We hot-footed it down the street to Big Daddy's Body Shop. But the sign advertising the specials of the day wasn't out, and the place was dark and closed. Terri banged on the door, and frantically rattled the knob. When he turned back around, it was with a steely determination that I hadn't seen before.

"We've got to go to Simmons's house in Mendocino right now."

"That's exactly what I plan to do. Except I'm going alone."

"Like hell you are," Terri growled, seeming to have more Jack Russell than French poodle in him.

"It could be dangerous, Terri. I don't know what I'm going to find."

"Which is exactly why you need me along. I can be a useful diversion."

I glanced at his curly blond wig, blue tapered shirt, and black leather pants, and had to admit he was probably correct.

"You have to let me help you, Rach. I'll never be able to forgive myself, otherwise."

I knew all too well how that felt. Besides, I didn't want this plaguing him for the rest of his life.

"I'll let you come if you promise not to argue with me, but do exactly as I say. Agreed?"

"Agreed." He fervently nodded, as a few last tears slipped from his eyes.

It was precisely because I didn't want a heated discussion that I opted against calling Santou and revealing my plans. As good as he'd been so far, Jake still liked to play by the book, and this was no time to defer to a bunch of tight-ass rules and regulations. Not when Lily's life was possibly at stake.

We hurried back to the Ford, where Terri tossed me the keys. Then we raced across town and over the Golden Gate Bridge, driving smack into a marshmallow fluff of fog so thick I wondered if I'd ever really woken from my dream. It swallowed the bridge, holding us captive for a while, before grudgingly spitting the Explorer out on the other side. We wasted no time but hastily sped away, trailed by the wail of a fog horn floating hauntingly in the air like a rhapsodic aria.

Neither of us spoke as the Ford burned up the miles, chasing a few stray rays of sun that dared pierce the clouds. However, even those beams faded like a distant radio signal as we swung off the highway and made our way toward the coast. There an angry rainstorm rumbled toward us, brutally pelting the windshield. The tempest pursued us through the redwood corridor, along Route 1, and past Mendocino. It

followed all the way to the old Baker property, where I
turned onto the gravel road and parked in front of the gate.

"Stay here. I've got to cut the padlock," I ordered.

I grabbed the bolt cutter under my seat and ran out into
the downpour, where the No Trespassing sign beckoned like
a beacon through the fog. Once there, I positioned what I
liked to call my own personal master key around the don't-
mess-with-me lock. The only difficulty was that I kept losing my grip while trying to wipe the rain from my eyes.

I must have had a guardian angel watching out for me, as
the problem was miraculously solved. Though the rain persisted to fall all around, it suddenly stopped pummeling my
head. I turned to discover that my angel was none other than
Terri, who stood holding an umbrella over me.

"Yeah, yeah. I know. I've committed the ultimate sin by
not following your orders and getting out of the car. But I
consider this to be a supreme fashion crisis that overrides
everything else. I hate to tell you this, Rach, but you look
more like the winning contestant in a wet T-shirt contest
than you do Holly Golightly being glamorously drenched by
the rain. So just cut the damn lock already and let's get back
inside the Explorer."

I grinned and did as instructed. One good snip and it fell
to the ground with a satisfying thud, allowing the gate to
swing wide open. The Ford chugged through, happy to be on
its way.

The gravel road rapidly deteriorated into a muddy path bor-
dered by a picket fence, its gray wooden planks resembling a
row of chipped, uneven teeth. We followed where it led.

The trail ended at a Gothic house precariously perched on
the cliffs. The rain slowed to a drizzle as I pulled up next to
what I imagined must be Simmons's car—an old turquoise
Thunderbird bearing a license plate that read DARK AGE.

Terrific. Another insight into Big Daddy's psyche that I didn't find terribly comforting. Then I remembered having spotted the car on Ashbury Street last night.

"Now what?" Terri asked, apprehensively looking around.

"I'm going to see if anyone's home. Do you want to stay here and wait?"

"Not on your life," he replied, and scrambled out of the vehicle.

The rain had finally come to a halt, leaving the ground as wet as a sponge. The moisture permeated my shoes and squished between my toes, causing my soles to squeak like a pair of chattering mice. We slogged through mud and grass, careful to avoid the edge of the cliffs, not wanting to slip and fall.

I trudged up the lopsided porch steps and approached the front door, listening for any unusual sound. But the only thing to be heard were waves crashing against the rocks, like the persistent baying of a dog.

"Jeez. Quite the place to live, huh? It's not exactly conducive for weekend get-togethers and parties. One false step off this wreck of a porch and you can kiss your *tuchus* good-bye," he said, voicing exactly how I felt.

I bolstered my courage and knocked loudly on the door. The surroundings remained quiet; all except for the waves which continued to scream, *Go away! Go away!*

The only other noise was that of Terri's breathing, which had grown as rapid as a hummingbird's wings.

"I guess no one's home. Maybe we should leave," he suggested, sounding as breathless as Marilyn Monroe.

However, footprints near the door insinuated otherwise, although their muddy tracks were dry. I tried the knob. It turned effortlessly under my touch. The door creaked open with a yawn. I pushed it a little wider and entered. Terri carefully wiped the mud from his shoes, and followed me inside.

"Anybody here?" he called out.

The quiet was so profound, I could hear the echo of his question.

"Holy crap. This place is pretty creepy, don't you think?" he asked, pointing to a row of masks on the wall.

They glared at us with angry expressions, as if demanding to know what we were doing here.

"Just keep your eyes peeled for anything that might belong to Lily," I responded, not wanting to admit that I was beginning to feel a little freaked out, myself.

Though I said nothing, I was looking for more than just a DVD collection of the TV show *Buffy*. My mission had taken on a dual purpose. I was fully determined to find proof that Big Daddy was also Horus.

We scoured every room of the house searching for the least bit of evidence. But nothing of Lily was to be found. Equally odd, not a single specimen of a butterfly was around. The only thing clear was that Simmons lived here. The house was as filled with things as his place in the Haight.

I gazed out a window, wondering what to do now, racking my brain for some kind of sign I might have missed. Instead, the amorphous face which continually haunted my dreams rose to the surface, metamorphosing into that of Big Daddy. I cursed Simmons for being the monster I'd recognized too late, realizing he must have Lily hidden somewhere else.

"I haven't found a thing, Rach. How about you?" Terri asked, nervously twisting his fingers.

"Me neither," I admitted.

We wandered back outside where the sky appeared bruised, still marred by ashen clouds hovering overhead.

"Trepler said there were twenty acres to this place. I can't search it all, but I've got to try and cover as much territory as possible while we're here. I want you to wait for me in the Explorer."

However, rather than walk back to the Ford, Terri defiantly shook his head. "Sorry, but I can't do that, Rach."

I was afraid he might say something like that.

"Don't argue with me, Terri. You can't go tromping around in the woods. Look at the way you're dressed. You're going to mess up your good leather pants and Diesel shoes. Besides, we had an agreement. Remember?"

Terri derisively brushed off my comment. "They're just clothes, Rach. And as for our agreement? I'd have said anything to come along. You should know that by now. You would have done the same thing yourself."

He folded his arms across his chest, making it perfectly clear that he wasn't about to budge. How could I have been so crazy as to think he'd actually listen to me?

"All right. Let's get going, then," I said, feeling far too pressed for time to stand there and argue.

But Terri remained rooted to his spot. "I think we should split up."

I stared at him, completely flabbergasted. "Are you kidding? You don't know this area. You could get lost."

"Don't be ridiculous. I saw a roll of plastic yellow tape in your glove compartment. I'll mark a trail as I go along."

"And what if you get in trouble?" I fired back. "Do you also happen to have a weapon with you?"

"Who needs one when I've got my cell phone?" he retorted. "Just keep yours on, and I'll call if necessary."

It was as if Terri had rehearsed this routine on the drive up, armed with a snappy response for everything that I said.

"Too much can go wrong," I countered. "What if you stumble upon Simmons and he gets upset? Do you know what could happen?"

Terri's eyelids flickered and I wondered if he was blinking back tears. Instead he stubbornly jutted out his chin.

"You don't have any say in this, Rach. It's my fault that

Simmons slipped away in the first place. I'm going to help find Lily, and there's not a damn thing you can do about it. Besides, we can cover more ground this way. Unless you want to bring in the local police, of course. I'm sure they'd be delighted to rush out here and help you."

My nails bit into my palms, but it was already too late. He'd carefully laid his trap and I was beginning to waver. Terri knew the police would never get involved. There was no proof Lily was here with Simmons—never mind trying to convince them that she'd been taken against her will. He instinctively sensed my dilemma and went in for the kill.

"Face it, you need my help. What if something happens to Lily that could have been stopped, only you don't get there quickly enough? Then how are you going to feel?" he asked, expertly pushing my buttons.

Damn him for being so clever.

I walked to my vehicle, opened the glove compartment, and handed Terri the yellow tape.

"Just don't do anything stupid. Got that?" I instructed, so fiercely it came out as a bark.

I was furious that he'd played me this well. Maybe it was losing my mother only two years ago, along with memories of Rebecca and dealing with Santou's close call, that had me on edge. But if anything happened to Terri, I swore to God that I'd kill Big Daddy.

"Don't worry, sweetie. I haven't gotten this body of mine into prime physical condition just to screw it up now," he said, taking the tape from my hand and planting a kiss on my cheek. "Which way should I go?"

I pointed in the direction of town, figuring that should keep him out of trouble. Besides, he could always order a latte once he got there.

Nineteen

I watched Terri walk away before turning around and heading inland from the cliffs. Even so, I could still smell the salty tang of the Pacific, and feel its windswept spray sneak around to dampen my cheeks.

Soon I'd left the ocean behind, and was hiking among a grove of redwoods that rose like a chapel above me. Their fallen needles softly pillowed my feet. I came upon a fallen log that rose as high as my chest. The wood had been hacked open, exposing an interior so red that it looked like raw beef. Walking over, I placed my hand on the open wound.

Ba bump! Ba bump! Ba bump!

Its core beat like a heart against my palm, coursing up through my arm, until my entire body pulsed in rhythm with its vibration. I pulled away, frightened by what I had felt.

Keep your mind on Simmons and Lily, I warned myself, not trusting the lure of the forest, which blatantly tried to seduce me.

I caught sight of a faint trail off to my left and my curiosity instantly became aroused. I followed its path and soon found myself surrounded by rhododendrons bearing deep pink blossoms the size of my fist, as well as huckleberry bushes littered with luscious black berries. I carefully watched my step, having spotted redwood sorrel sprouting underfoot. Its clover-shaped leaves had folded up in the rain like a profusion of miniature parasols.

But it was what lay beyond this verdant wonderland that caused my heart to race. There stood another house. I quickly hurried toward it.

The structure was a one-level cabin. A large shed stood nearby, next to which a car was parked. Something about the vehicle seemed oddly familiar. I wandered over to find that its doors were locked. I glanced inside. Nothing on either the floor or seats set off my suspicions. Then I realized where I'd seen the car before. It was the same navy blue Ford Galaxy that Spencer Barnes had driven—the young man I'd met at Big Daddy's Body Shop. What in hell was *he* doing here?

I remembered he'd given me a slip of paper with his phone number on it. I dug around in my jeans pocket now and fished it out. Area code 707. Bingo! The code was for Mendocino County.

The discovery made me all the more uneasy. Simmons and Spencer were apparently closer than I had thought. Then again, maybe I was jumping to the wrong conclusion. After all, this place *was* on Big Daddy's property. So what if Spencer also had a house in Mendocino? It didn't necessarily mean this cabin was where he lived. Perhaps he'd merely stopped by to give Simmons more sketches for his tattoo clients. Only how could he have known Big Daddy would be here on a work day, when he should have been at his store in San Francisco?

The best way to get answers was to simply keep digging. I decided to start with the shed for one simple reason. It was locked, and unlike the Galaxy, there were no windows through which to peek inside. The only problem was that I'd left my bolt clippers back in the Explorer.

I studied the lock. It wasn't nearly as large and foreboding as the one used to secure the entrance gate. With that in mind, I pulled my Leatherman multipurpose tool from its sheath and set to work.

God, I loved this thing! I jimmied the lock in no time. The shed door opened with a submissive groan, as if resigned to spilling its secrets. A feeble ray of light tiptoed in ahead of me.

The first thing to catch my eye was a van much like the one that had run me off the road. The very thought made my blood go cold. I plucked a small flashlight from my back pocket and began to examine its exterior.

The passenger side was dented and bore long scratches, as if a fiend had furiously slashed back and forth across the paint job with a set of sharp nails. But that wasn't all. The front bumper looked as though it had been repeatedly smacked with a hammer. However, the real clincher were the flakes of dark green paint that I found embedded in the abrasions—they were very same color as that of my Ford.

I thought back to what had happened last night. How odd. It already felt like weeks ago. Big Daddy could easily have beaten me home to the Haight. He would have had a good head start after pushing me into the woods. But there was something else. Simmons had clearly just taken a shower upon my arrival, and had been reluctant to let me inside. I hadn't looked for a van on his block. But then again, why would I? There'd been no reason to suspect that Big Daddy was the road rage culprit.

The only thing screwing up my theory was the blue Thunderbird that sat parked outside the other house. Simmons couldn't have driven both the car and van back to Mendocino early this morning. The whole thing was starting to make me a little crazy. I decided to give it a rest and look around some more.

A large freezer chest stood against the far wall. I made my way toward it, my stomach beginning to twist with apprehension at what I might find.

You've got too vivid an imagination, Porter, my inner voice scolded.

Maybe so. But my hands felt numb and my mouth had suddenly become dry.

Please, let there only be deer meat inside.

Lifting the lid, I nearly breathed a sigh of relief to discover a mother lode of plastic containers, all neatly stacked and filled with hundreds of butterflies. They lay lifeless, apparently ready and waiting for buyers. Their wings were flawless, as if having never been touched by a net. Though this didn't prove that Big Daddy was in any way Horus, it certainly revealed him to be a liar. There could no longer be any doubt but that Simmons was still in the butterfly trade.

Another thing struck me as I looked around. The shed was absolutely immaculate. There wasn't a speck of dirt on the cement floor—not even the least bit of mud from off the van's tires. Not a trace of dust could be found. Likewise, nothing was thrown about. Rather, every item and tool appeared to have been carefully organized and hung in its proper place. Come to think of it, this garage was cleaner than my own apartment. Funny, since neither Simmons's abode in the Haight nor the other house up here were close to being this orderly. I'd never have fingered Big Daddy for a neat freak.

I turned to leave when a ripple of fear raced through me. Leaning next to the door was an object I hadn't noticed before: a large metal scythe, its blade sharp and gleaming. I couldn't take my eyes off the curved steel, its shape a disembodied grin, almost as if it knew something I didn't.

I skirted around it and quickly left the shed. Then I headed toward the cabin while pulling out my gun.

I didn't bother to knock. Just as at the other house, the

door was unlocked. I opened it and listened closely. There wasn't a sound. I didn't call out. I didn't ask permission. Instead, I entered the cabin of my own accord.

I knew from the first step inside that something was wrong. Or perhaps it was a reaction to the fact that the cabin was also exceptionally neat. No question about it. Anyone this compulsively clean had way too much time on their hands.

But all that flew from my mind as I started to walk down the hall. The walls were filled with charcoal drawings of teenage girls. My apprehension swiftly escalated. They were nearly identical to those I'd seen in the gallery and at Carl Simmons's apartment. Each girl conveyed the same sensual smile and bore no trace of a scar. And I suddenly realized who was responsible for the portraits. Why hadn't I thought of it before? It couldn't be anyone other than Spencer Barnes. After all, he was the artist who designed tattoos for Big Daddy.

It's the artist's vision. He likes to idealize all the girls. Simmons's words came back to haunt me.

Was this possibly Spencer's house, after all?

I shivered, remembering how his fingers had lingered over the jagged mark stretching across my throat, almost as if he'd been fascinated by it.

I continued on, my mind awhirl, my feet taking me where they chose to go. I entered what appeared to be the living room, its walls lined from top to bottom with museum-quality cabinets. Walking around, I began to open all of the drawers. Each held a display case exhibiting the most gorgeous butterflies that I'd seen so far.

The collection was absolutely enormous. There must have been nearly a hundred thousand perfectly preserved specimens; a larger collection than are in most museums. The butterflies were presented with surgical precision. Each had four tiny tags attached to one leg, much like those I'd seen at Trepler's place. The penmanship on the labels was precise and clear. Their scribe clearly had a penchant for collecting and organizing field data.

The only other furniture in the room were two high-back chairs, along with a coffee table. On its surface was a letter waiting to be folded and mailed. I usually had to dig through garbage cans and break into locked drawers to get my hands on private correspondence. I didn't think twice, but scooped up the letter.

Dear Brian,

Enclosed you will find a pair of Neonympha mitchelli *as requested, which are very hard to obtain. I hope you appreciate the time and effort and will send me the balance of money due immediately.*

I also want to thank you for the gift of those two Apodemia mormo langei. *I can't tell you how much such little blue butterflies excite me.*

A happy face was drawn after the sentence.

Concerning your request, I might consider teaching you my technique for finding and rearing Papilio indra kaibabensis *larvae. Of course, I would expect a cut of the profit from any future sales. I had such a prior arrangement with another breeder. However he fell by the wayside, having been pushed out of business. The only thing I demand is that you keep secret whatever I disclose. LOYALTY IS UTMOST TO ME AND MY TIME IS TOO PRECIOUS TO WASTE.*

Consider wisely and let me know.

Your friend,
Horus

It was exactly like the letters I'd found at Mitch Aikens's place. That's when an even stranger thought hit me. Could Spencer be the Horus for whom I'd been searching?

My question remained unanswered as my feet took me back down the hallway.

I next found myself in the kitchen engulfed by an aroma of ammonia and Lysol. The room was so clean, I could have eaten off the floor. In fact I wondered if anyone ate here at all. I decided to peek in the refrigerator and check out its contents.

I opened the fridge door only to have my heart spring clear into my throat.

Ch, ch, ch, ch, ch, ch, ch, ch, ch!

The sound was the stuff of nightmares; that of hundreds of nails frantically scratching within a coffin. Chills ran up my spine as I stared inside and realized where the unearthly din was coming from.

Hundreds of butterflies, still alive, were stacked on the shelves, each imprisoned in their own glassine envelope. The sudden burst of warmth and light must have jarred them from their semidormant state, because they now stomped their "feet" against the cellophane walls in a futile attempt to escape.

I grew sickened by the sight. These were newly hatched butterflies being kept alive until their internal fat metabolized. That way it wouldn't leak out and stain their flawless wings. Only then would they be thrown into the freezer to die and sold as perfect specimens, not having flapped off one single precious scale.

I now checked the freezer. No butterflies were to be found: only packages of artificial food for hungry caterpillars. Either Spencer, Simmons, or both were raising larvae to sell, as well as catching butterflies in the wild. I couldn't help but take one more look inside the refrigerator before moving on.

This time my pulse very nearly burst through my skin. I blinked, unsure that I could actually believe my eyes. There on the top shelf were four of the most delicate little butterflies. Each was an iridescent violet blue with a crenulate black border, and the softest white fringe.

I barely dared breathe. If this was a dream, I didn't want it to end. I'd seen this butterfly once before—as a pinned specimen kept inside a locked vault. These four diminutive beauties were still alive. There was no doubt in my mind but that they were the same exact butterfly. If so, then I'd found what many others had searched for and feared to be forever lost—one of the most sought-after butterflies in existence: the legendary Lotis blue.

This must be how it would feel to find the Holy Grail, I mused, my hand reaching inside the fridge.

I was sorely tempted to take the winged treasures and vamoose. Only there was more yet to do. I couldn't leave without first conducting a thorough search for Lily. Instead I closed the refrigerator, reluctantly shutting the butterflies back in their tomb, vowing to return as soon as I could. Continuing on, I entered the bathroom.

A delicate bouquet filled the air, making me wonder if a woman might not also reside here. A quick glance revealed the room was stocked with a fragrant array of bath soaps. There was lavender, lily of the valley, and honeysuckle, as well as scented candles and body lotions.

I caught a glimpse of myself in the mirror and leaned in for a better view. What do you know? My skin actually appeared to be slightly dewy. Either I was sweating or my fifty-dollar moisturizer was beginning to work. Then I took a closer look at the bathroom mirror. Something about it seemed unusual. It wasn't attached to a medicine cabinet, but set directly into the wall. I acted on a hunch, and placed my finger against the reflective surface.

Damn it to hell! My finger directly touched its image. If the mirror had been genuine, there'd have been a gap between my finger and its reflection. A two-way mirror had apparently been installed. The next logical question was, from where was the bastard watching? I walked back out into the hall.

A closet next to the bathroom was filled with jackets and sweaters, all in men's sizes. I pushed them aside and entered. Then I ran my hands along the cedar panels, trying to determine where the mirror on the opposite side of the wall would be. A peg on which an umbrella had been hung seemed to mark the spot. I figured it was at least worth a shot. I gave the peg a hard tug, and part of the cedar panel popped out. A window was exposed, just as I had suspected.

I closed the closet door and peered through the window to obtain an unobstructed view of the bathroom. It was the perfect peephole for a Peeping Tom. Either Simmons could add *voyeur* to his list of transgressions, or Spencer wasn't as angelic as I'd imagined.

Creeeaaak!

The sound reverberated across the floorboards, through the closet door, and straight into my heart. My stomach contracted into a tight knot. I gripped my gun tighter and tried to determine from where the noise had come. But the only sound to be heard was the noxious thrum of fear in my ears. Then the house let loose a low moan, followed by the closing of a door. I waited until I heard nothing more before poking my head out. The cabin was empty, as it had been on my arrival.

For chrissakes, Rachel. Stop scaring yourself to death, the braver part of me chided, knowing there was still one more area left to explore.

I walked down the hallway toward the last door, fully aware this must be the bedroom. However, nothing could have prepared me for what was waiting inside.

The first thing to catch my eye were the wooden beams running lengthwise across the ceiling. Eureka! I'd finally found a room that wasn't totally clean. Hanging down from the rafters were oddly shaped dustballs. However, far more curious was that they were all positioned directly above the bed.

I continued to stare, my curiosity gradually giving way to stunned disbelief, as the realization began to sink in. A shiver gleefully squealed, gliding up and down my spine on a surreal roller-coaster ride. I'd never seen anything so bizarre in all my life.

What looked like miniature cadavers wrapped in shrouds were taped onto the wooden ceiling beams. Only these little "corpses" were actually dozens of maturing chrysalides. This way, Spencer—or Simmons—could keep watch and pop the butterflies into the fridge as each emerged, before they had a chance to flap their wings.

I lay down on the bed and looked up, knowing that within each was a larva morphing into its final stage. Though unable to eat or move, they were undergoing the most amazing transformation, much like a fairy tale in which mice turned into footmen and pumpkins into gilded carriages.

A closer look revealed that some of the chrysalides had already become transparent. Inside were fully formed butterflies, their wings curled around their bodies, patiently awaiting the moment of rebirth. I dragged myself away, aware that I was also hoping for an epiphany of sorts—something, anything, that would tip me off as to where to find Lily. I glanced around the room, knowing that my search still wasn't complete.

A bureau stood against one wall, and I jerked open the drawers. They were filled with socks and shirts, all perfectly ironed, folded and stacked in pristine piles. I took out my frustration by ripping apart each batch. But it was when I reached the last drawer that my heart turned into a jackhammer, my eyes falling upon the contents. Inside were what could only be called trophies. There was a pink camisole top, a necklace with a wooden cross, bangle bracelets, ladybug earrings and dozens of panties and bras, along with other assorted souvenirs.

I flashed back to Dr. Mark Davis's profile of an obsessive butterfly collector. He'd characterized my target as a white male, unmarried, with a need to control—someone who takes pleasure in holding the power of life and death in his hands. It was the exact same portrait as that of a serial killer. I gazed in growing horror at the trinkets and keepsakes all neatly laid out like precious relics.

My apprehension accelerated into terror at the possibility of what I might be facing. I whirled around, having felt a breeze on the back of my neck. It was almost as if the house were alive and enjoying my predicament.

While turning, I caught sight of a slight movement and glanced back up at the ceiling. A chrysalis had split open and a butterfly was starting to emerge. It slipped out like a letter from an envelope and, unfolding its shriveled wings, began to pump them full of blood. A breeder would have thrown it into the fridge at this point. Instead, I watched in awe as the wings continued to expand with liquid protoplasm, knowing that the butterfly would soon take off and fly away.

I wished I could do the same, but there was still one last place in which I had to look. My only consolation was that the faster I finished, the sooner I could get out of here. With that in mind, I hurried toward what I felt sure was a clothes closet and flung open the door. Two items stood ominously facing me—a large hourglass and a pedestal holding a bible.

The same quaking that I'd felt in my dream last night now took hold. Only this was no tremor, but my legs shaking beneath me. I remembered the scythe leaning near the shed door. That, the hourglass, and pedestal were all part of the same statue—the winged figure looming behind the weeping maiden. Big Sam had referred to the statue as Horus. Simmons had called it the Angel of Death. The one thing I now knew for certain was that I was inside Horus's lair.

I took a deep breath and began to approach the pedestal when the floor grew oddly pliant beneath my feet. Another step and the wooden boards emitted a loud creak. Whipping the flashlight from my back pocket, I ran its beam along the ground. Revealed was the outline of a trapdoor that had been neatly cut and fit into place. I leaned down and pulled on the handle. It emitted a low moan as though a covey of tormented souls were being released.

All was silent after that, the quiet so acute that it reached up and clawed at my throat. I slowly began to descend a set of rickety wooden steps, my feet taking me where I didn't want to go—down, down, down into a crude dirt cellar.

I should have known there was bound to be a place like this hidden away in the cabin. Nothing is ever completely immaculate, and the upstairs had been far too neat. The world just isn't that orderly. The thought was punctuated by a sour reek as I reached the bottom step. It was an odor that I'd smelled before—the stench of decomposition.

I pulled out a tissue and held it over my mouth and nose, keeping the flashlight firmly gripped in my other hand. My eyes remained glued to the ground while I took a step forward and *Wham!* My head slammed smack into a beam. Wouldn't you know? I was in a crawl space with a ceiling so low that I was forced to bend over.

I took another step and a cobweb wrapped itself around my face, conjuring up visions of big hairy spiders. I could feel them crawling up my clothes and slipping inside my head to spin their odious webs. But all such thoughts fled as the flashlight's rays illuminated a dark corner.

On the ground were a number of cigar-shaped bundles eerily similar to the chrysalides upstairs, only much larger. They were industrial-sized rolls of shrink wrap. Even from this distance, I could tell there was something contained in each one. I dropped the tissue, tucked my gun away, and clutched the flashlight tightly in both hands. Then I tremulously approached, aiming its beam at the nearest roll. The light landed on a pair of wide-open eyes that stared back at me in stunned horror.

A scream raced up my throat but never made it out of my mouth, blocked by sheer terror. I wanted to race up the stairs and never come back. It was my demons that made me stay.

I took a deep breath and ordered my shaky hands to continue running the light beam down along the rest of the roll. Inside was a man's body that had begun to decompose. The remains looked remarkably like a butterfly pupa, already liquefying into a strange primordial goo. Only there'd be no rebirth in this crawl space. Death was the final stage for all of these bundles on the hard dirt floor.

I broke into a cold, clammy sweat and the room began to spin around me like a carousel ride.

Oh, dear God, don't let me pass out now, I prayed with all my might, wondering if these were possibly the remains of the Fish and Wildlife consultant, John Harmon.

I lowered my head and took another deep breath. Then I went back to the grisly process of shining my light on the rest of the plastic-wrapped occupants.

The bile rose in my throat as I caught sight of the first young girl. The same sense of terror filled her eyes, along with baffled confusion. It was as though she couldn't understand how her life had come to this. I'd witnessed enough death and killing of both animals and humans to know the answer. There's such a thing as pure evil in this world.

What sounded like the rustling of dry leaves on pavement

suddenly sent my blood pressure soaring, disrupting the vacuum of silence. I jumped, so filled with fear that I tried to bolt for the stairs, only my feet refused to run. Then my eyes witnessed the impossible. One of the bundles had begun to move, as though its contents were shifting.

I held the flashlight as steady as I could, trying to ignore the rush of liquid dread that pulsed through my veins, afraid of what I was going to find. Forget about werewolves and vampires. I was surrounded by something far worse: a chamber of the living dead.

My flashlight landed on yet another young girl who stared back at me in unspeakable fright. Only there was something different about these eyes that made me linger. They weren't yet frozen in death. At the same time, I spied the ugly red scars marking her neck. The pent-up cry inside me now came rushing out, fueled by the desperate hope that I had found Lily.

Afraid I'd reached her too late—that I'd failed yet again, that someone else would be lost because of my inadequacies—I flicked open my Leatherman and began slashing through the sheets of shrink wrap covering her face tight as elastic. Finally I pulled off the very last layer. Her body was warm, yet I couldn't feel a pulse. Equally strange was that Lily's eyes remained open, though she seemed to be unconscious and barely breathing.

I quickly gave her mouth-to-mouth resuscitation and pounded on her chest. But neither managed to revive her. Instead she stared straight ahead like a zombie, as the flicker in her eyes grew dimmer. I set back to work, frantically redoubling my efforts, damned if I'd lose the girl now that I'd found her. I continued until I thought I'd pass out.

My endeavors finally paid off as she sharply inhaled, as if having been pulled back from the entrance to the netherworld. I took a deep breath myself, and then tore the remaining shrink wrap from her body.

Lily lay silent for a moment, as if surprised to still be alive. Then her hands reached up and began to rub her eyes. That set off a chain reaction, as she broke into heart-wrenching tears. I raised Lily into a sitting position and wrapped the girl in my arms, holding her tight, wanting to make us both believe that everything was all right.

"It's okay, Lily. Don't worry. You're safe now. I've got you."

"How do you know who I am?" she asked, nearly choking on her sobs.

"I'm a friend of your father's. He's been searching for you. Let's get out of here and you can tell me what happened."

I helped the girl to her feet and tried to guide her to the stairs, but she pulled back as if not yet ready to leave.

"He's not up there, is he?" she asked, in a voice thick with fear.

"No one's here but us," I assured her, anxious to get Lily out of the stench.

We slowly maneuvered the steps and exited the closet, careful to avoid the hourglass and pedestal. I gazed up at the beams and saw that three more butterflies had emerged and were furiously pumping their wings. I didn't stop, but led Lily into the living room and sat her down in a chair. The girl continued to whimper and nervously glance around.

"Who brought you here, Lily?" I asked, hoping to extract some useful information. "Can you tell me that?"

"Horus. He wanted to show me a pretty blue butterfly. He said it was beautiful and that I could be just like it," she revealed, hugging her thin arms around her body. "That's why we went into the woods a little while ago. Because Horus said it was time."

"Time for what?" I asked.

But Lily rambled on as though she hadn't heard. "I was looking for butterflies when something suddenly stung me and then I couldn't move. But Horus said it was all right and that I shouldn't be scared. It was all part of my transformation. Then he carried me back to the cabin and took me downstairs."

The rest of her words were drowned in a fresh onslaught of tears.

"Are you talking about Big Daddy, or Spencer?" I asked in frustration.

Lily wordlessly shook her head, too choked up to speak.

So that's why the cabin door had been unlocked upon my arrival. I'd been roaming around upstairs while Lily was in the cellar being rolled in shrink wrap like a mummy. Had I not gone down into the crawl space, she'd surely be dead by now. A shiver rippled through me. Horus must have left through the front door while I was in the closet uncovering the peephole. Either he didn't yet know I was here, or this was a game of some sort and he was still lurking around. In any case, a madman was on the loose and had to be found. It was then that I thought of Terri.

I pulled out my cell phone and quickly punched in his number. The response was the resounding echo of nothing. Damn. We were obviously in a dead zone. I looked around, but there was no phone in the house from which to call. I grew sick with worry, knowing that I somehow had to warn him. The problem was, what to do about Lily?

"Do you know how to use a gun?" I asked, pulling out my .38.

The girl's hands grabbed onto it like a lifeline. "Yes."

I didn't bother to question how or why she knew. At this moment, I didn't care.

"All right, then. I'm going to get my vehicle. I'll be back

to pick you up. In the meantime, if anyone comes inside the cabin, shoot them," I instructed.

Lily solemnly nodded, and I knew she'd do whatever was necessary.

Good girl, I thought and took off.

Twenty

I began to search around the grounds, but couldn't get my mind off what I'd found in the cellar—human cocoons all lined up in a row, each filled with indescribable terror. A different kind of chill now snuck up from behind and grabbed hold of me—one that vilely whispered in my ear.

There are worse things in this world than those that go bump in the night. Terrors beyond any you have ever imagined.

Though I tried to block the voice, it deftly burrowed deep into my head, producing darkly horrifying images. My only defense was to try and concentrate as best I could on what was around me. The effort paid off.

I spied a pair of fresh footprints near the shed, their tracks defiling the earth. Too large to be either mine or Lily's, there was no question but that they were those of a man. A metallic taste filled my mouth as I saw where they led: back in the direction of the main house. More than anything I hoped that Terri hadn't stuck around but was in Mendocino sipping a latte.

I followed the footprints until they vanished, swallowed up among the tall blades of grass. The fog had reappeared, making my task all the more difficult.

I passed the same rhododendrons and leathery green huckleberry bushes that I'd seen earlier. Soon everything familiar was consumed in a blanket of fog so dense that it felt as if I were floating. I continued on, no longer sure of where I was going. The only thing certain was that the forest was closing in around me like a spooky fairy tale.

I was about to turn back and try again, hoping to regain my bearings, when a ray of light filtered down straight ahead. It was almost as if God were nudging the foliage aside and pointing me in the right direction. I stumbled toward it, slipping and sliding on the matted vegetation.

Damn! What was I stepping on, anyway? I wondered, and glanced at the ground cover beneath my feet.

A layer of diminutive lotus plants, gaily topped with pretty yellow and purple flowers, led the way toward a bog. I followed along what appeared to be my very own magical yellow brick road.

The air was so dank and wet that beads of water began to drip off the tip of my nose.

Just think how good this is for your skin, I tried to convince myself, feeling more like a bedraggled hound than some hot, gorgeous model.

But all such musings ceased as I stopped and stared in wonder into a stream of soft, filtered light. Dancing in the fog and mist were violet-blue butterflies fluttering about like a troupe of tiny ghosts.

My heart began to race, my pulse to pound; the rest of my body turned to stone. Mesmerized, I watched each little butterfly flit through the air with the grace and ease of a ballerina. I scarcely breathed, barely daring to hope. Could it be? Had I possibly tripped across the last colony of Lotis blue butterflies in existence?

I softly cried out and began to approach, afraid if I looked away for even a moment they would vanish. Another few steps and I was tantalizingly close. A bit farther and I could very nearly touch them. These were the butterflies that lepidopterists had dreamt of and which collectors lusted to possess. They were legendary, part of that growing roster of species referred to by scientists as the living dead.

My hands trembled and my legs grew jittery, realizing I'd become privy to a highly guarded secret. I just wondered how many others were members of this elite club.

I drew still closer, wanting definitive proof that these were no phantoms but actual creatures. I didn't take my eyes off them for a second. As a result, I was caught off guard as my feet bumped against something large and I tripped, flying headfirst without any wings to save myself.

The ground raced up to meet me, but I didn't crash to earth. Instead, I landed on what felt like some sort of cushion. Only this pillow gurgled, followed by a deep drawn-out death rattle, as if bones were being shaken about in a box. The sound scraped against my soul, prompting the web in my head to spin furiously out of control, until it grew convoluted as a labyrinth. I looked down and the earth fell out from under me. A body had softened my fall. Then a sickening smell filled my nose and I knew I was being embraced by death.

I quickly rolled off and stared at what had once been a face, the skull having been crushed in by a rock. A wave of nausea rose up as I gaped spellbound at the body, unable to turn away. My eyes followed the line of an outstretched arm that doubled as a human canvas. Displayed on the mottled skin was an ornate tapestry of exquisite butterflies in flight.

I was gawking at the corpse of Big Daddy.

"I was hoping you'd come out and play."

The voice encircled me, soft as a velvet-covered garrote. My stomach lurched as I whirled around to find Spencer Barnes standing there.

"You saw them, didn't you? The Lotis blue?" he asked in near ecstasy. "They're my pride and joy. It's a trick of light, you know. Their wings aren't really blue at all. It's an optical illusion created by refractive ridges built into each of their tiny wing scales. Absolutely amazing, isn't it?" he chattered, as if it were perfectly normal that Carl Simmons should be lying there dead between us.

I watched as Spencer's angelic face slowly began to transform into one I hadn't seen before.

"I've kept their existence a secret for years. That's why your colleague, John Harmon, had to be stopped. He would have destroyed everything I've worked so hard to maintain. Word was bound to get out. Then collectors from all over would have swooped down like locusts and wiped out the colony. I had no choice but to protect them. I'm sure you understand."

I understood, all right. Barnes was apparently an eco-terrorist who'd gone over the edge.

"Then Simmons was the butterfly dealer, Horus," I reasoned, assuming that's why he'd been eliminated.

"Of course he wasn't," Spencer calmly corrected me. "I am."

My theory instantly went up in flames.

"But I thought your objective was to preserve the butterflies," I replied in surprise.

"It is," Spencer responded with a cherubic smile. "I believe in protecting my investment, the same as any good businessman. If collectors find this spot, they'll try to catch and breed them. That would cut into my market. It's all a matter of supply and demand. The more Lotis blue butterflies there are, the less money they'll command. As it is, I keep careful control over what's sold. My buyers believe they're obtaining one of the last Lotis blues left in existence. That way the price doesn't drop. You can't really blame me. Think about it. These butterflies are like gold. When something's that precious, you have to keep its location secret."

"That's why you killed Aikens," I hazarded a guess.

"I had no other alternative. He demanded money not to betray me. Besides, he began to get sloppy."

My eyes were drawn again to Big Daddy. "And what about Simmons? I thought he was your friend."

"Far from it," Spencer retorted, and impassively glanced down at the body. "The man was my foster father."

The news hit me with the strength of a punch. That meant Spencer had been the boy who'd brought charges against him—the one Big Daddy had pulled from a burning car.

"But why?" I asked, the question hitching a ride on a gasp.

"Any number of reasons. Let's see. Which would interest you most?" Spencer smiled benignly, as though I were terribly naïve. "For one thing, Carl demanded I stop selling Lotis blue butterflies. He threatened to expose me to you, otherwise. I couldn't let that happen. It was this whole St. Francis thing he had going. He'd become very spiritual whenever the mood hit him. Obviously, it didn't kick in when he left my mother to die in that car crash."

Spencer's eyes turned cold, and his lips grew thin and pinched.

"Then there were the girls, of course. Carl kept wondering what happened to them. He liked to believe they'd simply gone home. I'm afraid he discovered differently this morning. Still I might have let him live, if only he'd attempted to grasp what I'm capable of doing. Instead, he refused to understand."

"What do you mean?" I asked, unable to mask the quiver in my voice, remembering what Simmons had told me about the statue.

"Those girls were scarred, the same as you," Spencer said, motioning toward my neck. "I explained they could undergo metamorphosis just like butterflies and have a second chance at life—one in which they'd be beautiful forever."

Was it possible he really believed such crap?

Spencer studied me and sighed.

"Only I'm afraid that might not work in your case. The problem is, you're more of a moth than a butterfly. Otherwise, why would you be so attracted to danger, and knowingly fly into the fire?" he plaintively inquired, as if expecting an answer.

"You're completely out of your mind," I uttered, queasy at the thought of how many young runaways he must have already killed.

"What say we find out?" Spencer sinisterly suggested. "There's a game I like to play with the girls. It's my own version of hide-and-seek."

His cherubic façade now morphed into the face staring at me through the window in my nightmares, having become one more creepy, crawling predator.

Snap!

My nerves leaped at the sound and my eyes darted around, hoping Terri wasn't about to stumble upon us.

"My goodness, but you're jumpy, aren't you?" Spencer softly noted with a chortle. "You should be mindful of that. Don't you know a high stress level will kill you? Oh by the way, if you're looking for your friend, please don't bother. He's already been disposed of."

The garrote twisted tighter around my neck cutting off all breath. I began to reel, not wanting to believe that anything bad had happened to Terri.

Get hold of yourself! Don't let him see that he's gotten to you. Otherwise you'll never be able to get out of this, and there's still Lily to consider.

But I couldn't expel Terri from my thoughts. Spencer continued to leer at me, appearing calmer than ever.

"Tell you what. I'll be a good sport. I'll even give you a head start," he said, and visibly trembled with delight.

Spencer clearly loved playing the game, and I knew it

must be some form of sexual turn-on. That was enough to
stoke my fury. Each face in that crawl space popped back
into my mind again, their terror-filled eyes demanding retri-
bution. More than anything I wanted revenge for what he'd
done to Harmon, to all those girls—and possibly to Terri.
There was no way in hell this bastard was going to get away
from me.

Just calm down and try to think logically.

My guess was that Spencer must have a weapon of some
kind, although I hadn't yet seen one. Otherwise, how could
he act so cocky? Even so, the idea of physically beating the
crap out of the man was becoming incredibly appealing.

I was about to make a move when common sense inter-
vened. Hand-to-hand combat could prove to be risky. The
safest thing was to go for my backup gun.

I swayed, as though feeling dizzy. Then, doubling over, I
began to reach for the ankle holster.

"Don't even think of it," he warned.

I glanced up to find Spencer aiming a gun at me.

"I don't know what you're talking about," I tried to con.

"Oh, please. Give me a bit more credit than that. Don't
you think I watch cop shows on TV just like everyone else?
Carefully remove your weapon from that ankle holster and
slide it on the ground toward me."

Every nerve in my body throbbed, knowing I had little
choice but to do as instructed.

"Very good. Now we can start the game. It's easy. Just do
as I say and run."

I stared at Barnes, uncertain if he was actually serious.
What was this turning into? Some sort of sick, sadistic hunt?

"I told you to run!" he screamed at the top of his lungs, as
if the rage inside him were bursting.

A rush of adrenaline screamed through my veins as I
turned and took off, unsure of where I was going. Light no

longer filtered through the canopy. Rather the fog embraced me. Limbs slashed at my face and my feet stumbled over tree roots as I blindly ran through the forest. Was this how a deer felt while being stalked by a hunter closing in for the kill? If so, there was nothing either spiritual or sacred about it.

I struggled to catch my breath, not knowing what to do next. It was impossible to tell whether Spencer was still behind me. All I heard was the rush of blood in my ears, the rest of the world having become wrapped in a cocoon of oppressive silence.

Maybe I've lost him. Perhaps he's not as good at the game as he thinks, I repeated like a mantra, desperately wanting to believe it.

A tangy burst of salt air suddenly filled my nose, and I now understood where I'd been heading all along. But it was too late to do anything about it. I came to a lurching halt, having caught sight of the massive gray rocks looming in the water below. They sat hunched together like a group of judges deciding my fate.

Snap!

There was that sound again. Only this time, I knew what it was before I even spun around. Spencer was standing as close to me as I'd been to the butterflies, his gun raised and leveled at my body.

Thhhnnk!

Something shrieked through the air and a stinging sharp pain bit into my neck.

My hand flew up, expecting to feel a gush of warm blood, only to find a pencil-thin projectile embedded in my flesh. It remained lodged just above the collar bone. How strange. I glanced down and found it was decorated with pretty blue feathers, much like those that I'd seen on the front seat of Spencer's car in San Francisco.

Oh, shit.

I looked again at the weapon in his hand and the realization now hit. Spencer was holding a dart gun.

My arm dropped like dead weight to my side, and my legs buckled under me, as the paralyzing drug swiftly kicked in. I fell to the ground, my limbs having turned to lead. Muscle, tissue, and sinew were overcome by a tingling sense of numbness. But far worse were the fear and disbelief that rampaged inside my head.

I couldn't move; I couldn't speak. Yet, I was still able to see and hear everything perfectly around me. I now knew that's what those eyes frozen with dread had tried to relate. They'd lain in that crawl space immobilized, having been turned into living zombies, forced to die a thousand deaths before finally managing to suffocate.

I wanted to kick. I wanted to scream. But all I could do was to helplessly watch as Spencer now approached. He knelt and his fingers gently traced the scar along my neck.

"You know what's happening, don't you? The drug is coursing through your veins much like embalming fluid. Only you're not a cadaver. Rather, you're fully awake. You're experiencing something I truly envy; what it's like to slip little by little into death."

I summoned up every ounce of fury and glared at the man, wanting Spencer to know how much I'd love to help him reach his goal.

"It's too bad, really. I'd love to make you part of my little collection, but I already have a Fish and Wildlife employee in the crawl space. Besides, I'm running short of shrink wrap."

My rage boiled over in the only way it could. Tears streamed from my eyes in rampant frustration. For chrissakes, I couldn't even blink. Instead, Spencer had to wipe away the drops for me.

"Don't cry. Think of it as entering another phase. Who

knows? Perhaps you'll even come back as a butterfly. But right now, we really need to bring this to an end. How would you like to go for a nice swim?"

My nightmare intensified as he stood up and the world began to inch past me. I was slowly being dragged toward the edge of the cliffs.

Fight back! I screamed at myself, still refusing to accept defeat.

But no amount of anger could force my limbs to work. That fact was underscored as Mister Softee's jingle now began to play in my head.

Spencer scurried around and, turning to face the ocean, lined my body up along the ledge. Then he began to push.

I must have started to roll off, because the sky was no longer in my line of vision. Instead I found myself staring at white caps churning maddeningly beneath me, their rage exploding in a furious roar.

I began to pray as hard as I could, hoping that death would be quick and merciful. Then I felt myself leave this earth as the world started to blur and spin. That was when I learned the power of prayer. For rather than crashing onto the rocks below, the sky was suddenly above me once more. It was as if a hand had reached down and pulled me back from out of nowhere.

All I could see was an imposing figure looming in the mist as Spencer whirled around and gasped out loud. It was as if he knew what stood there waiting for him. Shrouded in the haze was his very own Angel of Death.

A shriek reverberated inside me as a large, curved scythe suddenly sliced through the fog and hung poised above his head. Then Big Sam swiftly lowered the sickle down onto his victim. The last thing I heard was Spencer's ungodly scream, followed by a flood of silence.

Epilogue

Eric and Lily sat close together on my how-many-lumps-does-this-thing-have Salvation Army couch, with Terri positioned nearby. Three out of four of us were being held captive, strong-armed into drinking large cups of home-brewed herbal tea.

"Finish that up and I make you some more," Mei Rose promised, claiming it would purge all remnants of the paralyzing drug from our bodies. She was probably right. Nothing could have survived tea that tasted this vile.

"And don't think of trying to pour it onto that plant, either," Santou warned us, motioning toward a pathetic-looking ficus tree on the floor.

"Why not? It might actually help the poor thing," Terri cracked. "Something's got to save it from Rach's nurturing touch."

I grinned at my friend, fighting the urge to get up and hug him again.

Terri sat wrapped in a stylish satin robe with a pair of pink fuzzy slippers dangling from his feet. He'd also been darted and left temporarily paralyzed. Apparently, Spencer had planned to drag him down into the crawl space after dealing with me.

"Of course he'd want to add me to his collection," Terri

had wryly remarked. "I'm like a one-of-a-kind designer gown. I'm totally unique."

Though it had been only a few days since the confrontation, it already seemed like a lifetime ago. It was clear that neither Terri nor I would be sitting here right now if it hadn't been for Big Sam. He'd pulled me back from the brink of death and then had swiftly dispatched Barnes.

"Don't worry," he'd rumbled, his voice as soothing as a lullaby to my ears. "You'll be all right now, and so will your friend."

Then my guardian angel had vanished as abruptly as he'd appeared.

Only later did I learn the police had received an anonymous call soon after the attack. A male voice informed them where both Terri and I could be found. By the time they'd arrived, the paralyzing drug had just started to wear off. That's when their interrogation began.

The police spent hours questioning me as to who had killed Spencer. I doggedly stuck to my story and did what I knew in my heart to be right. Though I'd seen the vague outline of a figure, I never managed to get a look at the face. Then I steered the police toward what I felt held far more importance: the bodies that were lying in the crawl space. After that, they'd quickly swarmed the house, removing the remains of John Harmon and five runaway girls.

But the case wasn't over for me yet. There was still one last thing to be dealt with, and for that, I needed to return to Mendocino. Santou had agreed to accompany me. He was feeling much better these days, having kicked the pain pills and started back with physical therapy.

"You better watch out, chère. I'll be joining you in Krav Maga class before you know it," he liked to joke.

I told him that I was counting on it.

We left our friends in Mei Rose's care and took off, promising to return before dinner. Settling behind the wheel, I drove straight to Spencer's cabin, determined to face down the nightmares that had been plaguing me since the attack.

I couldn't get that sound out of my mind—all those little legs scratching inside their cellophane shrouds, struggling to be set free. Those were the images that haunted me; hundreds of butterflies in a state of limbo, held captive in the cold and dark. That, and Spencer's face, which continued to stare at me through the window every night.

I'd come to realize just how vague the boundary between life and death can actually be. In addition, I'd learned the depths of a human being's capacity for rage and cruelty. I'd managed to hold my demons at bay by staying close to those I love while focusing on my main goal: making certain the earth's creatures don't vanish without a fight.

That's why I decided not to report what I'd found to my superiors. Perhaps the Lotis blue would stand a better chance of survival without further meddling of any kind. Especially since Santou and I were now the only ones who knew of its existence.

We entered the cabin and the ghosts raced out, ecstatic to escape their prison. Going into the kitchen, we opened the refrigerator door and gathered up all the butterflies slumbering inside their glassine crypts.

I led the way to the bog where so much had happened to change my life forever, and silently said good-bye to Rebecca. Then Santou and I set each butterfly loose, watching until the very last Lotis blue disappeared into the fog.